BUYER'S REMORSE

With a heavy heart, I called the number he'd given me. He answered on the first ring. "Mr. Kidd? I am listening," I said.

"Oh, I . . . um . . . Well, I have a bit of a problem, and I was told you were an expert in such matters."

I had to laugh. The human penchant for understatement never fails to amuse me. "No, sir, you do not have a 'bit of a problem.' You made a pact with demonic forces. You sold your soul to the devil, and now you want me to get it back. This qualifies as a huge problem."

It always takes people a moment to recover when I put things so plainly, and in the silence I added, "I will meet you at the Chino's across the street from your hotel. You have one hour to convince me."

A DEVIL IN THE DETAILS

A JESSE JAMES DAWSON NOVEL

K. A. STEWART

A ROC BOOK

ROC

Published by New American Library, a division of
Penguin Group (USA) Inc., 375 Hudson Street,
New York, New York 10014, USA
Penguin Group (Canada), 90 Eglinton Avenue East, Suite 700, Toronto,
Ontario M4P 2Y3, Canada (a division of Pearson Penguin Canada Inc.)
Penguin Books Ltd., 80 Strand, London WC2R 0RL, England
Penguin Ireland, 25 St. Stephen's Green, Dublin 2,
Ireland (a division of Penguin Books Ltd.)
Penguin Group (Australia), 250 Camberwell Road, Camberwell, Victoria 3124,
Australia (a division of Pearson Australia Group Pty. Ltd.)
Penguin Books India Pvt. Ltd., 11 Community Centre, Panchsheel Park,
New Delhi - 110 017, India
Penguin Group (NZ), 67 Apollo Drive, Rosedale, North Shore 0632,
New Zealand (a division of Pearson New Zealand Ltd.)
Penguin Books (South Africa) (Pty.) Ltd., 24 Sturdee Avenue,
Rosebank, Johannesburg 2196, South Africa

Penguin Books Ltd., Registered Offices:
80 Strand, London WC2R 0RL, England

First published by Roc, an imprint of New American Library,
a division of Penguin Group (USA) Inc.

First printing, July 2010
10 9 8 7 6 5 4 3 2 1

To Aislynn, for being;
to Scott, for believing;
and to Janet, for doing the hard stuff

ACKNOWLEDGMENTS

Thanks to my agent, Chris Lotts, for fishing me out of the slush. To my editor extraordinaire, Anne Sowards. To my beta slaves: Janet Yantes, Geoff Glover, Jesse Philips, Lori Diederich, Jessica Vaughn, Jenn Wolfe, and Will Sisco. To Auggy, for being beta, webmaster, and pet code monkey all in one. To Dr. Gita Bransteitter for being my part-time medical consultant and my full-time best friend. To the Rogue's Row at the back of the Metro bus, for always making me laugh. To Zak, Beth, and Badger of Badger Blades (www.bad gerblades.com) for making Jesse's swords a reality. To the AW Purgatorians for commiserating when I was down and for kicking my butt to get me back up again. To Aislynn, who keeps insisting my books need more dragons. And to Scott, without whom there would be no Jesse Dawson at all.

1

There's a certain sound the human head makes when it hits the trunk of a tree. Meatier than a "crack"; not quite as hollow as a "thunk"—it's unmistakable. And when it's my head, I tend to take offense.

I leaned against said tree and glared at my opponent until my double vision returned to single and the world swam back into focus. "That one's gonna cost you, Crabby." If looks could kill . . . well, first off, my life would be a lot easier.

On the other side of the clearing, what looked to be a mutant crab-scorpion crossbreed rattled and hissed at me in annoyance as it tried to wipe the thrown dirt out of its stalky eyes. The silver light gleamed off its knobby black shell, giving it a metallic sheen. Its right pincer, large enough to neatly sever my thigh, clicked and clacked loudly. A drop of venom hovered at the tip of its thick segmented tail, the dangerous appendage arching high over its back and weaving like a snake in thrall.

Taking a deep breath, I tossed my thick braid back over my shoulder, out of reach of grasping nasty things, and adjusted my grip on my sword. My breath and the cold night air combined to create frost in my beard, and I wiped it away with my free hand, flinging aside the pellets of ice. The crab creature got its vision cleared and gave a threatening stab of its tail in my direction.

Now, I'm a believer in the power of positive thinking, but do you ever just have a sneaking suspicion you're not winning?

The distant whump-whump-whump of a helicopter broke the silence as it patrolled the camp's perimeter and kept the paparazzi and innocent bystanders at bay. Any sane person or animal had long since fled the chill and the noise, which left just me and my definitely questionable grip on reality. The full moon was up in the sky somewhere, casting the world in blue-white serenity, while down here under the tree canopy I did the tango with . . . that.

What I had here was a class-two Scuttle demon, the category so named (by me) for the way they . . . well . . . scuttled. Only one rung up from primordial ooze on the demonic ladder, most times they were easily confused and taunted into carelessness. None of them would ever be a candidate for Mensa.

Lack of intelligence didn't mean lack of speed, however, or lack of armor. I was having a helluva time getting past that thick carapace. My blade already held quite a few nasty nicks from the attempts. Marty was going to kill me for hurting one of his precious swords.

Still, the crab-demon had a few wounds. Intangible dark energy, which passed for blood amongst demonkind, slithered across the forest floor with eerie sentience, coalescing into a ball of black nothingness behind the creature. I'd heard that essence called void-blood, nether-essence, or some other poetic-sounding crap. To me, it was just blight, and it would suck the life out of whatever it touched.

I gave the demon the universal "Come get some" gesture and pushed off the tree to resume a fighting stance. The crab scuttled left, testing me, and I carefully placed my feet on the uneven terrain as I shifted right. It was impossible to feel my way through the thick soles of my boots, and I couldn't afford to take my eyes off the demon. My armor jingled faintly, sounding like macabre sleigh bells, and the crab hissed and snapped its pincers in return. Not for the first time, I questioned the wisdom of wearing only chain mail and leather for protection. I'd found that I simply could not move well enough if I added plates to it, but was mobility worth it if I couldn't stop a crushing blow?

Lightning quick, the demon charged, spiny feet carrying it across the clearing in an explosive crackle of dead pine needles. At the last second, I calmly side-stepped right, avoiding the massive claw and dodging the poisonous stinger, bringing my sword down at the juncture of one chitinous leg. The twiggy limb snapped with a gunshot report, and the crab-demon screamed in inhuman outrage. The severed leg dissolved, and dark energy poured from the wound, billowing into the night air to join the rest that had escaped. Slowly it began to swirl, forming the beginnings of a portal.

You don't really kill demons. You can only wear them down until they lose the strength to hold on to this plane. Thanks to the crab's armored form, the fight had already gone on longer than I would have liked, and the trick would be to see which one of us was going to tire first. Next time—if there was a next time—I hoped for a fluffy bunny demon, something pink and easily dispatched.

I let my momentum carry me past and away like flowing water, again finding myself across the clearing. Now, I'm a fairly athletic man in the prime of my life, but we'd been at this for the better part of forty-five minutes, and the running back and forth all night was getting old. "Come on, Crabby. I'm too old to play tag."

The Scuttle demon limped in awkward circles for a moment, as if the now-missing leg had been the rudder keeping it on a straight path. Its eyestalks swiveled to keep me in sight, and it chittered something furious at me. I'd reduced it to babbling. It wasn't even bothering to speak English in its fury.

The next charge wasn't quite so coordinated. Twice on that pass, my katana glanced harmlessly off the black shell with a jarring clang. I felt it all the way to my shoulders. As I moved to spin away from the tail again, the demon whirled and slammed that massive pincer into my left hip. I went tumbling head over heels into the leafy forest litter, barely managing to keep my sword. The pungent smell of crushed pine needles filled the air.

It wasn't broken. Broken hips happen to old people, not to strapping young men of thirty . . . -ish. But it was going to bruise, and I could feel links of chain digging through my jeans and into my skin where the padding beneath gaped. I didn't have time to ponder the state of my armor or the severity of my injury. I didn't even have time to get up off the ground.

Crabby barreled over me, screeching at the top of its . . . lungs? There was no strategy to its attack. It had succumbed to rage, flailing wildly as it tried to stampede me. I could only curl up and try to protect my poor head. Even so, my braid caught on a spur of carapace, wrenching my neck despite my efforts. I aimed a kick at one leg, trying to make it list harder to port. In retaliation, one of those spiny appendages speared straight through my right calf like a shish kebab. I'm not ashamed to admit I screamed. The crab howled, too, triumphant.

Funny how you can notice key things when you're about to be skewered by a tap-dancing crab-demon— important things, such as how soft and squishy the underside of the thing looked. Its belly was silvery gray, and pulsated with every grotesque movement. In fact, it looked rather like the raw oysters I'd eaten at a black-tie gathering a few years ago. Yeah, I wouldn't be eating those again.

I consider myself a philosopher, an educated man. But there are times when learning and culture are simply not applicable. And should you ever find yourself being trampled by a demonic crustacean, when in doubt, stab the squishy spot.

Apparently, Crabby didn't have eyes on its underside, because it was having a hard time finding me, all tangled up under its legs. And while I was safe from the stinging tail, I was still in real danger of being bludgeoned into mush. A joint cracked against my head as

I tried to squirm enough to reach my boot, and colorful streamers darted past my eyes for a moment. My katana was all but useless in close quarters. This is why I carry a plain old skinning knife in my right boot. It may not be pretty; it may not be elegant; but the pointy end goes into the other guy, and that is all I need.

With both hands, I slammed the blade in up to the hilt, then did a little jerk and wiggle for good measure. Instead of oozing, wriggling innards, blight poured out over my hands, which instantly went numb clear to the elbow. I lost my grip on my knife in the frantic roll to keep the void energy from touching my face and chest. Deep in some primitive, instinctive place, I knew that stuff would kill me if I let it wash over me, and no amount of training can erase the first primal imperative to survive.

The crab-demon shrieked and spasmed above me, losing all interest in pursuing an attack. Staggering first one way, then another, it jibbered and chattered in some pitch approaching supersonic. There was no mistaking the sound of abject terror, even in some language I would never understand.

It occurred to me, perhaps a bit late, that being under the thing in its death throes was not wise. I took the easy exit on hands and knees, out through the hole left by the missing leg, not too proud to scuttle myself when the situation called for it.

The blackness beneath billowed up, a dark fog that flowed over the forest floor to join the rest, the portal growing larger, more defined. The crab-demon continued to shriek and twitch even as I watched its own black carapace collapse inward with a sickening crunch, its will draining away with its strength. First the spiny legs dissolved and flowed away, and then the shell, inch by inch. The tail stabbed at nothing in the leaves, one last reflexive effort to save itself. The creature's voice dwindled into a pathetic wail, then into nothingness. The last to go was the giant pincer, clacking to the end, and it finally poofed into an ominous black cloud and flowed into the gaping hole in reality.

The portal itself was a dark mirror, three feet off the ground, as big around as a fifty-gallon drum. It shimmered briefly, the surface going from black to silver to clear in a matter of heartbeats. A faint odor of sulfur tainted the crisp night air, and just out of my range of hearing, something screamed, high enough to make my teeth ache. As always, I tried to get a glimpse through that portal, to see what lay behind. I got no more than a sense of immense heat and terrible soul-killing dread before it vanished with a faint blip and the vague tingle of static electricity. Oh well. I'm probably better off not knowing, anyway—curiosity and the cat and all that.

The only thing left in the battle's wake was silence. In the distance, some brave night bird sent out a questioning chirp. The breeze was cold enough to sting as I gulped air, trying to will my pulse to slow, to keep my blood from pumping out and down my leg.

You never realize how hurt you are until the adrenaline starts to fade. I flexed my hands until the feeling returned to them. My bruised hip screamed with every beat of my heart and, oddly, hurt worse than the pierced calf. Of course, that could also have been the blood loss talking.

I limped across the clearing to pick up my knife. Though it looked clean, I wiped it on some dead leaves and sheathed it in my boot. That put me close enough to examine my calf. I was pretty sure I could poke my finger through the hole and wiggle it on the other side. I didn't. Even my stomach wasn't that strong. I needed bandages and something to stop the bleeding. Beneath the copper scent of my own blood, there was something else, an odd chemical odor. I didn't know what it was, but it couldn't bode well.

My body moved on autopilot, bending to collect my katana. I cleaned it as well, though the blade was likewise spotless. There were three new nicks in the edge. Marty was going to have purple kittens when he saw it. You wouldn't expect a blacksmith to be so damn touchy. I forced myself to stand upright, centering my body a moment before sliding the sword into its scabbard.

Only then did my gaze go to the three men waiting in the tree line. The two on either side, in their identical black suits and earpieces, tensed as I hobbled my way toward them. I couldn't fault them for that. It was their job. But the part of me that loved inappropriate humor wanted to giggle. *Big bad men in black, scared of a scrawny, beat-to-shit samurai.* I had to give the guys credit, though. They'd just seen things that weren't supposed to exist, and it hadn't even fazed them.

It was the man in the middle I focused on. He had salted hair, the lines of many cares on his face, and a suit that probably cost the taxpayers a pretty chunk of change. He pushed his left sleeve up and stared in unabashed amazement at the unblemished skin on his inner forearm. I thought I even saw him blink tears from his bleary eyes. Finally, he shook himself, reached into the breast pocket of his tailored suit, and produced a long envelope.

I snatched it with no remorse whatsoever. The medical bills on this one were going to be a bitch, and he could more than afford it. "Thank you, Mr. President. Your soul is your own again. Try to take better care of it this time." My right foot was overly warm. Somewhere in the back of my mind, I knew my blood was pooling in my boot. I didn't have time for pleasantries.

"Thank you, Mr. Dawson, for . . . Well, thank you."

"Here." I produced a card from inside one of my leather bracers, trying not to smear blood on it. It's a simple card. I print them myself—just white card stock and black letters, JESSE DAWSON, CHAMPION, and a private cell phone number. "If you ever find anyone else in your situation, you can tell them I might be able to help them. Make sure they mention your name."

He took the card, looking it over carefully, then tucked it away. "Will I be seeing you again, Mr. Dawson?"

"You'd better hope not." As far as I was concerned, that concluded my business there. I turned to limp toward the paved road, invisible through the trees. Will, my best friend, was out there in a rented car, waiting to take us both home. He was an EMT. He could patch me up until I could get to a hospital. Then they'd call my doc, and she'd fly out to collect my sorry ass. And there would be the lecture. I hated it when she lectured me. Better the doc, though, than my wife. Will should call her, I thought, and let her know I was okay. I was okay, wasn't I?

Dimly I recognized the rambling of my thoughts as a bad thing. I tried to concentrate, to mentally catalogue the symptoms of blood loss, but anything coherent kept flitting away, just out of reach. I staggered to a halt amidst the trees, disoriented, and wondered whether I was really still walking toward the road or whether I'd gotten turned around somehow. The moon shone on my back, casting my shadow long over the ground. The shadow was a rather handsome fellow, tall and almost too slender, a long braid of hair hanging down past his stooped shoulders. He looked injured. *Poor guy*. I decided to follow him, since he looked like he knew where he was going.

Okay, maybe a hundred-yard walk through the trees was not one of my more brilliant ideas, but in my defense, I didn't expect to be bleeding so badly. The chemical smell had invaded my taste buds, and I had nothing left in my dry mouth to spit with. By the time I could see the car, and Will, silhouetted in the moonlight, my body was prepared to go on strike. The moonlight reflected off Will's glasses, giving him an owl-eyed look. I think he said something then, maybe called my name. Most likely, he said, "Dude?"

The last thing I recall was hitting the dead leaves face-first and wondering idly whether there was any poison ivy about.

Farewell, Camp David. We'll always have the memories.

2

Spring in Missouri is wonderful . . . for about a week. During that week, the sun comes out in all its glory, and the brisk mornings warm up to pleasant afternoons. Most important, there are very few insects out. Then, in the blink of an eye, we have the heat of Death Valley, the humidity of the Everglades, and mosquitoes the size of large poodles come out to carry off small children and family pets. And we have tornadoes. Never forget the tornadoes.

We were still enjoying that blissful week of true spring as I sat meditating in my garden. It wasn't a large garden, or elaborate. It took up one corner of the backyard, leaving plenty of grassy space open for whatever. Around the small pond, a stone "river" flowed through the landscaping, white pebbles interspersed with cream and black. I had finished moving my bonsai trees, my pride and joy, back out from their winter shelter just a few days prior, and already I could see the rich green of the leaves taking hold in the bright sunlight.

The cheerful trickle of water into the shallow pond (no koi, sadly; we have raccoons) seemed to provide background music for the early-spring birds in the tree branches above me. I toyed with a pair of white river pebbles, turning the smooth stones over and over between my fingers. The soft clicking sound was sooth-ing. Three yards over, I heard a lawn mower start up. It was a comfortable addition to the ambient sounds of the neighborhood. It was the perfect kind of peace, suitable for meditation.

I sat cross-legged in the sun, wearing my favorite pair of sweatpants and no shirt. The sweats, hanging low on my hips, were baggier on me than they had been; I was still regaining the mass I'd lost in my three-week ICU stint. Hospital food sucks, and the weight drops off fast. Building it back up took time, and I was never what you would call bulky to begin with. Some would call me scrawny. I prefer wiry.

The sunlight glowed a cheery red through my closed eyelids, and I smiled to feel it on my face. The morn-ings were a bit chilly still, and it was interesting to feel the sun chase the cooler shadows across my skin. The hint of warmth was soothing on my aching muscles. They didn't hurt nearly as much after two months of recovery. I'd even been doing the physical therapy for my leg, like the good doctor told me, in addition to my usual katas and workouts. All right, she didn't tell me to do it in *addition* to, but . . . what she didn't know wouldn't hurt her.

I had chosen the works of Tsunetomo Yamamoto for my meditation of the day. In his written works, called *Hagakure*, he lists four vows that a samurai should re-cite every day. The fourth of those is "to manifest great compassion and act for the sake of man." That was what I focused on for the day, turning it over in my mind as I examined all possible meanings and oppositions. I like to think such mental exercises keep me keen.

Behind me, I heard the sliding glass door open. "Jesse, the phone's ringing." Ah, the dulcet voice of the love of my life, my wife, Mira.

Without opening my eyes, I answered, "Can you please take a message?"

I don't know if I'm the only husband with this talent, but I can actually tell when my wife is gritting her teeth just from the tone of her voice. "The *other* phone is ringing, Jess." Oops. Mira did not follow the *bushido*, so I doubted I'd get great compassion for the sake of man from her at this moment. In fact, she was more likely to throw something at me.

"Coming." I opened my eyes and bowed from the waist to the little Buddha statue in my garden. No, I'm not Buddhist. He just seemed to belong there, and I hated to leave without at least acknowledging him. Courtesy, you know.

The remnants of morning dew soaked my bare feet and the cuffs of my sweats as I crossed the yard. Stepping up on the brick patio, I grabbed my discarded T-shirt off the lawn furniture and slung it over my shoulder. It gave me a chance to eye the beginnings of a tan. I'm out at night a lot. Add that to the pale blond hair and blue eyes, and I am the poster boy for white and pasty. I was more likely to burn than tan, but every spring I hoped for the best.

The only thing that wouldn't tan would be the scars, starting just below my left armpit and disappearing beneath the waistband of my sweats. These particular ones were a lingering souvenir from a Skin demon. It had been a hulking white-furred creature, with long grasping arms and talons the length of my forearm. Towering a good four feet over my own six-foot height, it reminded me of a prehistoric sloth. There had been nothing slow about it, however, and even though I won that fight, I most certainly had not walked away from it. When I had nightmares, it was what came at me out of the dark with silver claws and glowing red eyes, killing me night after night.

In my mind, I still called it the Yeti, because the weak attempt at humor was all that kept me from going screaming mad in terror.

My other scars, peppered over my shoulders and arms, were inconspicuous next to the Yeti's spectacular marks. I could name most of them. The small spattered burns on my forearms belonged to an explosive Snot from two years ago. The horseshoe marks on my shoulders, the size of fifty-cent pieces, were left behind by something leechlike nine months back. I was never sure whether it counted as a Snot or a Scuttle. The tiny scar at the right corner of my mouth, mostly hidden by my goatee, was my own doing. I had cut myself shaving in my youth.

Sure, I had more than my fair share for a man my age, but if anyone noticed that my scars had strange shapes and occurred in odd places, they never said. They pretended to believe they were knife wounds, and I pretended I believed they believed that. It worked out well for all concerned.

Mira was bent over, her head stuck in the dishwasher. She wore a pair of short cut-off jeans and a tank top, her thick mane of sable curls temporarily confined in some kind of twisty clip that probably had a name known only to women. All right, I'm a pig, I admit it, but I stopped to let my eyes wander up the slender column of her legs, over her nicely rounded behind, across the curve of her back . . . to find her green eyes staring at me over her shoulder. She raised one brow, and I shrugged with a sheepish grin. "You can't blame a guy for looking."

"Go answer the phone!" She hit me in the chest with a damp dish towel. At the same moment, a hard object collided with something lower down and much more precious to me. No combat training in the world can prepare you for the toddler-head-in-the-junk attack.

"Oof!" I looked down to find the culprit grinning up at me, all red pigtails and blue-eyed innocence.

"Daddy, your phone is ringing," she informed me in all her five-year-old seriousness.

"I know, button. Lemme go so I can get it, 'kay?"

"Annabelle, go pick your toys up out of the living room, please." At the sound of her mother's voice, she was gone, her bare feet thundering down the hallway like a small herd of buffalo. It was amazing how much noise one small child could make.

The phone—*that* phone, anyway—never brought good news, so I took my time sauntering down the hallway, smelling the faint incense Mira had burning. Our house was nothing spectacular. I think the real estate agent called it a single-level ranch, three bedrooms, one and a half baths. I called it mundane suburban. Pale yellow vinyl siding and an unfenced yard completed the picture. The house was light and airy, and the maple hardwood floors almost glowed when the sun crept in through the tall windows. We've lived here six years already. I guess that means we're going to stay.

I could hear Annabelle in her room as I passed, giggling fitfully as she tried to hide under her huge stuffed rabbit. We simply could not convince her that snickering madly was not a good way to stay hidden. "You'd better get moving before your mom finds you, kiddo."

In my den—a walk-in closet, in a former life—the shrill chirp of my cell phone ceased just long enough for the person on the other end to hit REDIAL, then started up again. I closed the door behind me, encasing myself in my own personal haven. My desk and chair were against the far wall, the short wall. Two tall bookcases towered at my left, laden with everything from ancient Japanese philosophies to the latest bestseller from my favorite author. The right wall was adorned with my tie-dyed Jimi Hendrix wall hanging, right next to a Japanese silk print of two samurai battling. *Home, sweet home.*

I settled into my old desk chair, one left over from Mira's college days. The abused leather felt sticky against my bare back, and I had to be very careful not to lean on the right arm, because it would fall off and dump me on the floor. It was my favorite piece of furniture in the house.

I examined the still-ringing cell phone before I answered it. Eighteen missed calls already. It was a local number, but not one I knew. Whoever it was, was persistent. I had to give the person that. "Hello?"

There was a moment of confused silence on the other end. Since a simple hello so confounds my callers, I always wonder how they expect me to answer the phone. "Mr. Dawson?" It was a man's voice, older than I if I had to guess; in his fifties, maybe.

"Yes." There was a long, uncomfortable pause again, and I just waited, letting him squirm. What can I say; I'm not good with small talk.

"Um . . . a friend of mine recommended you. . . ."

"Who?" I picked up the handy-dandy pen and notepad I kept on my desk.

"Walter Brandt. He said you might be able to help me."

"And where can I reach you?" He rattled off the name and number of a local hotel, which I scribbled down with a frown. I don't like it when they go ahead and invite themselves to my city, just assuming that I'll take up their cause. It was a strike against him, whoever he was. "And your name?"

"Nelson Kidd."

I had to pause in the middle of writing that down to blink. "Nelson Kidd, the Arizona pitcher? Mr. Perfect-Game-in-the-World-Series Kidd?"

"The same."

Well how d'ya like them apples? I confess I'm still a bit starstruck at some of the people I wind up working for. But I remembered my professionalism enough to keep from squealing like a fan girl. "I will call you back in twenty minutes, Mr. Kidd." I hung up before he could protest. I know people hate that, but it gives the left-over rebel inside me a great deal of pleasure.

The first thing I did with any new client was touch base with his reference. I learned the hard way not to just take folk at their word, and I've got the scars to keep the memory fresh. Walter Brandt's name was in my phone book (under *B*, even!), and I dialed him up.

A woman's bored voice answered. "Lexicon Industries. How may I direct your call?"

"Walter Brandt, please."

"I'm sorry, sir, he's in a meeting. May I take a message or forward you to his voice mail?" It was said with a tone of "I'm only doing this until my acting career takes off, so I won't bother to treat you with more than indifference." I could picture her snapping her gum and filing her nails. Do secretaries still do that? Oh wait, I'm sorry—administrative assistants.

Whatever she was, she irritated me. "Interrupt the meeting and tell him it's Jesse Dawson. He should be expecting my call." I had no doubt that Walter Brandt would move hell and high water to take my call. His assistant, however, was apparently not aware of my privileged status.

Her sigh fairly dripped with exasperation—*God forbid I make you do your job, lady*—but in the end she just put me on hold. I was treated to the plaintive strains of an orchestral version of Prince's "Purple Rain," followed by something that might have been "Hazy Shade of Winter" before it was butchered—a damn travesty. Finally, the line clicked live again.

"Mr. Dawson?" The words were deep and gravelly around the edges, the voice of a whiskey drinker and lifetime smoker. This was my man.

"Mr. Brandt. How have you been?" I hadn't seen Walter Brandt since my job for him almost three years ago. He was one of my early ones. I wondered if he still had the same graying handlebar mustache, but I couldn't think of a tactful way to ask. I envied that mustache, but Mira had sworn to divorce me if I even thought about copying it. I had to make do with my beard in the winter and be clean shaven the rest of the time.

"I've been . . . doing well. The cancer is officially in remission. But somehow, I doubt this is a standard follow-up phone call."

"Did you give my card to someone?"

His voice lowered, though I knew he had to be alone in his office. "Yes, I did. Nelson Kidd." He nearly whispered the name, as if we were trading state secrets.

"And you truly believe he has come to see the error of his ways?" It mattered, you know, at least to me. I wouldn't help someone just looking for the easy way out. That's how they usually wound up in trouble in the first place. Maybe I hadn't mastered my great compassion for the sake of man. I'd have to work on that.

Brandt hesitated before he answered, thinking it over. I'd have called him a liar if he hadn't. "I believe so, yes."

"You know the rules. Is he going to check out?"

"I . . . think so. Truthfully, he didn't go into a lot of detail. He is ashamed."

"He should be." I rocked the chair back into its upright position. "That's all I needed to know. You have a lovely day, Mr. Brandt."

"You, too, Mr. Dawson. God bless." We hung up. I suppose I didn't mind the blessing so much, despite not being a religious man myself. He meant well.

My fingers traced slowly over Nelson Kidd's name on my notepad, and I sighed in disappointment. It was one thing for Joe Schmoe businessman to fall, but somehow baseball players should have been exempt. They were the true heroes of my childhood. I still had most of my original card collection, and though I didn't get to play anymore, I still followed the season avidly.

Nelson Kidd had been a star in his day, leading the league in almost every category a pitcher can. But, like all of us, he got old, and his arm started flagging. Teams traded him four or five times in one year, always for someone younger and faster. Everyone labeled him as done, and there was talk of moving him to the minors if he didn't retire.

Two years ago, he made his miraculous comeback. It ended with a World Series title for his Arizona team, and the first perfect World Series game since Don Larsen in 1956. It was made even more spectacular when he tested clean for every steroid and enhancement drug they could think of. The fans, the newspapers, the agents went wild, and despite his age, he was suddenly able to name his price wherever he wanted to go.

I knew now how he'd done it. I think I would have preferred the drugs. *Nothing is sacred anymore.*

With a heavy heart, I called the number he'd given

me. He answered on the first ring. "Mr. Kidd? I am listening," I said.

"Oh, I . . . um . . . Well, I have a bit of a problem, and I was told you were an expert in such matters."

I had to laugh. The human penchant for understatement never fails to amuse me. "No, sir, you do not have a 'bit of a problem.' You made a pact with demonic forces. You sold your soul to the devil, and now you want me to get it back. This qualifies as a huge problem."

It always takes people a moment to recover when I put things so plainly, and in the silence I added, "I will meet you at the Chino's across the street from your hotel. You have one hour to convince me."

3

I hung up the phone, and it immediately rang in my hand. Then it hit the floor with a clatter, where it proceeded to buzz itself in happy little circles under my desk. Okay, yes, there was a bit of flinching, but you see how manly you are when a giant joy buzzer goes off unexpectedly. Mental note: Take the cell phone off vibrate.

I fished it out, banging my head on the desk only once, and checked the caller ID. This number was also unfamiliar, and not local. I eyed it warily. I'd never received a request for two jobs in one day before, but I supposed anything was possible—possible in the same sense that, yes, I could get struck by lightning four times in the same week.

No matter how I glared at the little device, it refused to offer up any more of its secrets. I was finally obliged to answer it.

"Hello?" Retrieving an elastic tie from my desk, I gathered my shoulder-length hair into a ponytail. I was still getting used to the shorter length, but the longer hair had become a liability.

"Dawson. Good morning."

I winced and held the phone away from my ear. "Ivan?" With that thick Ukrainian accent and booming baritone voice, it couldn't be anyone else. I could barely make his words out over the unmistakable clamor of an airport in the background.

"*Tak.* It is much good to be hearing your voice." The man had been traveling in and out of the United States for the better part of thirty-five years, and his English was still horrible. I loved it.

Out of habit, I checked my desk calendar. "I don't have to check in for two more weeks, so to what do I owe the pleasure?"

"Rosaline was to be calling me." I frowned and had to wait for the next part of his statement for clarification. Okay, maybe the broken English wasn't so much fun, sometimes.

"And?"

"And she is not to be hearing from Miguel for two weeks past."

Translation, for those who don't speak "Ivan": Rosaline had called, and she hadn't heard from Miguel for two weeks. I frowned harder. Sure, the business takes us out of contact sometimes, but I have never failed to call my wife for two weeks straight. If I ever did, I'd never be able to come home again. She'd kill me.

"Did he miss his check-in?"

"*Ni,* not yet. But it is to being most unusual for him." Ivan sounded worried. I think that bothered me more than anything. When the old man is worried, deep shit is going down.

"And his weapon wasn't delivered to you?"

"*Ni.* Have you to been speaking with him? Did you know of his most recent mission?"

"I haven't talked to him in a couple months. Rosaline doesn't know where he was going last?"

"I am to be flying into Mexico City later today. I will be finding out what I can."

"Yeah, Ivan, keep me posted. Let me know if there's anything we can do from here."

"The phone lines there are not to being stable, and they are not to having a connection to the Internet. Perhaps I will to be having you relay messages to Grapevine, when I am able to be making contact?"

"Yeah, I can do that. Hey, you be careful down there, okay?"

"*Tak*, I will be doing that. May God be keeping you safe, Dawson."

After we hung up, I wondered if all these blessings were going to jinx me.

We called ourselves champions. I didn't choose the name; it had been that way longer than anyone could remember. We shared no race, no country, and our reasons were as varied as our backgrounds. Men—and women—like us had been fighting the good fight for millennia.

Some were warrior-priests, tied to the church. Some were holy men, shamans who drew power from the land. We were mercenaries, and monks, and everything in between. We battled with blades and hammers, pipes and bats—whatever we had that we were comfortable with. Most—in fact all save me—also had that little something extra. Call it faith; call it voodoo—the religion doesn't seem to matter. Hell, even the atheists of the group have it. There is magic in the world, and it gives a champion the ability to hold his own on a mystical level.

Except me. I'm the mule of this circus. No wonder they keep expecting me to drop dead at any moment. I could feel magic. I know when it's present. But trying to touch it myself is like grasping at smoke. It goes right through my fingers.

I picked up the clear crystal from my desk, turning it over in my hand. It was small, a perfectly shaped quartz. It was marred by a single milky flaw in its depths.

Ivan gave it to me years ago. He insisted my magic wasn't gone, just dormant, and when I finally found a way to reach it, I would see some sign in the crystal. So far, it hadn't even twitched. Day after day, it lay on my desk, flawed and inert—like me. *Sorry, Ivan.*

Sometime before I became a champion, back when I was still chasing cheerleaders in high school and sneaking beers from my parents' fridge, a champion named Ivan Zelenko decided he was tired of fighting that good fight alone. Using the technology that was still in its infant stages then, he set about finding all who had fought Hell's minions and won.

He found us through newspaper clippings, hospital records, village legends. I can only imagine what it was like for the first person he contacted, having this enormous stranger appear on his doorstep. I wonder, did he just come right out and say, "Excuse, please, you fight demons?" The thought always made me chuckle, but it was most likely the truth. Ivan wasn't known for subtlety.

He worked for years, doing research, traveling, gathering us all. He connected men and women from all over the world with others who understood the things we could never explain to those closest to us. With Ivan keeping track, never again would a champion's death go unnoticed, his soul lost to the blackest abyss. Never again would one of us die unremarked and unknown, our deeds fading along with our memory. We were tagged and catalogued, like any other endangered species, our names and locations held in one secured database called Grapevine. When one of us disappeared now, at least someone would know.

Ivan never talked about his life before being a champion, and you don't really ask things like that. If I had to guess, I'd say he was military. The dramatic side of me says KGB, but there's no way to know. I do know that he has survived longer than any currently living champion, with more kills under his belt than several of us put together. Now easily into his fifties (hey, I'm not asking him his age, but you can if you want), he doesn't fight anymore. But he still watches after the rest of us, a combination of drill sergeant and father.

My fingers traced the framed picture on my desk. Frost-haired Ivan stood on one side of a bride and groom, towering over them both, his shoulders as broad as two of me. Mira and I stood on the other side of the dark-haired, dark-skinned couple. Both were smiling at each other more than at the camera. The photographer had captured Rosaline's wedding veil fluttering in the breeze, as if it might suddenly spring to life in the photograph. Miguel gazed down at his new wife, dark eyes glowing in that way unique to a man in love.

"She is everything to me, Jesse. I could pass to Heaven

happily, knowing I had been in her presence for only a few moments. To have her as my wife . . . God has blessed me."

At the time, I had chalked Miguel's poetic sense up to a young man's true love. But now something seemed darkly prophetic about those words, and they settled somewhere low and cold in my gut. It was the place where disaster lurked, where misfortune was quite comfy. Mira called it premonition, insisting that it was my one claim to magic. I called it common sense, and I just couldn't bring myself to believe in a happy ending for this one.

Leaving my den for the bedroom, I chose the day's attire carefully, mindful that I was meeting a client. My blue jeans had no holes in them, and my black T-shirt said I'M A GEEK in big white lettering. The sleeves were short enough to show off the tattoos down both biceps, each one a string of kanji quoting the first two lines of the *Tao Te Ching.* "The Way that is spoken here is not the eternal Way. The name that is spoken here is not the eternal name." The outfit was complete with the combat boots that had no visible bloodstains. Dress to impress; that's my motto.

Mira had managed to capture Hurricane Annabelle, and the redheaded imp was currently seated at the kitchen table with chocolate pudding smeared from ear to ear. "Daddy! Hugs!" Those fudgy fingers reached for me, and I had to laugh despite the pall that had descended over my day.

"Not a chance, button. You're a mess." I did carefully lean down to kiss the top of her pigtailed head, though, then took a moment to wrap my arms around my wife and just hold her.

She tucked her head neatly under my chin, proving yet again that we were perfectly matched in every way. Her hair smelled like strawberries.

In the ten years I'd known her, she'd gone from a plucky, headstrong girl to the most elegant, graceful creature I had ever laid eyes on. Even after childbirth and eight years of marriage (which translates as eight years of putting up with my shit), she was not only beautiful in body, but in spirit. The mere thought of being without her was enough to make my stomach clench painfully, and I squeezed her tighter.

We stood for long moments in each other's arms before she asked, "What's wrong?"

That's why she's so perfect. I don't have to tell her; she just . . . knows. "Ivan called. Miguel is missing."

She leaned back so she could look up at me, her green eyes going dark with concern. "Oh goddess . . . Rosaline?"

"Ivan's on his way. He'll call when there's word." I offered her my cell. "I know—normally I say don't answer it, but . . . If it's not Ivan, just tell them to call back tomorrow."

She frowned, eyeing the hated phone as if it might bite, but finally she nodded and tucked it into her hip pocket. "I'll work a protection spell for both of them later. They gave permission." My wife, the witch.

I'd known she was Wiccan long before I had ever known about the reality of magic. At one time, her offering to cast a spell would have been the same as someone's saying, "Good luck!"—well meant, but ultimately useless. It was only later, when I wound up in the middle of this mess, that I realized how powerful her spells could truly be. If I had no magic, Mira made up for it in spades. She believes that's why we were drawn together; that we are stronger together than we are apart. I kinda like that idea.

"You're going out."

"Yeah. Just a meet and greet, I should be back later." The look on her face made me pause. "What?"

"It's just . . . a little soon, isn't it? It's only been two months, and you were hurt so badly. . . ." She worried her lower lip between her teeth.

"Hey, I'm fine! Bench-pressing cars and leaping over tall buildings, even." I gave her what I thought was a rakish grin. "Besides, it's just a meeting. I'm not going to whip out my sword and go to town right then and there."

Somehow, I don't think she was convinced of my prowess. Still chewing her lip, she took a wet rag in hand and went to try and uncover my child from somewhere under an explosion of chocolate.

We'd been over this before. I mean, Mira understands what I do, and she supports me. But I always worry that at some point, she is going to get tired of waiting for that phone call from Ivan, the one that says I'm not coming home. I guess I'm lucky she's put up with me for this long.

She finally sighed heavily, indicating that her internal conversation was over. "Well, don't forget you have to work this afternoon. And you still have to get a present for your mother's party on Saturday."

Crap. I eyed the schedule stuck to the fridge, and

yes, she was right. Why do I even pretend to doubt her?

My mother's birthday party was the event of the year in my family; never mind Christmas or Thanksgiving. The reigning matriarch of the Dawson clan would be celebrated, and woe to he who thought otherwise. And trust me, I don't care if Evelyn Dawson is only four foot eight; I'm scared of her and you should be, too. She's a short firebrand of pride and old-fashioned Scottish temper. She raised my brother and me with an iron fist inside a satin glove, and to this day I hold the highest respect for all women because of it ('cause if I didn't, she'd know, and she'd find me).

"I'll probably go to work straight from my meeting, then. I can go shopping after, and I'll be home in time for dinner."

Mira snorted. "Sure you will. You just don't want to be here to help me with the house cleansing."

Well . . . there was that, too. I grinned. "Sorry, honey, the life of a busy man and all." If I missed the yearly smudging of the house with sage bundles, so much the better. I love my wife, and I respect her abilities and her religion. I just wish it didn't involve so much smoke.

I was getting into my truck when she poked her head through the kitchen door, Annabelle settled on one hip. "Jesse?"

"Yeah, baby?"

"Be careful. Please?" Those lines of worry had formed around her eyes again. She didn't have those four years ago—a lifetime ago.

Normally, I'd have had some flip answer for her, but

it occurred to some higher level of my brain that this might not be the right time. "I will, baby. I love you."

"Love you, too."

"I love you, too, Daddy!"

She hit the garage opener for me, and I backed out into the noonday sun.

Now, you have to understand that I have a very exclusive list of things I love in my life. Sure, I love my mom and dad, and my brother, yadda yadda. But topping the list were three things: my truck, my daughter, and my wife. Not necessarily in that order, but . . . I love my truck almost as much as I love my wife.

It's a steel gray '94 Mazda B-4000. It leaks every fluid it has, the power steering has this horrible whine to it, and it hasn't had air-conditioning for the last six years. But she's paid for, and she's never let me down. Every time Mira threatens to shoot her, I go out and buy her something pretty like seat covers or a new gear shift knob. The truck, not Mira. And there is a certain thrill to riding down the highway at "Drive it like it's stolen" speed, hair blowing in the wind from the open windows. Man, I couldn't wait for summer.

The only thing that could dampen that bright thought was the lingering worry over Miguel. There are only a double handful of men (all right, and one woman) in the world who do what I do. And when one of us goes missing, it touches us all. I hoped Ivan was able to find something. If that old man came up empty-handed, there was nothing to be found.

At the very least, he would be able to take care of Rosaline if the worst was true. *Damn, they haven't even been married a year yet.* I'd had Mira and Anna long before I'd taken on this duty, but looking back, I don't know that I would have married at all if I'd have known what was ahead.

Maybe Miguel was just stuck somewhere without communications. Maybe he was even injured, but fine. Maybe . . . Maybe he was dead, and his soul was in Hell, being tortured by a whole slew of fiends he'd sent back there himself. The lead in my stomach told me just which of those options I truly believed.

I didn't want to think about what Hell was really like. I mean, sure, I tried to catch a glimpse now and then, but that was purely morbid curiosity. I suppose I believe we all have our own personal Hell, full of the things that frighten us the most. Mine, I'm sure, would force me to watch unspeakable things happen to my wife and daughter, over and over again, while I stood there helpless. And there would be zombies. I hate zombies. Yes, I know they're fictional creatures, but so are demons, and we see how that holds true.

Dammit, Miguel, what did you do? This wasn't supposed to happen. Not to him. Not with a new wife, and so many years ahead of him.

Even driving, I can manage to meditate, and I took a few deep breaths to find my center. *The cares of the world pass through me and around me. I am a willow in the wind. I bend and am not broken.* Worry for Miguel would have to wait. I had a client to interview.

From my house to the airport was only about a twenty-minute jaunt up the highway. Convenience was part of the reason I liked it here in Kansas City.

It was urban enough to have all that culture and stuff that people think is so great, and still rural enough that people went out of their way to be courteous and help one another.

And Kansas City, north of the muddy Missouri River, was booming. Sprawling housing developments and retail expansions blossomed on both sides of the six-lane I-29. I saw at least three new hotels, a couple large-scale hardware places, and countless restaurants where there had only been muddy lots a few months ago. *Ooh, hey, they're opening a new Hooters!*

Of course, to punish me for my impure thoughts, the powers that be chose to make me forget my exit was coming right up. I saw the sign about thirty yards too late. "Aw shit!"

My poor truck lurched and groaned in protest as I downshifted faster than recommended and cut across two lanes of traffic. The rumble strip vibrated under my tires and horns blared around me, but I managed to swerve down the exit ramp in a feat of dexterity that impressed even me. "Crap! Sorry . . . sorry . . ." The driver behind me was not so impressed and gave me the finger. I waved an apology and kept my head down, hoping the red light didn't catch me at the bottom of the ramp. I'd rather be safely away from the guy in the Volvo I almost ran over, thank you.

Mira's always lecturing me about road rage and how many crazy people there are in the world. Sadly, she's right. You never know when that guy next to you just found out his wife is cheating on him with the pool boy, or maybe he just got Diet Coke instead of regular at the drive-through. You never know what's going to make someone turn on a fellow human being. And as much as I love my truck, I didn't think she'd stop a bullet.

There are times (usually when I'm having trouble with my compassion for man) that I wonder why I bother helping people. Humans, as a group, aren't known for their inherent goodness. We run the very large gamut from true evil to insignificant pettiness, but as a rule, we're not a kind species.

It is also possible that I am jaded by the population I deal with on a regular basis. I get to see the worst of them—the greedy ones, the vain ones, the ones who reached for just a little more and got their hand caught in the trap. Now, I'm not saying that no one has ever sold his soul for a good cause. But typically, I don't get those folk knocking at my door. Sure, the ones I get are sorry for what they've done, regretful and contrite. But . . . Well, I don't know about you, but I personally think there had to be something wrong with them to entertain the devil's offer to begin with.

So, why do it? Why put myself on the line for people I don't know, and like even less? Because it needs to be done. It's not even a choice for me. A samurai who turns his back on those in need is no better than any other common thug. He should protect the weak and advocate for good over evil. Shirking that duty would be a great act of dishonor. And that's just not who I am.

4

The darkness inside Chino's Sports Bar was an abrupt contrast to the blinding sunlight outside, and I had to blink my eyes for a few moments before they'd adjust. It was fairly busy, for the Monday lunch crowd. I'd counted on that. Businessmen in suits chatted and told dirty jokes over their on-the-company steak lunches. One group of construction workers was loudly cheering on an arena football game at the bar. Three tables in the back were taken up by off-duty security guards from the airport, killing time before or after a shift change. Quiet places are no good for private talks. You need noise to muffle the conversation.

I glanced over the tables, looking for Nelson Kidd. It was a sure bet he'd be in a ball cap and sunglasses. Famous people always think that hides their identity, like Clark Kent with his glasses. Kidd would also be wearing a long-sleeve shirt or jacket, despite the beautiful spring weather. It would hide his mark of shame.

Sure enough, I spotted a man who fit the criteria sitting in the farthest back corner of the restaurant—an older man, with a cap for the local ball team, probably purchased at the airport or hotel gift shop. He wouldn't dare wear his own team's logo, not for this. He had on a sweatshirt and khakis, and he watched the restaurant with short nervous glances but never made eye contact. That was my man.

Waving the hostess off, I headed that way. Mr. Baseball Cap and Shades looked up as I got closer, and despite the dark glasses, I could almost see the wheels of his mind working as he compared this man walking toward him to the description he'd been given. Six foot two? Check. Blond ponytail? Check. Scruffy red beard? Check, and if I didn't shave soon, Mira was gonna get grumpy.

He was still uncertain until I walked up and stuck my hand out to shake. "Mr. Kidd."

"Mr. Dawson." He shook my hand finally, but he still made my name sound like half a question. You know, one of those "Please God, is this really the man I'm waiting for?" sort of questions. I was pretty sure it was the T-shirt that really worried him.

I slid into the empty side of the booth without being invited, then nodded toward his left arm. "Let me see."

He took the time to remove his hat and glasses first, stalling as long as he could. He looked older than he did on his television appearances, the lines on his face carved deeper and longer by stress and constant exposure to the sun. His face looked downright leathery. His hair had more silver strands than blond, but you'd never be able to see it in the bright sunlight. One day, he would look up and have snow-white hair, as though it snuck up on him. It was buzzed into the same crew cut he'd probably had since high school.

My steady gaze seemed to make him uncomfortable. Honestly, that's why I do it. Funny how the soulless always seem afraid to meet another person's gaze, as if they're afraid we can tell, just by looking. Most of the time, I can. It's something in the eyes.

He finally rolled the sleeve of his sweatshirt up, taking care to keep his inner arm turned away from anyone's wandering gaze.

I took firm hold of his wrist so I could get a good look and ignored his meek attempt at a protest. The mark was there, burned stark and black into the skin. It could easily be mistaken for some tribal tattoo, so popular just a few years ago, but I knew better. Sinuous curves led into sharp angles that didn't quite follow the laws of physics. It seemed to ripple as I looked at it, my eyes simply not designed to grasp all they were trying to take in. If I stared at it long enough, I'd end up with a blazing headache. I released him and sat back in the seat.

Some of the sigil I recognized; some of it was new to me. That's not to say I can actually read the demon script, only that I'd encountered similar things before. He was someone's property; one in a herd of cattle, no doubt. His was fairly complex, indicating first the strength of the demon he was bound to, and second the number of convolutions involved in his contract. Kidd must have struck a helluva hard bargain. That tattoo would have hurt like hell, burning in (no pun intended).

"All right, the way this is going to work is you're going to do a lot of talking, and I'm going to do a lot of listening. Then I'm going to do a lot of talking, and you're going to do a lot of listening, okay?"

Kidd only nodded mutely as the perky waitress came by, and he pushed his sleeve down quickly.

"Hi. Can I get you guys started with drinks or an appetizer today? We're having a lunch special on boneless buffalo wings!" Her name tag said BRIT. She looked like a Brit, with bleached blond pigtails and way too much enthusiasm about her menial job.

"A Coke to drink. And I'll have the rib eye, medium rare, with fries." Hey, I had to go to work right after this, and I hadn't eaten yet. Besides, Kidd would be picking up the tab. If I hadn't had to work, I'd have ordered a beer, too. My theory is, if you can see your hand through the beer, it's too light, and Chino's had a great dark ale from their microbrewery.

Waitress Brit jotted it all down, nodding like a bobblehead. "And for your second side?"

"More fries." I'm a simple man. I like French fries.

"And you, sir?" She looked to Kidd expectantly, and he kept his face turned toward the window. I wanted to tell him that the odds of Waitress Brit recognizing him were slim, but who was I to deny a man his delusions of his own fame? After all, I'm a legend in my own mind.

"Just coffee, please. Regular." At the bar, the construction workers broke into raucous cheers, and Kidd flinched.

Waitress Brit didn't seem to notice. "Right, one coffee, wired. I'll be right back!" She bounced off, her pigtails bobbing behind her.

We sat in silence until she brought our drinks, and then I waited longer as Kidd added sugar and cream to his coffee until it turned a nice pale mocha color. "All right. Tell me what happened."

The old ball player stirred his coffee and finally sighed. "Are you a baseball fan, Mr. Dawson?"

"I am. Since I was a kid, actually."

"Then you know me and my career. You are not new to your business, as I understand. I am sure you can already guess what happened. I was getting old. The new players coming in every season were younger, stronger, faster. Arizona was the first team to keep me for more than two months, and the only one to let me do more than warm up in the bull pen. All I ever wanted to do was play ball, and nobody was going to let me anymore." He sipped from his cup.

"One night, I was standing out on the mound after a game, just watching the empty stadium and contemplating whether I would retire or take the bump to the minors. All I could hear was the echo of the grounds crew, already back in the tunnels, and the hum of the lights. It was so still. . . ." For a moment, he was lost in the past. I had seen that look many times, on many faces. "I thought I was alone, but then this man walked out of the visiting dugout. He had on a suit, clean-cut. I just figured he was someone's agent or lawyer. He had that look." Kidd paused there, and I could see a shudder run through him.

"And then he started talking. It was like his voice was piercing right into my skull. Like . . . there aren't any words to describe what it was like." His eyes, when he finally looked at me, were wide and shocky.

Even now, years after he must have made his bargain, that memory threatened to unhinge him.

"Drink your coffee, Mr. Kidd." I pressed the cup into his hands, and he clutched it like a lifeline. "I know what they sound like." I had spent more time conversing with demons in the past four years than I wanted to think about. The voices stayed with me long after I banished their physical forms. It was like an oil slick in the mind, a sickly rainbow taint gliding over crystal clear water. No amount of showering would get rid of it, but I'd tried, in the beginning.

"You ever just suddenly realize that someone isn't human, even though that should be impossible?" He shook his head, dropping his gaze again. "Yeah . . . I suppose you have."

"And he made you an offer you couldn't refuse." It's cliché, yes, but it's amazing how often it applies.

Kidd seemed to think about that before shaking his head again. "No. I could have refused. I mean, that's what free will is about, right? There's always a choice? I chose what I did with full knowledge of what I was doing. At the time, I thought, hey, I'm not a religious man, so what does it really matter? And my game came back, and we went to the series and it was everything I dreamed it would be."

"So what changed?" Normally, they came to me when they were sure they were dying and only had Hell to look forward to. I get a lot of cancer patients.

"My daughter had a baby about seven months ago. My first grandchild. A little boy." He smiled faintly, and I had to return it. What can I say—my daughter is the light of my life. I understood completely. Kidd's smile faded, though, quickly. "He screams when I try to hold him. He's inconsolable. My wife keeps trying to tell me that's just how babies are, but . . . He knows, doesn't he, Mr. Dawson? Just a baby, but he knows."

The conversation paused as Waitress Brit brought my lunch and refilled Kidd's coffee, though he hadn't had more than a sip. I cut into my steak to make sure they'd cooked it right—I loathe overcooked steak—but it was perfect and red in the center. "Yeah . . . he knows," I said, talking around my first bite. "Children and animals, Mr. Kidd. They're not fooled by all the masks and shields. They know. If it's any consolation, by the time he's about fifteen or so, he'll be just as jaded as the rest of us, and it won't matter anymore." The fries were good—hot and seasoned perfectly. I didn't even bother with ketchup.

Kidd watched me with a dazed look as I wolfed down the food. I knew the feeling. Once upon a time, I couldn't have eaten while discussing these things, either. Now . . . I'd grown a bit more practical.

"So, now you have decided that you don't want to go through with it. You want your soul back. Realize, once we start this, there's no going back and you only get one shot." He nodded, gazing deeply into his coffee. "Here comes the part where I do all the talking, so listen carefully."

I nibbled on my food as I talked. I'd given this speech before. I think it's even gotten better over the years. "I have a wife, Mr. Kidd, and a five-year-old daughter. My wife runs her own small bookstore, and my daughter is starting kindergarten in the fall. I tell you all this so you understand my motivations for what I'm going to say next."

Although he still wouldn't look right at me, he was actually listening. You can tell when someone isn't.

"My base rate is a hundred grand, paid up front. And it goes up from there if things get sticky. This is nonnegotiable." Before you start thinking I'm a total dick, let me tell you that it is only nonnegotiable for people who *have* the money to begin with. I wouldn't turn down someone who couldn't pay, but those who can . . . well, they can share the wealth.

Unfortunately, too many of my recent clients fell into the "no pot to piss in" category. Kidd's hundred would be just enough to pay off the last round of hospital bills and get us back on an even keel.

"I charge money so that I can put a third of it in an account to support my wife and child when I get killed. Make no mistake, I will die one of these days. It may be tomorrow; it may be ten years from now, but it will happen." Well, ideally that's what I would do with it. In practice, most of my fees tended to go to cause number two.

"Another third goes into an account to cover my medical bills, because this job comes with crappy health insurance, and I *will* get hurt. I have yet to be challenged to a game of tiddlywinks.

"The rest goes into maintaining my weapons and armor, because that stuff isn't common, or cheap." I sopped up some of the steak juices with my fries. Damn, those were good fries.

"What I want you to understand, and I mean *really* understand, is that you are asking me to risk my life because you made a mistake out of greed or vanity or pride. If I die, my wife is a widow, and my daughter is fatherless, all because of you. Your job, over the next twenty-four hours, is to think that over real hard. You have to decide if you can live with yourself after something like that." I wiped my mouth and tossed the napkin on the table. "I'll call you tomorrow afternoon to get your decision."

Waitress Brit popped up with that "Do you want dessert" grin on her face, and I just shook my head as I slid out of the booth. I swear, her pigtails actually wilted. She was crushed. "Bring him the check." I glanced to Kidd. "And you'd better tip well."

The clock above the bar said one thirty. I had to be at work by two.

As I passed the bar, I noticed the construction workers had vacated, and the television had gone from arena football to the weather. A round fellow in glasses gestured wildly at a map with arrows all over it. "This looks like the largest storm front in the last ten years. We can expect high winds, damaging hail and lightning, and possible tornadic activity, starting early Friday."

Damn. That was going to ruin Mom's party.

The bright sun seemed determined to make a liar out of the weatherman, and I felt compelled to whistle a jaunty tune as I walked to my truck. Then I noticed a man standing by the back bumper, obviously waiting for me, and my musical urges died between one step and the next.

He stood up straighter as I neared, but it didn't hide that he was a good five inches shorter than I. He was clean-cut and baby faced, and his gray suit probably cost as much as my house payment. He seemed young, and when I checked his shoes, sure enough he was wearing loafers. I always assume people do that when they're not old enough to tie their shoes yet. The thought made me smirk to myself, and the man gave me a puzzled look.

"Mr. Dawson." He offered his hand, which I ignored, and a plastic smile, which I did not return.

"Don't lean on my truck."

"Sir?"

"Don't lean on my truck." I proceeded to do that very thing. "I don't know you, so you don't get to touch her." Okay yeah, I made the first hostile move. But he looked like a lawyer. I hate lawyers.

"Ah." He eyed the truck warily but took a step away, wiping his hand on his trousers as if she'd contaminated him somehow. *Losing points left and right, my boy.* "My name is Travis Verelli. I represent the interests of Mr. Kidd." He offered me his business card, which I took and read carefully. Ugh, he was worse than a lawyer. He was an agent.

"And is there a reason you're lurking out here by my truck, Mr. Verelli?" I had to squash the urge to call him something snide. Junior and Skippy were the two favorites at the moment.

"Mr. Kidd asked that I wait outside while he met with you."

"Good puppy. What do you want now, a treat?"

The smile he was fighting to keep wavered at the edges. "I would like to ask you to leave my client alone."

That earned him a raised brow. "And does Mr. Kidd know you're out here asking me that?"

His smile turned into a distasteful grimace. "Mr. Kidd is well aware of my opinions of his . . . situation."

I crossed my arms over my chest and shook my head in amusement. "And just what do you grasp as his 'situation'?"

His eyes hardened, and I mentally tacked another five years onto his age. "My client is no longer a young man, Mr. Dawson. And at times I believe he is . . . confused about certain things. This would make it easy for someone unscrupulous to take advantage of him, and I intend to prevent that."

I couldn't help but snicker. "Let me get this straight. You think he's going senile, and you are protecting him from the big bad world. Doesn't hurt that your income is protected, too, so long as no one knows the old man's gone batty."

"I have my client's best interests in mind. You, on the other hand . . ." A bit of petty triumph gleamed in his eyes. I wanted to smack him. "I have done some investigating into your background. I have connections, Mr. Dawson. You have minimal discernible employment for the last four years, and yet you consistently deposit large sums of money into several bank accounts. You have been hired repeatedly as a 'security consultant' by people who have had their own security forces for years, and you seldom remain on the payroll longer than a month. It leaves me to wonder just what services you are performing."

"I give windows a sparkling, streak-free shine." I said it with a straight face, and he glowered.

"I have been dragged all over the country in the last few months, dealing with Mr. Kidd's . . . we'll call it a dilemma. I do not now, nor will I ever, believe these delusions of his, and if you will not stop feeding them, I will be forced to take legal action." He said it with the same menace I might use when threatening to run a sword through someone's guts.

Did I mention I don't like being threatened? "You take whatever action you like. I'm doing nothing illegal, and you're going to make me late for work. Good day, Mr. Verelli." I slid into the truck and slammed the door before he could answer. *Slimy little weasel.* He'd piss himself if he ever saw the things I'd seen.

I gave him a finger-fluttering wave as I pulled out of the parking lot, and I could feel his scowl all the way down the block.

5

I had to walk seven blocks from the designated employee parking lot just to get to work. I'd be so much happier once they finished the new parking garage, but that project had languished in limbo since the early freeze last fall. I personally believed the contractors had made off with the money, never to be seen again. Management kept insisting that construction would resume in the summer, but in the meantime, we were left with a roofless shell of a garage, piles of rusting construction supplies, and rivers of yellow clay mud every time it rained. When it wasn't raining, the wind blew clouds of dust into all the shops, coating everything in a fine yellow powder. I mostly watched the weather to see if I was going to be slogging through muck or eating grit on any given day. So much for Sierra Vista, the latest and trendiest in outdoor shopping meccas.

Don't ask me why a shopping mall in Kansas City, Missouri, was named Sierra Vista when there isn't a mountain in sight for hundreds of miles. I wasn't consulted. I suppose the faux sandstone façades and orange clay tile roofs could be reminiscent of a quaint Hispanic village. Y'know—one with a Starbucks on the corner and a Japanese steakhouse at the end of the block. I passed a day spa, a Victoria's Secret, two competing comedy clubs, and the garish neon sign proclaiming the newest restaurant to be named Moonlight & Roses. The hot pink moon and violently purple roses were bright enough to sear through eyelids, even in the daylight. I was never going to get the ghastly sight out of my head.

Even though it was an early Monday afternoon and school didn't get out for summer for another four weeks, the place was crawling with teenagers. I had to wonder if their parents knew they weren't in school. That's the father in me talking. It's an attitude I'm cultivating in preparation for Annabelle's teen years.

The music from It, the place where I worked, pulsed through the soles of my feet long before I passed the chain bookstore and overpriced ice-cream shop next door. The sign propped out on the sidewalk proclaimed IT'S SPRING CLEARANCE! and I cringed inwardly. Just as I expected, the small store was packed solid. I squeezed my way through the door, nodding slight apologies to the tattooed and pierced customers in my way.

The roar of confined life-forms echoed off the ductwork in the unfinished ceiling above, tripling the noise level in an instant. People were stuffed into every conceivable space between the already cramped clothing racks. Strobe lights and black lights flickered everywhere, promising headaches to the unprepared. Behind the artfully arranged display merchandise, the black brick walls were splashed with fluorescent blobs of color, glowing happily under the strange lighting.

"Hey, old dude!" Kristyn's voice carried over the heavy metal music somehow, and I realized she was actually standing on the counter to see over the crowd. Her hair was dyed raven black again, with streaks of hot pink fading into a deep purple. Two days ago, it had been green and blue.

"Nice hair, Kristyn!" The music thumping through the speakers changed to "Voodoo Child," and I waved to whoever was deejaying in acknowledgment. We all have our theme songs, and that had been deemed mine because they knew I liked Hendrix. (I suspect it was also the oldest music they could think of. Most of the kids I worked with were too young to remember the eighties, let alone Jimi Hendrix.)

By hook or by crook, I skirted the ever-rotating tower of body jewelry (for the piercing of your choice) and worked my way to the back and the relative sanity of the break room. I lingered only long enough to dump my wallet into my employee locker and grab my lanyard with my name tag and assorted snarky buttons. The name tag, too, said OLD DUDE. At thirty-two, I was the oldest employee in the district. Even Kristyn, ostensibly my boss, came in a few years shy of thirty.

Between the back room and the front counter, I handled three questions on prices, and one on fashion (which is *such* a bad idea, trust me). Abe was manning the stereo at the back of the store and trying to keep the shoplifters from making off with our CDs. I stopped long enough to have him nod me toward a couple he was keeping a particular eye on, then moved on. I finally arrived at the register to find that Kristyn had made a new friend. The dark lanky teen gave me a sullen look as he leaned against the wall.

"Rook for you to train, old dude." Kristyn gave me a wicked grin. "This is Paulo. Paulo, this is old dude."

I stuck out my hand to shake. I'm not totally devoid of manners. Paulo took it, glaring at me from under a mop of shaggy black hair and squeezing harder than was strictly necessary. Ah, so that's how it was going to be. I held his grip, sizing him up. There was a distinct lack of piercings and tattoos about him, unusual for employees of It. He was of a height with me, all lean whipcord muscle, but there was no tone to it. Most likely he was a runner; maybe he lifted weights in a high school gym class. But he didn't move like a fighter. I wasn't worried. "Nice to meet you, Paulo."

"*Encantada.*" It was said with a sneer of sarcasm, but the accent of a native Spanish speaker. I made a mental note to have Mira brush me up on Spanish cuss words. Never hurts to know.

"Now, don't let his age fool you," Kristyn advised Paulo. "Old dude is a baaaaad man. He works security consulting on the side. All kung fu and stuff." Well, at least she *thought* that's what I did on the side. It was as good an explanation as any for why I left town abruptly and came home in bandages on a regular basis. I even had permits and licenses to make it all official, thanks to Ivan.

If Paulo was impressed, it didn't show.

Kristyn was rapidly getting swamped, and I slid into the register next to her. "I didn't know we were hiring."

"Chelsea no-called again today, and I'd had it. Then Paulo walked in. It was like destiny!" My punk-haired boss gave me a cheeky grin, and I could only chuckle.

"Does he at least have some retail experience?" I hated training rookies from scratch, and she knew it.

"Nah," she said, and my heart sank. "But he's hot, and that's what the girls want." True enough, our young, brooding Latino was getting more than his share of admiring looks from the panting throng.

"If being hot is a hiring requisite, how the hell do I still have a job?"

Kristyn gave me a wink as she handed a customer's card back. "You're hot in an old-hippie kinda way."

"Gee, thanks." I smirked, bagging up some purchases to hand across the counter. "You do realize I'm about thirty years too young to have actually been a hippie, right?"

"Bah, hippie's in the soul."

Well, if hippie was the worst thing in my soul, I was doing pretty darned good.

Between the two of us, we managed to clear out the mob, one rabid customer at a time. By the time the crowd thinned, the other five employees had arrived for the monthly employee meeting.

Chris—a gargantuan teen whose six-foot-oh-my-God height allowed him to see most of the store at a glance—took over the register while the rest of us gathered around Kristyn. Paulo found a clothing rack to sulk against. I was starting to wonder whether he could stand up unaided. Maybe the sullen slouch was a medical condition.

The first announcement was the hiring of Paulo, prefaced by Kristyn's assertion that "Chelsea will not be joining us again for the rest of her life. She pissed me off for the last time." The dark boy gave everyone the same indifferent glower by way of greeting. Good to know it wasn't just me.

"Spring Clearance will run through Sunday, and on that day we'll have an extra ten percent employee discount tacked on." Kristyn shuffled through a stack of e-mails, while the kids murmured amongst themselves. I eyed some of the clothing racks myself. You could never have too many T-shirts with witty sayings such as SOULS TASTE LIKE PEEPS. That one always made me laugh, but I'm pretty sure some of my clients wouldn't have shared my amusement.

"And Sierra Vista management has asked me to review storm procedures with you, since we're hitting tornado season again, and they're predicting a bad front moving in this weekend." Everyone groaned. "C'mon, guys, I gotta do this. Cut me some slack." Kristyn gave a long-suffering sigh, and the rabble quieted.

"*In case of a tornado warning, which means that a tornado has actually been sighted on the ground—*"

"The exits are herehereherehere anywhere!" The kids cracked up as Abe channeled Aladdin's genie and Kristyn swatted him with her papers.

"Okay fine, smart-ass, you do it." She shoved the e-mails into his hands.

Abe cleared his throat solemnly and proceeded to read the instructions in what was possibly the worst British accent I have ever heard. "*Please direct customers to the designated storm shelter areas, and lock the doors to your businesses. All public restrooms and storage hallways are to be considered storm shelters. Once there—*"

"Put your head between your knees and kiss your ass good-bye." Leanne tossed in her two cents that time, and Kristyn threw up her hands.

"I tried. If you all get blown to Oz, it isn't my fault."

The meeting was dismissed to a chorus of "I'll get you, my pretty!" Poor Kristyn. She's actually a good manager, but riding herd on that bunch of miscreants was nearly impossible when they were all together. Such were the hazards of a relaxed work environment.

She caught my eye and gave me a tired smile. "You'll take care of them, old dude, right?"

"I always do."

For the record, upon my death, I want to be nominated for sainthood. I'm not Catholic. I'm not even sure I'm Christian. But it might do the church a world of good to admit a beer-drinking, brawling, hippie samurai into their ranks. And after I spent the entire afternoon trying to train Paulo on a register, getting no more than a grunt or two from him in response, I damn well deserved some recognition. Thankfully, Kristyn shooed Paulo out the door at six, and after that, my evening was infinitely better.

As Mira predicted, I wound up working past my shift, helping Kristyn and Leanne with the mad clearance rush. Believe it or not, I like my job. I get to listen to all kinds of music, see interesting people, and I don't have to wear a tie or cut my hair. It's perfect!

No one blinks if I have to take off with no notice, and I can usually give them at least a day or two. They're used to my coming back on crutches or otherwise injured, and it's not really a physically taxing job when I'm limping around. And the kids, bless their little hearts, believe every lie I tell them about what

I've been doing. Nothing like a bunch of teenagers to swallow your BS story hook, line, and sinker.

And if I am being wholly honest, I don't do well taking orders from people I don't respect. That particular tendency of mine tends to limit my long-term employment options. I have an extensive list of "You just didn't work out" dismissals to prove it, not to mention that a BA in philosophy doesn't open a lot of doors. Yeah, I had strikes against me from all directions.

On my break, I borrowed the store phone to call and check on my girls. It was a nightly tradition to tell Annabelle good night as Mira tucked her in.

"When are you coming home, Daddy?" I could hear the sleepiness in her little voice. She was fighting to stay awake even now.

My heart always breaks when she says things like that. "You'll be asleep when I get home, button. Daddy has to work."

"Can you stay home tomorrow? I miss you."

"I'll see what I can do, sweetheart. You go to sleep. Have sweet dreams." She passed the phone to Mira. "Has she been good tonight?"

"Of course. She helped with the smudging. Then we had a tea party with her stuffed animals."

I smiled wistfully. "Wish I could have seen that. Anything else of import happen?"

"We got a notice from the hospital." My stomach dropped. It definitely wasn't her "good news" voice. "The insurance company denied that last claim again."

I sighed and rubbed my temples, a faint headache

springing up. "I was afraid they were going to do that. What's the damage?"

"A little more than two grand."

I felt like banging my head against the wall. Damn bureaucracy. "Well, at least we have it. I'll just pick up a few more shifts here for the next couple months to make up for it. I'm sorry, baby."

"Can't be helped. We'll find a way." That's my girl, ever the optimist. "I'll leave dinner in the microwave for you."

"Thanks, baby." I worked because I had to, but sometimes I felt I was missing my daughter's life.

"Hey, old dude. You still need Saturday off?" Kristyn was poring over next week's schedule as I came back out of the break room to straighten the shelves.

"Yeah, it's my mom's birthday. I'm a dead man if I don't show up."

"You get her a present yet?"

I eyed her suspiciously. "You been talking to Mira?"

She grinned under her punk bangs. "Would I do that?"

"Yes."

"You still don't have a present, do you?"

"I'll do it! I'll do it tomorrow." Or the next day, maybe. It was only Monday, for Pete's sake. I had until Saturday.

We closed at ten. I didn't leave the store until almost eleven. There was one car I didn't recognize in the parking lot, a dark-colored Escort, and I waited for the girls to get in their cars before I took off. I could see the featureless silhouette of the driver, just sitting there, and though I couldn't tell if it was a man or a woman, I operated on the assumption that my own male presence was enough to ward off trouble.

Kristyn laughed at me. "It's not like every strange car is a serial killer waiting to pounce, old dude."

I only shrugged and stood next to my truck until they pulled out onto the street. Sure, the odds of Jack the Ripper jumping out of that particular car to wreak havoc were slim. But slim isn't impossible, and an honorable man takes care of those around him. If I didn't do it, I wouldn't be who I am.

I turned out toward the highway, and happened to see the Escort pulling out of the parking lot, too. See? It was just an employee of another store going home for the night like the rest of us.

My usual route to and from work involves minimal highway exposure. There are several quite serviceable back roads that point toward home, and I don't have to deal with the traffic. No one in his right mind would cruise the steep hills in the dark when he could buzz along at light speed on the freeway. I guess no one ever pointed out that the joy is in the journey, not the destination.

When I glanced back to see another car leave the highway right behind me, I was understandably surprised. Encountering another set of headlights on this stretch at this time of night was unusual, to say the least.

Mostly out of mild curiosity, I kept checking my rearview mirror, waiting to see where it turned off.

There were many residential additions on the way, and I kept expecting the car to duck into one of them at any moment.

Instead, it seemed intent on catching up to me. And if I considered my speed on the dark, narrow road unwise, this guy was downright suicidal. I watched with ever-growing concern as the car continued to edge up on my back bumper without regard for anyone's personal safety.

I let up on the gas, thinking that he'd pass me if he was in that much of a hurry. Wrong idea.

At first, I didn't understand why I felt a sudden shudder through my steering wheel. Only on the second thud did I realize there wasn't something wrong with my truck. The bastard behind me was actually ramming my bumper! "What the fu—" My teeth cracked together as he hit me again, and I gripped the steering wheel tightly to stay on the narrow road. "Are you out of your fucking mind?"

Seemingly in answer, the small dark car nudged my truck again, and I fought the wheel to keep the front end pointed south. Tree branches scraped down the side of the truck and I felt the loose soil on the side of the road give way. I yanked hard on the wheel, swerving into the other lane to avoid the ditch. "Buddy, if you dent my truck . . ." What the hell was this asshole's problem? With one hand, I reached into the door well for my knife and laid it on the seat beside me.

I know, they always say don't get out of the car in a road-rage incident, but I'd be damned if I let this guy run me off the road, then sit there unarmed, waiting for him to come back with a gun or something.

There was one little lonely stop sign out in the middle of god-awful nowhere. As I barreled toward it, I frantically begged anyone else out driving in the night to be anywhere else. Fate or whatever was with me, and there was no one there as I blew past the sign without stopping. All four tires left the road as we jumped the top of the steep hill.

As close as he was, and with the headlights glaring, I couldn't see the plate number. Even the color eluded me, in the absence of working streetlights. *Would it kill the city to put some lights out here?* The streets ahead were better lit, however, and I sped up, anxious to get the car behind me into the light. I most definitely did not want to stop out here in the dark with no witnesses.

Of course, getting to better lit streets involved staying *on* the street in the first place. The next hit almost put me in the ditch again despite my best efforts. If I could just make it to the top of the next hill, there would be people below—and lights. And maybe cameras at the intersection to get this jackassery on tape.

Whoever the guy was, he was obviously not ready for his close-up. As we crested the last hill, the brightly lit intersection below us, he whipped into the oncoming lane and zoomed around me. The light turned red, and he barreled through it to the tune of honking horns, leaving me to slam on the brakes and skid to a stop. There was no license plate on the back of the little car, but it was definitely a dark blue Ford Escort. *The one from the parking lot?*

The light cycled slow enough that I was almost done shaking by the time it went green again. I couldn't even think of any suitable curse words, I was so unnerved. *Freakin' drunk sonsabitches.* Damn high school or college kids, probably, thinking it was some great prank. Little jerks were going to kill somebody like that. I thought about calling the police, but it seemed futile without a plate number. Finally, I resolved to call my brother-the-cop in the morning, and let it go at that.

I'd be lying if I said I wasn't watching behind me as I drove on toward home. Last thing I needed was some little punks egging my house or breaking my windows or something. Not to mention I'm pretty sure scaring the hell out of Mira would be hazardous to their continued well-being. But there was no one back there, and I arrived without incident.

Climbing out of the truck in the garage, I immediately went to inspect for damage. The corner of the license plate was a little bent, but that could have happened long before. Other than that, there wasn't a mark on her. "Atta girl." I patted the fender affectionately, some of the tension going out of my shoulders. At least my baby wasn't hurt.

The house was dark when I got inside, and it smelled of sage and enchiladas. It figured that I'd work late. She hadn't told me it was enchilada night.

Mira, the most perfect woman in the world, left me a plate in the microwave. Her enchiladas were even better reheated, and I wolfed them down as quickly and quietly as possible, lurking in front of the bay window in the living room. Nothing stirred outside; no cars, no people, nothing. Somewhere, there was an owner of a small dark car who was no doubt congratulating himself on giving some perfect stranger the scare of his life.

I put the plate in the dishwasher, then did my usual house walk before bed, checking the doors and windows. Stopping to eyeball the street again, I watched one lonely car trundle up our block until it reached the end and turned out of sight. It wasn't the mysterious car that followed me from the highway; I recognized it as belonging to a house a few blocks down. The light came on briefly in the neighbor's yard to our rear, and I heard her mumbling to her dog to hurry up his business. Blocks away, another dog started barking, to be silenced by its disgruntled owner. On the surface, things were as they should be.

As I walked down the hall toward the bedroom, I heard the softest of sounds from Mira's sanctuary.

While I got the former closet as a haven, Mira had claimed the spare bedroom and converted it into her own little hideaway. The spare bed was shoved negligently into the corner and buried under piles of books, mostly research on things Mira wanted for the shop. Bundles of dried herbs dangled from hooks in the ceiling (an entire weekend's work for me, to get those just how she wanted them), giving the room a pungent, earthy smell. Only Mira knew what they all were, and their purposes. To me, they just looked like dead weeds. A wreath of grapevines, woven into a pentacle, hung on the wall, and beneath it rested a small altar, all the implements of Mira's faith set in their precise places.

Frowning, I poked my head in.

The candles were lit, one for each cardinal direction, lending a cheerful glow to the hardwood floor. The air in the room felt heavy, like the thickness before a lightning storm. A large metal basin sat in the center of the floor, filled with some kind of milky liquid. And on the far side, Mira sat huddled, arms wrapped around her knees and her face buried as she sobbed quietly.

"Mira?" Alarm sent my heart thudding into my throat again, and I stepped into the room, only to stop short when she flung her hand out toward me.

"Don't! Don't break the circle!" Hurriedly, she wiped tears from her face, crawling back to the basin. "You have to see this."

I moved as close as I dared. Somewhere between us was a thin film of Mira's own will, holding in her magic or keeping foreign magic out (I was never quite sure about the mechanics of it). I craned my head to see what she was working with.

"I was setting protective spells for Miguel and Rosaline, and it occurred to me that I could try a scrying, see if I could locate him." Mira's voice held steady as if she hadn't just been crying her heart out, her hands making quick and efficient movements over the bowl of milky liquid. Ever practical, that's my girl. "Here, watch."

The flickering candlelight made vision difficult, and I strained my eyes to see what Mira saw. The liquid in the bowl—heavily salted water, if I had to guess—swirled in response to my wife's graceful gestures, clouds of white following her hands like a magnet.

Once she had them swirling in a very nice whirlpool, she withdrew her hands, and the water took on a life of its own.

At first, it was no more than streams of white through the water, caught up in the vortex momentum. But gradually, the lines began to diverge and congregate, solidifying into something like the reverse of a black-and-white movie. The first thing I recognized was the shape of a man, and as it grew clearer, sharper, I was able to recognize Miguel in negative, his black hair stark white in the reversed image.

But what was he doing? It looked at first as if he were going through katas, the same exercises I did every morning to practice my fighting skills. But Miguel wasn't a martial artist, and as far as I knew, he didn't work through forms like I did.

He lunged with the weapon in his hand and chopped hard to the right. *That's not his machete*, I thought, and I leaned as close as I could to look. In fact, it looked suspiciously like a baseball bat. *What the hell?* No one in his right mind used a nonbladed weapon unless he had no choice.

Next, he spun to the left, aiming a low block at some invisible enemy. Then his left shoulder jerked back in response to a blow I could not see. Before he could bring the weapon around again, something hit him hard enough to spin him in a circle. The bat went flying out of his hand and out of view. The grimace of pain was visible on the tiny dark face, even in the dim light. This was no kata, and I was only getting half the scene.

"Why can't I see what's there with him?"

"I only have something of his. The salt in the bowl is bound to the salt in his body." Glancing away from the disturbing images playing out in the water, I saw her fidget with something tiny in one hand.

Miguel's negative image doubled in half, taking some kind of blow to the stomach, and then dropped to his knees. The next strike came to the back of his neck. I knew it even before his body sprawled on the ground, simply because that is what I would do to a kneeling opponent. For long moments, he lay there; the salt-image wasn't precise enough to be able to see if he was breathing. Finally, one arm jerked upward at an awkward angle.

"Is this happening right now?"

Mira shook her head, eyes fixed on the basin. "No, it hasn't changed in the last two hours. This is just the last thing I can see before he was taken beyond my sight." *Being dragged*, I realized. Whatever had taken him down was slowly dragging the body off . . . somewhere. "Beyond your sight. Dead?"

"I don't know. I can't see any more. Something just . . . ends it." The salt abruptly dissipated, the basin clouding over into murky water. The item in her hand dropped free, clattering across the floor. It crossed the barrier of her magic circle and came to rest against my foot. A wooden bead; I recognized it from a choker Miguel always wore.

Mira curled up again, hiding her face against her knees, and I immediately crossed the broken circle to gather her into my arms. She wrapped her arms around me and held me as tightly as she could, shaking. "Shh . . . You did good, baby. You did real good."

Her skin was ice-cold. I could feel it through the thin fabric of my shirt. God, how many hours had she been sitting here, just watching that horrible image replay into infinity and holding that thread of magic as it drained her strength? And I, like a jerk, stopped to eat dinner in the kitchen first. "You shouldn't have done this. . . . It wasn't worth this, baby."

"We had t-t-to know." One small sob shook her; then she took a deep breath to gather herself, just as I knew she would. "Are you going to tell Rosaline?"

I looked at the bowl of salted water and shook my head. "No. We don't know that he's dead, and . . . there's no need for her to know this." Hell, I wished Mira didn't know it. "Come on, let's get you to bed."

I got her to her feet with some urging, then scooped her up into my arms. She didn't even protest, providing evidence of the incredible exhaustion caused by her efforts. I got her tucked into the bed with some extra blankets, but she still shivered visibly. "Check on Anna p-p-please?"

In her room, Annabelle was sprawled in her big-girl bed in one of those positions only kids and cats can sleep in. I tucked her in and kissed her forehead before returning to Mira in our bedroom.

She barely stirred as I undressed and crawled into bed beside her, but the moment I was under the covers she turned to snuggle tightly against me. Her entire body was almost frozen, and I pressed her close to take advantage of my body heat. Big magic takes a lot out of you, or so I'm told. She'd be freezing and exhausted for hours.

I kissed her forehead. "Go to sleep, baby."

She was probably asleep before the words left my mouth. I lay awake a little longer, just listening to her breathing in the dark. After a while, I could swear our hearts beat in unison. The house did its nightly creaking and groaning around us. Down the hall, I could hear Annabelle mumbling in her sleep. She gets that from me.

My big secret—probably not that well kept—was that I hated Mira's magic. The passive spells were one thing. The protective stuff on the house, some hocus-pocus on my armor, was simple stuff. It lay in wait to be triggered. But the active spells, such as the scrying she'd done tonight, drained so much out of her.

If I hadn't come home, how long would she have held that circle closed? There were horror stories, things I'd gleaned from Ivan and others, of magical addicts, casting and casting until their life was literally drained away into their craft. I didn't think Mira would go that far, but I worried. I never wanted her to sacrifice so much for me. I wasn't worth it.

Regardless of what I'd seen in Mira's salt scrying, there was nothing I could do for Miguel at this exact moment. And with a job on the horizon, I would need all the rest I could get. But oh how I dreaded sleep.

The dream came like it always does. Well, not always, but a good seventy-five percent of my nights are spent fighting old battles.

I'm not sure where I was. It was dark. It's always

dark in my dreams. Snow crunched under my boots, and I could smell pine needles. Maybe I was back with the president again, my blood draining into the soil of Camp David.

I didn't feel injured, though, just cold. And everything was so quiet—quiet enough that I could hear the breathing to my right. The breaths were large, pumped through massive lungs. I knew those breaths. I'd felt them on my face, over my chest. And if they got that close again, the pain would follow soon after. I reached for my katana to find my hip bare. I was unarmed.

"I know you're there." My voice echoed as if I were inside a jar—or a cave maybe. I'd never fought underground, but who said dreams had to make sense?

I was answered by a low rumbling growl, distinctive in pitch and tone. It's the one sound in the world that makes my guts turn to water and my legs go all quivery. I turned to keep it in front of me—or where I thought was in front of me. I couldn't get my bearings in the all-consuming blackness.

"Just get it over with. I don't like playing games." It did, though. I knew it just as surely as I knew what waited out there in the dark. It would play with me, even after it got its claws on me. It would toss me in the air and bat me around like a cat with a mouse.

The growl came again from the front, but the attack came from the rear as I had known it would. Even knowing it, I couldn't turn fast enough; I couldn't strike hard enough. The red eyes and silver claws seemed to float from the endless night, and swept toward me in a beautiful and deadly arc. And there was nowhere for me to go when the Yeti struck home.

To my credit, I no longer lurch from bed yelling and waking the whole house up, so my eyes merely popped open, following the slow spin of the ceiling fan as my heart pounded in my ears. In her sleep, Mira snuggled close, perhaps sensing my distress, but when she found my skin sweat-soaked, she frowned faintly.

"Shhh . . . Sleep, baby. It's okay." That seemed to be all the reassurance she needed, and the creases on her brow smoothed. For my part, I lay awake for another hour, counting revolutions of the fan and waiting to see if the Yeti would pay me another visit.

The night officially sucked.

6

The cannonball landing in the middle of my bed announced dawn's arrival. Annabelle giggled, proud of herself. "Mommy, come turn cartoons on for me!"

Keep in mind, my daughter is quite capable of manipulating the television on her own. I'm pretty sure she could program the DVR. But it is always more fun to have Mommy or Daddy do it for her.

Although she could barely keep her feet, Mira slid out of bed before I was fully awake, and my girls disappeared down the hallway. I struggled out of my short nap, intent on at least trying to help Mira with breakfast this morning.

Pulling on a pair of loose sweats, I grabbed a ratty T-shirt and shambled my way out through the kitchen. Mira's eyes were ringed with dark circles, but she threatened me with a spatula when I tried to go near the stove. "Out. I have this."

I debated for several long moments before relenting. If she said she was all right, then she must be all right. I kissed her gently, and then Anna, before I headed out to the backyard. The cold dew on my bare feet served to wake me up quite nicely. Of course, it was a thousand times better than the subzero midwestern winter we'd just passed, so I wasn't about to complain.

The sun was barely up high enough to shine over

our neighbor's privacy fence, casting my long shadow across the yard. I kept my face to the light but closed my eyes as I set about going through my morning katas. It allowed me to feel the warmth as it seeped into my stiff muscles, feel the life flowing into my limbs without the distraction of sight.

I could do every kata I knew without thought, simply moving through the forms for the exercise, but that wasn't my preference. Each gesture, each step had a purpose and a function. The graceful wave of my hand here could snap bone at speed. This step to the left would block a low kick and bring me inside an opponent's guard. Each movement was at once beautiful and potentially lethal. Something like that should be contemplated. Before a person does something he should always have a full awareness of his capabilities and where his actions might lead.

I follow the *bushido*, the Japanese code of honor and conduct dating back to the thirteenth century and possibly before. The samurai believed in loyalty, frugality, mastery of oneself and one's art, and most important, honor. You might wonder how in the world one comes to call himself a modern samurai.

Well, I wasn't always the fine upstanding member of society you see today. I had a temper, as a child. Oh, who am I kidding? I still do. But at fifteen, it was fueled by all the usual teenage angst, the slings and arrows of a misspent youth. I traveled with a pack of like-minded degenerates and malcontents, and we left destruction and violence in our wake. I wasted more nights than I like to think about, blitzed on whatever

drug we could easily get our hands on, gleefully causing mayhem in the name of whatever entitlement we
felt we had. I was headed down that long road that so
many travel and very few escape.

The best thing that ever happened to me was getting arrested for chucking cinder blocks through business windows. Sure, you might say I was a juvenile,
and therefore pretty much untouchable, but you didn't
grow up in my little Missouri town. They still believed
in straps behind the woodshed back then.

There was no getting out of it. The cops caught me
red-handed while my supposed friends bailed out
over the back fence. I remember standing there in the
flashing blue lights, fists clenched, ready to take on the
world simply because it existed. These days, a kid like
that would get shot, but I grew up in a different time. It
probably saved my life.

The second-best thing to happen was coming before
Judge Carter, a staunch advocate of alternative punish-
ments. It was his idea to stick me in a court-mandated
martial arts class, saying it would teach me discipline
and control. (His opponents insisted it would teach me
only a more efficient way to cause havoc, and he re-
tired under pressure shortly thereafter. I still send him
a Christmas card every year.)

I hated him, at the time. I hated the class. I hated
the sensei, and all the other clean-cut, bright-eyed
students. I sulked my way through, feeling they were
lucky I even showed up. Any effort on my part was
just gravy.

While I would like to tell you there was a tiny little

Asian man in my life, a Mr. Miyagi to set me on my path, there wasn't. Instead, I had Carl. Carl Bledsoe was as large and as black as they come. As a teenager, I had to crane my neck upward to look into his face, and he seemed an immovable mountain of solid obsidian. As an adult, I still do, and he still is. Every once in a while, I go spar with him and get my ass handed to me. I'm getting closer to beating him, though. Maybe someday I will, when he's old and in a wheelchair or something. (Hell, he'll probably just run over my spine with it.)

He worked out in a cut-off sweatshirt and Gi pants, his thighs as big around as my waist, and his biceps bulging like cantaloupes about to burst. Back then, I had no doubt in my mind that he could squash me like a bug and laugh while doing it. He told me so himself. Trust me—he cut me no slack. If I wasn't on the ball, I paid for it. But amidst the sparring and the humiliation, he would also spout sayings and ruminations that sounded really cool, things I'd never heard in my sleepy redneck town. He would say, "For a warrior whose duty it is to restrain brigandage, it will not do to act like a brigand yourself." I even went and looked up brigand, just to see what it meant. I liked the idea of being a warrior instead of a punk kid.

I was way too cool at the time to admit I was intrigued, of course, so I mocked Carl and called him some names I refuse to repeat now. But I remembered everything he said, and I wondered where he'd learned it.

One day, after my usual halfhearted efforts, he tossed me a video as I headed out the door.

"What the hell is this?" I wrinkled my nose, turning the case over in my hands. It was some old black-and-white movie, and I sneered.

"Kurosawa. *The Seven Samurai*. Watch it. It's in Japanese, but it has subtitles."

"You give me a movie, then expect me to read?"

He grinned, white teeth flashing against his ebon skin. "Trust me."

I watched it, just so I could tell him how lame and stupid it was. Then I watched it again. After about the fifth viewing, I knew parts of it by heart. My favorite scene involved the samurai who masqueraded as a monk to disarm an enemy with his bare hands. My mom told me *The Magnificent Seven* was based on it, so I had her rent that and watched it, too. It wasn't as good, in my opinion, but I could see the parallels between the two movies, the themes that carried over. Here were men with honor, who used their powers for good (so to speak). I was fascinated.

When I took the movie back to Carl at my next weekly class, I felt so educated and worldly. After all, I'd watched a foreign film! Carl quickly proved me wrong.

"If you want to truly understand *bushido*, and the way of the samurai, you have to read—a lot. Samurai were educated men, not just trained thugs."

The first book he gave me was *Hagakure*. He quizzed me over it as we sparred, forcing me to use my mind and my body at once. I can honestly say, I got so caught up in learning about this foreign and exotic culture, I forgot to be a hoodlum.

Once we moved past hand-to-hand techniques and on to weapons training, he gave me *The Book of Five Rings*, and my studies continued. They still continue. Every time someone comes out with a new translation of one of the classic texts, I'm there. Sometimes, someone even writes something new, relating *bushido* to modern life. Countless businesses cite it in their ideals, alongside Sun Tzu's *Art of War*.

I admire people who try to keep the code. Honor and duty are fairly good concepts, no matter what credo you maintain. But I am the only practicing samurai I know. Even Carl can't say he ever used his training in actual combat.

The world has changed a lot since the days of the samurai. The rules have changed. So what does being a samurai mean for some gangly white boy in today's modern America? It means when in a darkened parking lot, the samurai takes the extra moment to see that a young woman gets to her car safely. It means he watches a lost child until her mother returns for a tearful reunion. It means he sees to it that the local vandals are caught and prosecuted. Yeah, the neighborhood watch took on a whole new meaning when I moved into the area.

I still study the notable names of Japanese *bushido*. Every day, I choose some quote or teaching to meditate on, most lately revisiting the works of Miyamoto Musashi and his *Book of Five Rings*. I practice *battōjutsu*, the art of drawing and sheathing a sword. Don't laugh; it's harder than you think. I practice *kendo* and *jujitsu*, both for combat and for exercise. I also practice down-

and-out redneck brawling. It's the one thing enemies never seem to expect from someone they view as a trained combatant.

But most important, I practice honor. All I want is for my little girl to say, "My father was an honorable man." I've seen people aspire to less.

For nearly two hours, I put my body through the rigors of my own training, as well as the physical therapy assigned by my doctor. I stretched to cool down, feeling the scar tissue down my left side pull slightly. After almost four years, it rarely bothered me anymore. No one could guess that something had tried to carve my heart out through my rib cage.

My left hip was aching when I finally sat down to meditate, and the angry muscles in my right calf were twitching spasmodically. Neither had healed as I would have liked. I was lucky to still have the right leg at all. I had never dreamed that the Scuttle could inject poison through its legs, too, so it hadn't occurred to me to negotiate around it. I wouldn't make that mistake again.

I cleared my mind, moving past the pain to a place of peace, and focused on my breathing. The sun was higher, beaming over my bare shoulders. It promised to be the first truly hot day we'd had this year. Spring was nearly over, brief as it was.

My quote for the day came again from the *Hagakure*. "There is a way of bringing up the child of a samurai. From the time of infancy one should encourage bravery and avoid trivially frightening or teasing the child." I thought on that quote a lot—pretty much every time I looked at Anna. Yamamoto said that parents shouldn't make their child afraid of the lightning, or dark places, because cowardice was a lifetime scar. But I knew what was waiting in those dark places, and I had a hard time coming up with a justification to leave my daughter ignorant. Granted, at five, she was too little to understand. But when she was older, if I was still around, what would I tell her? I had yet to figure out the answer.

I don't know how long I'd been sitting in meditation, working the white river pebbles between my fingers, when I heard the scrabbling of claws on stone. I opened my eyes to find a bold squirrel sitting atop a rock not three feet from me. It looked to be a healthy little thing, all fat and sassy, with slick red fur and gleaming button eyes.

I tilted my head to the left. It mimicked the movement. I tilted my head to the right; it did the same. With a sigh, I raised my right hand and flipped it the bird. It repeated the gesture and burst into little rodent snickers. I threw one of the stones at it, and it ducked.

"What do you want, Axel?" My peaceful meditation was officially over.

"Just paying my usual morning visit." The squirrel scampered off the rock and zipped over to perch on my water bottle, guaranteeing I wasn't going to reach for it. "I hear you're working from home this week."

The first time I'd seen this trick pulled, I'd expected it to speak in squeaks, like the cartoon chipmunks. Instead, the squirrel's voice was a pleasant tenor and sounded too much like my own. It was creepy. With a groan, I pushed myself to my feet. "I have a client in town, yes."

"Any chance you're wanting an edge? A little boost to put that victory in the bag?" The creature's eyes gleamed an unnatural red for just a moment. "Just a little wiggle of the fingers, a little mojo extraordinaire, and you can be the demon hunter you've always wanted to be."

"Shame on you, Axel. Selling out one of your own?" The eerie little creature followed me as I grabbed my T-shirt off the patio table and pulled it on. A glance through the glass door told me Mira and Anna had disappeared into the depths of the house, and I placed myself where they couldn't see the possessed squirrel if they came back to the kitchen. There are things I'm just not ready to explain to Anna.

"Spilled milk. You're worth it." It zoomed up the back of the wrought-iron chair, tail flicking spastically.

"First, they won't accept my challenge if I don't have a soul to offer. Second, you know I'm not going to take you up on it. Don't you have something better to do than annoy me?"

"Nope. You're it. As long as I'm hounding you, I don't have to do anything else." I swear, the squirrel grinned. I didn't even know squirrels had those muscles. "And I am, if nothing else, a being of leisure."

Now that Axel was off my water bottle, I retrieved it to take a long drink. "That's the same as being lazy, right?"

The squirrel pouted. "You are an uncultured cretin, you know that?"

"That's the rumor."

Axel hopped to the top of the patio table. "It's my move, right?"

The top of the table was worked in a checkerboard pattern. I hadn't picked it out on purpose, but it turned out to work quite nicely as a chessboard. The pieces were stone, heavy enough that a breeze wouldn't knock them over. I'd been playing against Axel for a couple years now.

He knew very well that it was his move. After a few moments of studying the board, he nosed a bishop forward a few spaces. "Your turn!"

Damn. He'd put me on the defensive with that one move. I was going to lose this one if I didn't start paying attention. "I'll think about it."

Vicious barking broke out on the other side of my neighbor's fence, and the possessed squirrel flinched. The thick boards shuddered as the mastiff on the far side tried to smash its way through to get at the demonic presence in my yard. "Tybalt, stop that! Get back over here! Sorry, Jesse!" my neighbor called over the fence.

"S'okay, Ellen. Have a good day at work."

"Filthy smelly mongrel . . ." The squirrel's eyes began to glow red again, and I thumped him on top of his furry little dome with one knuckle. Axel gave a very squirrelish yelp of pain, then zinged under the patio table to glare at me, rubbing his head.

"Ahht! You know the rules, no touchy. You don't want the dogs to chase you, quit possessing the local wildlife."

"I could always visit you in my true form. I could eat that dog's heart and spread its entrails over their trees like garland. Think your neighbors would like that?" He was angry now; his tail was twitching all over the place. He really hated dogs. They felt the same about him.

"I think if you don't want me to have Mira ward the yard, you'll behave." After the talking cockroach incident, she put protective wards on the doors and windows. Axel hadn't come anywhere near the house since.

The squirrel burst into a stream of profanity in both English and Demonic, ran a couple laps around the patio, then fell over dead as the demon vacated its little body.

"Dammit, Axel!"

Just once, I'd like to start my morning without having to bury some furry corpse. I'm running out of places to stick them in the yard, and I secretly harbor the fear that they're all going to get up some night and come knocking on the sliding glass door à la *Pet Sematary*. Like I said, I don't do zombies.

The neighbor's dog fell silent the moment Axel disappeared, proving that the demon really had departed. I went in search of a shovel.

We had a strange relationship, Axel and I. His job was to con me out of my soul, something he went about with the bare minimum effort. And my job . . . I liked to think it was to make his life even worse than Hell. We enjoyed baiting each other, playing the occasional game of chess. Sometimes, we even talked philosophy.

I can't even imagine how old he is, but it gives him an interesting perspective.

His name isn't really Axel, of course. It's a "Sympathy for the Devil" reference, and he really didn't strike me as a Jagger. I don't know his real name. I never want to know.

I didn't know his true form, either. He was too intelligent to be a Scuttle or a Snot. The most Snots could manage was the occasional menacing belch. I was pretty sure he was a Skin; possibly even a Shirt. The beast and humanoid demons were equally nasty to deal with, for various reasons, but Axel could fit either profile.

I've been told there is a fifth class of demon, above even the Shirts. Those would be the actual angels who fell from Heaven once upon a time. I don't know anyone who has seen one. It may be our own champion version of an urban legend.

This of course begs the question, do I believe it? Y'know, I can probably believe there's a God out there—big G and everything. But why he'd want to take a close personal interest in this ant farm down here, I don't know. There are demons, so I suppose at least at one time, there had to have been angels. But this is Missouri, the Show Me state. So until I see it, I'll file it in the maybe pile.

Regardless, Axel was no angel. I was certain of that.

Mira was getting shoes on Hurricane Annabelle when I finally made it back inside. I frowned a bit. "You girls have big plans today?"

"I'm going to work with Mommy!"

Mira nodded. "Yes, but we're not going to color in anything but our coloring books this time, are we?"

The red pigtails bobbed as Annabelle nodded. "I promise."

I scrubbed the dirt off my hands in the kitchen sink. "Mir, I could probably take her today. You can just sit behind the counter at the store and rest. Dee could do the heavy stuff." I should know better. Nothing is going to get my wife to stubborn-up like my implying she can't do something.

"I'm fine, and Anna and I are going to have a fun day." It was that "Are we clear?" voice. You know, the one that does not invite further argument. "What are your plans for the day?"

"I guess I'm going to head over to Marty's, see if he's got my gear ready. I'll probably have to go out late tonight, too."

"You still need to get your mother a present, while you're out," she reminded me.

"I'm gonna call Cole, see what he got her. I don't want to duplicate." If my baby brother had ponied up for something big, maybe I could just split the cost with him and it could be a joint gift. I really suck at this whole gift-giving thing.

I got the girls out the door and on the way to Mira's bookstore, but I really wasn't happy about it. Mira should have stayed home and regained her strength today. Nice to know my wife listens to me.

I went to pull on some real clothes and get my hair under control. The day's T-shirt said I'M MEAN BECAUSE

YOU'RE STUPID. Add jeans and a ponytail, and you had the all-purpose uniform. I tucked my cell phone into my pocket. Ivan hadn't called back, and I was starting to get worried—well, more worried than before. The scrying was ominous, at the very best, and no matter what I'd told Mira, I didn't think Miguel had survived that battle.

I was no shrink, but even I knew that worrying without action accomplished nothing. Since I could take no action at the moment, I decided to run errands instead. Regardless of Miguel's fate, work was still work and staying alive was pretty high on my priority list. I'd start that process by getting my gear back from Marty. The rest . . . Well, everything else pretty much had to wait until I touched base with Nelson Kidd.

I didn't figure he'd wimp out. It took guts to come so far and admit so much. People like that don't cave. I didn't expect *anyone* to back out once they'd asked me for help, but I always gave them the choice. Who knows, someday someone might surprise me.

To occupy my mind, I made a few more ticks on my mental to-do list. If Kidd was still willing to go through with it, I'd be summoning a demon tonight, and that required advance planning. You don't just walk into a demon summoning unprepared. I'd done that. To say it didn't end well is the edited-for-TV version. I'm damn lucky to still have my soul and all working organs and appendages.

7

Once upon a time, when Mira and I were still in college and we lived in the only ratty apartment we could afford, we had some bachelor neighbors. They were rowdy, uncouth, and basically good guys. Eventually, we got older, moved out of the mold-infested apartment building, started doing the whole grown-up responsible shtick. But we never lost touch. Marty and Will are still my two best friends in the world, and I exploit them shamelessly.

Marty is a walking anachronism. He's a welder by trade, but a blacksmith by passion. He wears a kilt whenever he can get away with it. The man doesn't even own a TV. I mean, do you know how hard it is to not only find a blacksmith, but one who knows more than horseshoes and yard ornaments? It's a dying art. We're a dying breed, both of us men out of our time. That's probably why I get along with him so well.

It was a fifteen-minute drive to his house, and in that time I crossed from neatly mowed suburbia into nearly rural territory. Yards in this neighborhood bordered on fields and pastures, and the once-paved streets had long since gone to gravel. The last event of note here happened last summer when some cattle got loose and spawned a seven-mile low-speed chase. (Rumors of my alleged involvement in that bovine escape are highly exaggerated.)

I parked in the front yard and waved to Marty's wife, Melanie, as she pulled out of their drive. "He in bed yet?"

She rolled down her window. "Nah, he's out in the shed. There're pancakes left in the fridge if you're hungry."

"Thanks, Mel!" I must look positively emaciated. People are always trying to feed me.

Marty worked nights, so I had even odds of catching him before he went to bed for the day. It seemed to be my lucky day so far. I could hear the static spit of the arc welder as I walked around the house to the workshop.

A detached garage in a previous life, the shed had been converted into the manliest of manly domains, a refuge for all who revel in testosterone. The back corner was largely taken up by the forge and anvil, but there were also four motorcycles and one lawn mower (don't ask) in various states of disassembly, an arc welder, and most important, a beer fridge.

I didn't bother to knock. He wasn't going to hear me.

Duke greeted me first. The young brindle mastiff rose from his pile of shop rags near the door and padded over, his tail swaying happily. He was the product of my neighbor's last litter, and Marty had been more than happy to take the runt. If Duke was the runt, I didn't want to see his siblings. At only seven months old, he was still growing to be the size of a large horse in short order. I couldn't wait to see what he weighed in at, fully grown.

Despite his impending hugeness, he had the sweetest temperament I'd ever seen in a dog. It never fazed him when Anna pulled his ears, crawled all over him, stepped on one of his enormous paws. The big wimp would turn and run from any unexpected noise, and he cowered at the sight of the Chihuahua next door.

His doggy breath was warm on my hands, and it was an effort to keep him from bathing me with that huge pink tongue. I scratched his ears, and he rumbled in contentment, leaning against my thigh hard enough to almost knock me over. "You spoiled thing."

Marty, bare chested but welder's mask firmly in place, was working over something I didn't even recognize. It takes a real man to weld with no shirt on—or an idiot. He was possibly both.

The welder threw off strobes of light, casting his extensive tattoo sleeves in strange dancing shadows. The stylized Celtic wolf on his right forearm almost looked as if it were snarling at me. I shielded my eyes from the glare, looking away. The welder hissed and spat a few more times until I heard the knobs on the power supply being dialed down. Marty, his helmet perched atop his head now, smirked at me when I dropped my hand. "Wuss."

"Bite me. You're wearing a mask."

"I've eaten, thanks." He laid the helmet and torch aside, then ran a towel over his shaved head. I still can't figure out why, when a guy thinks he's going bald, he shaves his head. It didn't keep me from seeing the hints of gray in his black beard. And he was two years younger than I. I resisted the urge to check my own facial hair for signs of aging. "Go lie down, Duke." Obediently, the mammoth mutt padded off to curl up on his bed again. "You're here for your stuff?"

"Yeah, if it's ready."

"It's ready. Not sure I wanna give it to you, though." He cast me a disgruntled look as he rose from his stool. He was built like a fireplug, short and stocky with muscle mass attributed to long years of work at the anvil. In all truth, although I towered over him in height, I wouldn't want him getting his hands on me in a fight. I firmly believed he could break me in half. "What the hell did you try to do—chop down trees with it?"

It is a fact of life. Marty's swords are his babies. Mistreat them at your own peril. "You knew it was going to get used when you gave it to me, man. And it's held up to everything I've thrown at it." Yes, Marty knows what I do. But he's never seen it. I think there's a large leap to be made between knowing and seeing. He couldn't fathom the things that sword had been through.

He grumbled under his breath and tossed a jingling duffel bag at me. It hit me in the chest hard enough to knock the breath from my lungs. "The chain was easy enough to fix. There's a set of new leg guards in there, too. Trying to see if I can get the plates whittled down enough to be useful."

I glanced into the bag long enough to be certain he hadn't affixed metal plating to the rest of my armor. "I can't move in that stuff, man. Binds me all up."

"Just try it out, okay? If it works, you won't have this problem with stabbing wounds anymore."

He had a point. Chain just wasn't meant to stop a piercing blow. That I'd survived this long was either a testament to my skill, or my pure dumb luck. I wasn't sure which.

Five swords of various styles rested in the rack on the back wall. I eyed a rather vicious-looking kopesh while Marty retrieved my katana. He brought it to me for examination, drawing it from its bamboo sheath with the same reverence I showed it.

Marty worked with 1075 high-carbon spring steel. The swords had full tangs and guards and pommels of either solid bronze or steel. With proper leverage I could bend a sword nearly in half, only to watch it snap back to perfect form every time. I'd seen him knock chunks out of his own anvil with a blade and never mar the finish on the sword. He took pride in his weapons.

"There were some bad nicks, but I got them worked out. I'm gonna start on a new one for you. Not sure how much more this one's gonna take. She's had a hard life."

Boy, didn't I know it. "How about that kopesh there?"

Marty snorted at me. "You couldn't handle that one. Stick with the katana." He perched himself on his work-table and picked up his twelve-string guitar, his burn-calloused fingers moving over the frets absently. It's what he does when he's annoyed. When he's actually playing, he's damn good.

He was right, of course, about the kopesh. I didn't know the first thing about fighting with one of the wickedly curved blades. Still, I could add that to my list of things I'd like to learn someday. "What do I owe you?"

He strummed a few bars of "Stairway to Heaven," and I threw a greasy rag at him in retaliation. No self-respecting guitar player plays that song. "I had all the stuff already. You buy the beer next Sunday."

"Done." The beer deal was the ultimate bargain between men. Marty puttered around the shop, bedding the place down for the day, and I leaned against the fridge. "Hey, what'd you get your mom for her last birthday?"

He glanced at me quizzically. "We all went in on a new flat-screen TV for her and Dad. Why?" Damn him. Marty-of-the-six-brothers—he could afford to do something like that.

"Having a barbecue for Mom's birthday on Saturday, and I still don't know what to get her."

He whistled lowly. "Damn, man. You'd better get on it."

Thanking him most profusely for his jewel of wisdom, I took my leave (paying my respects to Duke, too). I tossed the duffel bag into the back of my truck with a jingling thump and laid my sword nicely on the passenger seat. The sword got buckled in, even. Always show respect to your weapon.

I tucked my earpiece into my ear and speed-dialed my little brother as I pulled back out into traffic. It rang three times before he answered.

"Cole Dawson."

"Hey, little brother." Yes, my brother's name is Cole Younger Dawson. Mine is Jesse James Dawson. My father had an outlaw obsession, and for some unfathomable reason, my mother didn't veto his name choices. Don't call me JJ. Only one person gets to call me JJ, and you look nothing like my ninety-six-year-old grandmother.

"Hey, big brother. What's going on?" I could hear a police radio squawking in the background. He was obviously working.

"Calling to touch base with you about Saturday. You coming?"

"Yup, got the day off work. Steph and I are bringing Nicky and some pasta salad thingy."

"Cool, cool . . ." That would make Annabelle happy. She adored her cousin Nicky. "So . . . what are you getting Mom?" There was a long moment of silence that said so much. "Crap, you don't have any ideas, either."

"Steph said she'd find something." He sounded sheepish. I don't think cops are supposed to sound sheepish.

"Mira's making me do it myself."

He snickered at me. "Well, if you're lucky, that storm front they're predicting will move in and we'll have to cancel. Give you more time to shop."

"Are you kidding? Mom'll have us out in the yard with umbrellas to protect the grill and the cake."

His radio blared an unintelligible message, demanding his attention. "I gotta go, big brother. See you Saturday."

"See ya." I sighed and hung up. *Dammit!* And I'd forgotten to tell him about the belligerent tailgater from last night. *Crap crap crap.* Oh well, it'd wait another day.

I missed Cole.

Outwardly, my brother and I were a study in opposites. Sure, we both topped six feet tall, but where I was skinny to the point of scrawny, Cole had more bulk, earned on the police gym's weight benches. Instead of my blond, Cole's hair was chestnut brown with a hint of curl if he didn't keep it cropped short. We shared the same sharp nose and blue eyes, but Cole's eyes always seemed to fade more toward gray.

Aside from the few incidents as boys where we'd wholeheartedly tried to kill each other, we'd been close. Cole even credited his career in law enforcement to my brief stint with lawlessness. Even as adults, after we'd gone our separate ways, hardly a day went by that we didn't talk, and we always kept up our goodnatured competition. I got the first college education, but he landed the reputable career. I bought the first house; he bought a bigger one. He married first, but I had the first kid—that sort of thing.

Things changed, after Nicky came.

Even at barely five years old, my nephew was probably the strongest person I'd ever known. That child had been through more pain and suffering in his short life than any person should have to see in ten lifetimes.

I'm not sure the doctors know everything that's wrong with him yet.

He was six months old when they nearly lost him. I can't count how many nights Mira spent holding Stephanie's hand at the hospital. Twice, the priest was called, and even Mira gave her own form of last rites. It wasn't a matter of if; it was a matter of when.

That's when Cole made his deal. I couldn't tell you how the demon found him, but I'm willing to bet they haunt hospitals, places where people are at their most desperate. Looking back, I've always tried to figure out whether I realized Cole was gone extra long that night? If I'd gone to find him, could I have stopped it all? But I didn't, and it was done.

Within hours, Nicky's vitals had stabilized. They took him off the machines. He smiled for the first time. We were so happy with his miraculous recovery, it never occurred to anyone to ask how. Back then, who knew to be suspicious of unexpected good fortune?

I still remembered Cole coming to me one sunny summer day at Mom's. Nicky and Anna were just crawling, and content to play in the dirt. Dad and Mom were fussing over the placement of the checkered tablecloth, while Mira and Steph just set the table without waiting for the discussion to be resolved.

"Jesse?" That's what got my attention. He never called me by name. I examined his face closely and saw something dark in his eyes, something terrifying. He looked scared. My brother-the-cop was never scared, even when he ought to be. "I think I did something really bad."

He showed me the writhing brand on his left arm, the sigil that marked his soul as someone else's property. He introduced me to a world of demons and nightmares I hadn't even known existed. And he asked me if I knew any way out.

Now, realize that my wife is a witch, as in Wiccan. But her magical abilities are something separate and apart from her religion, and at that time, I had no idea this stuff existed. I accused Cole of getting drunk and tattooed. I laughed in his face. It took some time to convince me he was really in trouble. After that, though, it was on.

I mean, what was I supposed to do? He was my little brother, and he was in deep. He explained to me about the contract, what the tattoo meant. And it stood to reason that a demon that would make one deal would make another. In the movies, people made challenges with the devil all the time, right? Golden fiddles and shit. I didn't know all the rules, but I knew how to fight. It's one of the few things I've ever been good at. And I knew that turning a blind eye was worse than anything else.

I fought for his soul. I fully admit that I won only through sheer luck. It should have made us closer, surviving something like that. Instead, we drifted apart.

Maybe he knew I always harbored a faint disappointment in him. Maybe he couldn't handle my knowing his dirty secret. Maybe he just hated himself for not making a better deal when he had the chance. He'd bargained for Nicky to live, that one time, not for his continued good health. The demon got the better of

Cole. Maybe it ate at him. I don't know. Like I said, we don't talk much anymore.

I brooded on that way longer than I should have—most of the drive home, in fact. We'll pretend that's why I didn't notice the blue Ford Escort in more than a passing way until I was nearly home.

In all fairness to me, though, I had no reason to notice it. I mean, it's an Escort, right? The most innocuous car known to man. It wasn't driving erratically; it wasn't even that close to my truck. It was there, three cars back, the driver no doubt minding his own business and thinking things such as "Man, my hemorrhoids hurt." If not for the incident the previous night and the sudden feeling of ants crawling all over my arms (never a good sign), I never would have noticed it at all.

But once I'd made four different turns, and it was still back there, I started paying more attention. What were the odds that a blue Escort tried to run me off the road the night before, and now one had just showed up behind me again?

On a hunch, I took a random right turn, just to see what would happen. Not thirty seconds later, the plucky little car followed right behind me. "Okay, buddy . . . Let's see how serious you are about this." I sped up, soon doing forty through the residential neighborhood.

The Escort kept up, never farther than three blocks behind me. To my frustration, I couldn't make out any features of the driver. The sunlight bounced off the windshield, the glare blinding me. I took another right down a shade-dappled side street, hoping to get a better look, and screeched to a halt in the middle of the street.

The car pulled up at the end of the block and sat there for several long moments. I watched it in my rearview mirror, almost feeling the gaze of the silhouetted driver staring back. I was almost certain it was a guy. The hair was either close-cropped or slicked down, shoulders decently broad. I could hear the whine of a belt under the hood, and I filed that away as an identifying mark.

I don't know how long we stared at each other like that. It seemed like forever. Then the Escort floored it and squalled tires in the other direction.

"Oh, you think so?" I did an ugly U-turn myself, running up over someone's nicely manicured lawn, and was off in hot pursuit. The bastard wasn't man enough to face me directly, was he? It should be noted that this ranked pretty high on my "stupid me" tricks list.

I caught a glimpse of the car as it left the subdivision and headed east. *Toward the highway.* If I didn't catch up to him before he hit I-35, I'd lose him in the traffic. I shifted through gears as fast as I could, rounding corners at highly unsafe speeds. Where the tiny residential street met a four-lane thoroughfare, I lost sight of the blue car for just a moment.

Cussing under my breath, I glanced up and down, trying to guess which way he'd gone. The highway was to the left, but he could lose himself in more housing additions if he went right.

The sound of a squealing belt carried to me through the open window, and I smirked. *Gotcha.* Stomping on the gas, I turned left. I lost the belt whine in the roar of my own engine, but I knew he had to be just ahead of me. I topped a small rise, fully expecting to see the blue car just ahead of me, and fumed when it wasn't. *Where the hell . . . ?*

There was nothing there but a pale yellow VW bug, its engine wailing plaintively as it trundled over the next hill. "Dammit!" I glanced behind me, on the off chance that a blue Ford Escort would materialize on command, but there was nothing.

My gaze returned to the front just in time to keep me from annihilating a small ratlike dog as it ran into the street yapping at my wheels. I slammed on the brakes, and rested my head against the steering wheel until my heart stopped marching double-time in my chest.

Well, that rather eliminated any chance of last night being a random act of drunken stupidity. In a way, I was relieved. I mean, for whatever reason, someone was rather annoyed with me. But at least that meant there wasn't some maniac on the road, running hapless people into ditches. Mira was safe; the girls at work were safe. The question was, should I report it or not? I mean, if this was work related—champion work, not retail work—what would I say?

I concocted and discarded at least twenty different stories on the way home, and none of them were even remotely plausible. By default, I guess I would just keep it to myself—no use upsetting Mira.

My power steering whined as I pulled into my garage, mocking me and almost muffling the ring of my cell phone. "Hello?"

"Dawson." Ivan sounded as if he'd been gargling gravel. "It is being morning there, *tak*? I am not to be waking you?"

"No, no, I'm up. What's going on?"

I could almost hear him shaking his grizzled white head. "It is being muchly difficult here. And I am thinking that the news will not be good."

8

I rummaged through the kitchen to fix myself some kind of sustenance as Ivan talked. Surely any and all paranoia I was experiencing was a result of hunger. That was the ticket.

The leftovers were piled neatly in the fridge, dated and color coded. My wife is sometimes a bit anal, but I love her anyway.

"Miguel was to be entertaining a client three weeks ago. He was to be meeting them when he traveled north to visit family. A town called Mascareña. He was to be telling Rosaline this, but he was not speaking the name." Ivan's voice grumbled in my ear, sounding rather like a great disgruntled bear.

I didn't find Miguel's actions unusual. I don't tell Mira whom I work for, either, most of the time. I operate under the assumption that she's safer not knowing. "He didn't tell his brothers or anything? Not even where he was going?"

Ivan has a powerful frown. I could hear it over the phone, could picture the deeply creased forehead beneath his stark white crew cut. "There is to being some language difficulty here, but, I believe the brothers are not to be knowing. The family in the north; they are being afraid to speak, even to Miguel's family. It is possible they are not to be understanding that I mean no harm. I am told I am to being intimidating."

He was probably right. No one would ever mistake Ivan for anything other than military or law enforcement, and neither was popular in Mexico, especially near the border. Add to that his horrible English and their native Spanish, and it gave a whole new meaning to "language barrier." "Look, I have a client in town myself, but once I've settled him, Mira and I can fly down. She can translate for you." Mira was amazing with languages, and Spanish was just one of several she spoke fluently.

"That is not being necessary. We are to be making do with what we have. The family is to being most hospitable to me."

Of course they were. Miguel's mother often reminded me of my own. Every woman was her daughter and every man was her son, even if they already had white hair and wrinkles when she met them. No doubt, Ivan was finding himself mothered to death by the feisty Mexican widow.

"Well, is there anything we can do?" I pinned the phone against my shoulder so I could slap a few slices of leftover pork roast on some bread—good stuff.

He sighed heavily. While I joked about Ivan's being the old man, it occurred to me for the first time that he truly was getting old. He'd been battling demons longer than I'd been alive. No other champion had as many kills to his credit as Ivan. "His—what is word?—his weapon is not to being returned. I am to be worrying much about this."

"He uses a machete," I supplied absently. Not returning a weapon was against the rules.

I've never seen a losing battle, but from what I hear, demons don't leave bodies lying around. One of the first things Ivan taught us to negotiate was for some proof of death to be delivered. A head or hand is a bit macabre, so we usually opted for our weapon to be presented to the person of our choice. Beats a singing telegram.

"Miguel wouldn't have forgotten that clause. He's been at this longer than I have." Ten years longer, for all that Miguel was seven years my junior. It was a family matter, with him, handed down through the generations. He'd lost his father and one older brother to it already.

"*Tak*, I am to be knowing this. But it is not to be found all the same."

"Is it possible he isn't dead?" Mira's scrying hadn't been one hundred percent conclusive, though I'd never heard of a demon taking a hostage. They didn't worry about our fleshly vessels, just the sweet goodies inside. Maybe souls really do taste like Peeps.

"I am not knowing. I have never to be seeing this before." He hesitated a moment before going on. "Dawson, being careful, *tak*? Some things are to being incorrect. I am not happy."

I wasn't happy, either, for more reasons than I could count. "Yeah, I'll be careful. You know me."

"This is what is to be worrying me."

"You're just a regular comedian aren't you?" I had to smile, but I knew Ivan wasn't joking. I wasn't entirely sure he knew how.

"Is Mira being there?"

"No, she's at work," I mumbled through a mouthful of sandwich.

"When she is coming home, perhaps to be having her call Rosaline? I think she would like to hear from Mira."

"I'll let her know."

"I will be in touch." He disconnected the call before I could say good-bye. It really was rather annoying. I'd have to stop doing that to people.

I finished my lunch because I knew I'd need the energy later tonight, but it just didn't taste good anymore.

My next pass through the kitchen was business related. Nelson Kidd was never going to say, "Y'know what? I screwed up, so we'll just let the demon have my soul." And even if he did, I couldn't live with myself after that. Deep down, I knew this. So tonight, I would be summoning a demon for negotiations.

Your average denizen of Hell is just that—stuck there with only other demons and Jerry Springer reruns for entertainment. Sure, there are a few texts floating around the world with actual demon names, and every so often some amateur magician tries to summon one forth. (It does work, although it rarely turns out like the summoner intended.) Other than that, vacation options from Hell are pretty limited.

However, once in a very great while, a demon gets enough power to come across on its own. Then, they wander around, gather up souls, and solidify their power base until someone like me comes along and puts the hurt on them.

Regardless of how they get to this plane, they're usually rather pleased to be here. I'm guessing Hell's not that scenic, and the chance to get out and stretch their appendages is welcome. On top of that, they get a chance at another soul. Who wouldn't be happy to take the trip to the real world? But y'know how you always have that one tourist, usually sitting next to you on the plane, who just bitches and gripes about everything? They have those in demonkind, too, and they get real snippy about being ordered around.

Since I thought of myself as an air marshal on a demon's vacation flight, it was only fitting that I equip myself with all the necessary measures to control a rowdy passenger. And I was all out of demon-be-gone.

It's a simple recipe of Ivan's devising, and all the ingredients can be found in an average kitchen cabinet—well, at least in our kitchen cabinet. In truth, we're the only people I know who buy both cayenne pepper and cumin in bulk.

You take a bunch of cayenne pepper and a bunch of cumin. I operate on the idea that more is better, so long as it'll still spray through the spritzer thingy. Dump that into a bottle of water, attach a spray nozzle, shake well. Squirt your pesky demon like a bad puppy and it usually departs posthaste. Do *not* stand downwind of your spray. It hurts just as bad in your own eyes—not that I would know anything about that, of course.

No, I don't know why it works. Mira says those two spices are known to have protective properties even without magical additions. Good thing, since you could put all my magical talent on the head of a pin and still have room to spare.

I poured some into a refillable Mace canister on my key chain, amongst the rest of my strange collection of protective charms and antidemon gadgets. I tucked the larger bottle into my duffel bag.

My next task was to do a check of my armor. Perhaps it's disrespectful to my Asian leanings, but I prefer metal around me to bamboo. There's just something comforting about being encased in links of steel.

I hadn't always worn armor. That first battle I went into with a sword and rampant stupidity. I was lucky, that time. I never got the chance to be so lax again. The second time, I won, but I spent six months in ICU after the Yeti tried to eat my lungs. That's when I started charging fees and convinced Marty to throw together some protective gear. We've been tinkering with the armor ever since. He wants to put me in plate. I'm resisting.

The mail covered the big areas, chest, thighs, calves, upper arms. I wore thick leather bracers on my forearms, and steel-toed work boots. Beneath it all, I wore a layer of heavy padding, designed to keep the metal from ripping my skin to shreds. That alone added a good fifteen pounds to the already heavy outfit.

In the beginning, I had worked long hours to build up my strength to compensate for the extra weight. But the protection it offered more than made up for any loss in mobility. You can't fight when your guts are flopping around down by your feet.

The only thing I hated about it was the smell. No

matter what I did, my armor and padding always smelled of sweat and blood and sulfur. It wasn't the easiest thing to wash. Maybe, with the arrival of warm weather, I could try to wash the padding again and hang it out to dry. It'd take a couple days, though, and there was no time to do it now.

I dropped the tailgate on my truck and laid each piece out, looking them over for any imperfections, not that I expected to find any. Marty did good work. He had even oiled the leather straps and replaced one buckle that had started to wear thin.

My shirt looked like a wadded-up ball of steel until I shook it out into the supple, shining work of art that it was. It was dull, tarnished steel, though at one time, Marty had worked gold-tinted links into the neckline and cuffs of the sleeves. Most of those had been damaged and replaced over the years, and now it was an almost uniform charcoal gray. The newest links shone brightly against the dull chain of the original armor, but aside from that, the repair was seamless.

The new plated leg guards I eyed skeptically. Marty had cut the thin steel plates down to narrow strips, barely three inches wide, and attached them so they'd fall two on the outer calf, two on the inner. That left a lot of gap, covered only by chain. I wasn't sure how well they'd work, in practice. At the very least, I could run through some katas and see what they did for my range of motion. But that would be later—much later. I crammed them into the bottom of the duffel bag, and piled the usable armor in on top of them.

My sword got some attention next. I drew it and examined the edge closely. I'd never do that in front of Marty; I'm sure he'd take it as my questioning his work. It was wicked sharp, and the blade was as straight and true as the day it was crafted. Marty had rewrapped the hilt, using the dark blue cord I preferred. It made me sad to think of putting this one aside for a new one, no matter what piece of genius Marty might construct for me. This sword had been with me since the beginning.

To most, it might appear ordinary, even plain. The guard was an octagonal piece of bronze, and the pommel was a simple round knob. The blade was unadorned. Even the scabbard was merely functional as opposed to decorative. But I found beauty in simplicity, and she'd always been true to me.

I practiced drawing and sheathing it a few times, finding my center, and focusing on just what I was doing at that moment. I felt better with it in my hand. Sure, I could use other weapons, but I was most comfortable with the katana. It made me feel more balanced. I laid it again in the front seat of my truck, then went to attend to some of the more mundane aspects of my life.

Technically, I had another hour before Kidd's reflection period was up. He could wait while I threw some laundry in.

That's right, ladies. I do laundry. I figure it's a fair trade, since Mira actually works full-time and looks after Annabelle. I'd offer to cook, too, but face it: Mira runs circles around me there. If it were left to me, we'd have pizza rolls for every meal. I'd be okay with that, actually. She would not.

By the time I got the laundry sorted and a load thrown in the washer (how in the world does one five-year-old child go through that many socks?), I had three hours to myself before Mira and Annabelle came home. If I was going to call Kidd, I needed to do it now.

9

The phone rang so many times, I started to believe Kidd had packed up and left town. His agent had been most determined, after all. When someone finally answered, there was a jarring clatter as the receiver was dropped and possibly kicked across the floor in someone's haste.

"Wait, wait, don't hang up! I'm here!" The voice was distant, tinny, but the receiver was rescued, and I could hear Kidd's heavy breathing as he tried to calm himself. "I'm here."

"Run for the phone?" I received an affirmative grunt in reply. "Your time is up, Mr. Kidd. Have you reached a decision?"

He was quiet for a few moments. Maybe he was giving himself one last chance to butch up and take his punishment like a man. In the end, he sighed. "I cannot continue this way, Mr. Dawson. Please help me."

It was what I expected. "All right, here is the plan. Tonight, after dark, I am going to pick you up, and we're going to drive out into the middle of nowhere. Then, you're going to call your little friend's name, and he's going to come pay us a visit. At that point, we'll negotiate the terms of the challenge. The challenge itself won't happen tonight, but we'll lay the groundwork."

There was a long hesitation on his end. "How long should it take?"

"You have a date, Mr. Kidd?"

"No, I . . . My team is flying in tonight. We're playing a series here this week, and I'll need to report back to the hotel. They keep the players on curfew."

That might make things a bit tricky. Things would take as long as they took, and not a moment less. It wasn't something I was willing to rush. "I'll try to have you home before you turn into a pumpkin, all right?"

"Is there . . . anything I need to do? Or bring?" He got a few points for at least being willing to help.

"Just show up, and when I tell you to, speak the name."

"You want me to call it? Can't you—?"

"No." I cut him off right there. No way would a demon's name ever pass my lips. I didn't need that kind of attention. It was bad enough I had about a dozen of the vile monikers swimming around in my mind. Nobody should have to have that filth in his head. "I suggest you get some rest today, Mr. Kidd. We could have a long night ahead of us." I hung up without waiting for a response. Old habits are hard to break.

There was no telling how long the negotiations would actually take. The lesser demons, the Scuttles and Snots, weren't real picky about terms. The Snots rarely got past saying, "Rawr, me smash!" They just wanted a chance to fight, to work themselves up their brutal hierarchy, so they'd agree to something fast and dirty. It was the Shirts and Skins, the powerful ones, who could give lawyers a run for their money. They'd want every single detail nailed down, preferably to their advantage.

I'd have no way of knowing which I faced, until Kidd said the magic word and the demon made its grand entrance. I hate surprises.

And speaking of surprises, my doorbell rang. I answered it to find our across-the-street neighbor standing on my front step. I smiled. "Hey, Dixie."

Dixie is that neighbor who knows the neighborhood's story of the last fifty years and more. She can tell you the names of the original builders of most of the houses, she knows what happened to the grandchildren of a man who hasn't lived here in thirty years, and she can probably tell you what everyone on the block was having for dinner that night. Every neighborhood has a Dixie.

Widowed, her children grown and gone, she'd adopted Mira and me, and she doted on Annabelle worse than my own parents.

The white-haired woman smiled back, tucking a pair of muddy gardening gloves into her belt so she could shake my hand. "Hello there, Jesse. I was wondering if I could ask you a favor."

"Sure, anything."

"Jack's not going to be able to come by to mow the lawn until next week, and it's looking positively shaggy. Do you think you could . . . ?"

I chuckled. "Yeah, sure. Just lemme change clothes."
I was Jesse Dawson, champion of lost souls and amateur groundskeeper.

Appropriate lawn-mowing clothes donned and
sunblock applied (the last thing I needed was to try
and wear mail over a sunburn), I headed across the
street to mow Dixie's lawn. It wouldn't take long; she
had a nice riding mower and a yard the size of a post-
age stamp. The only problem was skirting the artful
but inconveniently placed flower beds. There were
four.

As I motored carefully around the yard, I became
aware of eyes on me. Glancing around, I saw only Dixie's enormous tabby tomcat perched atop the birdbath.
Garfield was an aloof creature, merely tolerating my
presence on a good day, but today he watched me with
uncanny alertness. Seeing that he had my attention,
the large cat flicked his tail once, and the eyes glowed
red for a heartbeat.

"Oh no no . . . Axel . . ." *Dammit*. "Come on, the
lady's cat?"

He gave a feline leap as I neared and settled his large
bulk quite comfortably in my lap. My skin crawled,
and it took everything in me not to chuck the creature
under the mower deck. "You said no more local wildlife," he said, in my voice. "This is not wildlife. This
is possibly the most disgustingly domesticated creature I've ever seen, besides you." It wasn't fair that he
didn't even have to raise his voice to be heard over the
mower.

The last thing I needed was for the neighbors to see me talking to myself. I muttered under my breath. "Yeah, but she's gonna be heartbroken when the cat keels over dead."

"I can leave it alive, if you want, when I vacate."

I looked down at the cat in my lap. "You can?" He nodded. It was an odd gesture, coming from a cat. "Then quit killing my squirrels, too!" I maneuvered around a large oblong flower bed in the middle of the yard.

"What's it worth to you?" My contempt must have shown on my face, because he chuckled. "You have no sense of humor, you know that?"

"I've been told. What do you want? You're not normally this clingy."

"Just keeping an eye on my favorite demon slayer." He actually began washing his ears in true catlike fashion, then blinked at his own paw. "Eugh, why do they *do* this?"

"You know, you can keep an eye on me quite well from the birdbath. Or from the house. Or from another state. Anywhere but from my lap." It was like Marty or Will crawling into my lap. Ew. Guys just don't do that.

"But I'd miss our little talks." I swear the cat pouted. "Don't you love me anymore?" I know I gave him a scathing look then, and he actually purred. "You're a collector's item, you know. A dying breed. Fewer and fewer of you all the time. It'll be a pity to see you all go the way of the dodo."

"Well, I don't plan on keeling over any time soon, so you can stop fretting your pretty little head." I wheeled around the heart-shaped flower bed, making a mental note to get the Weed Eater and finish trimming around it later.

"I'll bet your friend Miguel said that same thing to his wife, that last day."

I slammed the mower into park, torturing the motor and engulfing us in a cloud of acrid exhaust. I turned it off, eyeing the orange tabby suspiciously. "What do you know, Axel?"

"Nothing I'm willing to share for free." His fluffy tail swayed in a lazy rhythm, eyes half lidded in amusement.

"This isn't the time to start playing the 'I'll swallow your soul' game, Axel."

"Who says I'm playing? This is what I do, Jesse; I bargain." His purr went up about three notches, rumbling against my legs. "Just because you're a friend doesn't mean you get a discount."

I snatched the fat tabby up by the scruff of his neck, dangling him at eye level. "So help me, Axel, if you know where he is, or what happened . . ."

"Careful, Jesse. You don't want that sweet little old lady to come out here and see you abusing her precious puddy tat, do you?" The golden eyes gleamed red again. "I give nothing for free. You want to know what I know, let's talk deal."

"Tell me, and I won't snap your furry neck." I shook him once, and he answered with a low feline growl. Who knew Garfield had it in him?

"You can't hurt me in this body. You know that. What's it worth to you, Jesse, to avoid dear brave Miguel's fate?" The cat sneered at me, fangs bared.

"I'll dunk your furry ass in holy water—how about that for a deal?"

"I don't think I want to play with you anymore. You're not nice." He took a swipe at my face with a loud hiss. Startled, I dropped him before I remembered Garfield didn't have claws.

The chubby cat retreated to the shadow under the birdbath, tail lashing furiously. "Your arrogance will get you killed. When your soul is being tortured Down Below, remember I offered to help."

"Get back here, you conniving little—!" I lunged off the lawn mower in his direction.

Garfield the cat regained control of his massive body as Axel escaped, and he let out a caterwaul to end all caterwauls. Puffing up to twice his previously huge size, he streaked for the nearest tree. I didn't even know the lazy thing could move that fast. The cat huddled in the branches, visibly shaking.

Cussing under my breath, I put the lawn mower away and fetched Dixie's ladder to retrieve poor abused Garfield. I placed my feet carefully on the metal rungs, keeping an eye on the terrified feline, but my mind was on Axel.

The demon bantered, he taunted, but he'd never been nasty to me before. *He's a demon, you dipshit!* I cussed myself, too, while I was in a cussing mood. I was a million times an idiot for even half trusting him. I killed his kind on a regular basis, so what was I thinking?

The better question would be what was *he* thinking? Did he know something about Miguel, or was he just trying to trap me in my own curiosity?

No deals, no deals, no deals. I chanted it to myself like a mantra. Even minor bargains with demons could snowball. One tiny deal, one seemingly harmless trade only opened the door. Best not to start. But dammit, I wanted to know what he knew. That is, if he actually knew it. The conundrum was enough to scramble my brain.

A horn honked as I clambered down from the tree with a rather disgruntled Garfield wrapped tightly in my T-shirt. I waved as best I could to Mira and Annabelle. Anna was babbling a mile a minute as they got out of the Explorer, and she bounced her way across the street, clinging tightly to her mother's hand.

"Daddy! Is that Garfield? Can I pet him? Why's he in your shirt? Is Dixie home? Can I get a cookie?" It is possible that the cat was more afraid of my daughter than he had been of the possessing demon. With strength born of sheer terror, he struggled free and zipped inside the door as Dixie came out to greet us.

"Goodness, what's got into him?" She eyed her cat for a moment, and I wanted to tell her she really didn't want to know. Muttering about "that crazy cat," Dixie wandered over with a plate of fresh snickerdoodles. "I thought I heard my favorite cookie monster out here!"

"Can I have a cookie, Dixie?"

"Anna," her mother said, with that warning mother tone.

Annabelle immediately corrected herself. "Please?"

"Of course, sweetie. You can have as many as you want."

Mira and I exchanged glances over the elderly woman's head, and my wife managed to keep the cookie plunder to just one. When Dixie offered the plate to me, however, I couldn't resist taking two, and Mira gave me the look of death.

"Now, Mira, if those storm sirens go off, you get you and Anna over here to my house. We can settle in the basement and listen to the radio and such." Dixie waggled her finger at my wife.

Mira smiled. "I think we can probably do that. They're saying it's supposed to move through fast, not more than a day or so."

That was more than I'd heard. "It's gonna rain on Mom's party."

"It will be fine. We'll adapt somehow."

We gathered up the cookie monster and returned home for dinner. About the time Mira put Annabelle to bed, I'd have to head out again to get Kidd, but until then I could claim some quality time with my family.

Quality time included dinner, one round of horsey through the house (the hardwood was killing my knees by the end), and a rather boisterous bath, where the floor got cleaner than the child.

I lingered long enough to tuck Annabelle in, kneeling at the side of her bed to kiss her good night. Of course, that led to kissing the stuffed wolf good night, too, then the stuffed dragon, then the rabbit, then . . . She had a lot of animals wanting kisses.

"Will you be here when I wake up, Daddy?"

The question caught me off guard. "Of course I will, button. Why would you ask that?"

She gave me a sleepy grin and clutched her stuffed wolf to her chest. "Just checking."

10

The sun was just beginning its descent as I arrived at the hotel, and Kidd's watch-puppy was waiting in the hallway, still wearing a suit and tie (though it was blue this time). I had to wonder if the man even owned any casual clothes.

"Mr. Verelli."

"My client has a curfew tonight, Mr. Dawson. I expect it to be observed." He pushed off the wall to scurry after me, taking two steps for every one of my long strides.

"Or what?" I was dying to know, really. He would have a threat prepared, if he was any kind of legal eagle.

"Or I will call the police and report him abducted."

That brought me up short, and I burst out laughing. "Don't you think that's a bit much? Start small and work your way up, grasshopper. Don't just jump straight to the big guns."

He frowned at me, a crease forming between his eyes, showing what kind of bitter old man he'd become one day. "You are mocking me."

"Every chance I get." I turned to face him, blocking the hallway. "Look. I appreciate that you're trying to protect your client, even if I think you're more interested in your paycheck than his well-being. But this

'Chihuahua yapping at my heels' act is going to get old, real fast, so you may as well drop it now."

He sneered. It had been a while since I'd seen a good old-fashioned sneer. "Demon slaying, Mr. Dawson? You couldn't find a more believable scam? Phony tree-removal maybe? Shoddy roofing jobs?"

"The wooden nickel racket dried up."

"I deal with con men on a daily basis, Mr. Dawson. I can smell one a mile away, and you reek."

"Have you checked your cologne? That stuff can go bad, y'know." I could keep this up all night.

He nodded stiffly, straightening his tie. "Very well, as you like. Everyone has secrets, Mr. Dawson. It's just a matter of locating yours. If you don't want that to happen, you will walk away from Mr. Kidd."

I stepped closer and gave him my most evil smirk. I saw the moment he realized I had a good five inches on him. I may not be a bulky man, but I know very well how to use my height to my advantage. "Are you attempting to blackmail me, Mr. Verelli?"

I had to give him credit. He stood his ground, though I could see the faint sheen of sweat break out on his forehead. I was willing to bet he'd never been in an actual fight in his life. "I am merely educating you as to the consequences of any dubious actions on your part."

"Man, you haven't *seen* dubious yet." I loomed just long enough to make him really nervous, then stepped back. "Get outta here, kid. Ya bother me. And learn to tie your shoes."

I left him standing in the hallway behind me, fuming. I was almost positive he couldn't do anything to me. Almost positive. Seventy percent sure. Okay, I wasn't sure at all, and it was starting to worry me.

Sure, if I ran around telling the world I was a demon slayer, they'd lock me up and medicate me into vegetation. Hence, not doing that. I was okay with Junior's not believing. But it was going to be a royal pain in the ass if he insisted on interfering. Seeing how easily he'd come up with information on my employment history, I had no doubt that he could dig up (or trump up) something to make my life more complicated. The question was how to get rid of him.

"Pompous little pencil-pusher," I grumbled to myself as I knocked on Kidd's door. He joined me with little fanfare, and we were on our way.

The old man was quiet as we drove north up the highway. He didn't remark on my ratty truck, which was good, because he might have hurt her feelings. He even held my sword for me without question. There was a look of intense weariness around his eyes. I assumed he'd been arguing with Skippy the Chihuahua all day, so I could sympathize.

The sun was only a deep red glow on the horizon when we pulled off the highway. I tried to pretend it didn't look like blood streaming through the darkening sky. I'm not a man who believes in portents, but things were just too weird lately. I took a few quick turns from the service road, and we pulled onto a seemingly random dirt road in the middle of nowhere. Only then did Kidd give me a quizzical look.

"It's property that belongs to the airport. I did a

favor once, and the security people look the other way if I need to use the land." I didn't owe him an explanation, but I hate it when people think I'm doing something shady and I'm not. Now, if I *am* doing something shady, then it's all right for them to think whatever they want. What? I wasn't always an honorable man.

I hopped out of the truck long enough to unlock the gate and swing it open. Then we bounced and rattled our way past the row of screening trees and into a large open area filled with tall prairie grass. I suppose it could be called a meadow, but that always makes me think of Bambi, which then leads to visions of some demon ripping Thumper's head off and sucking him like a juice box. Until you've seen the things I've seen in the last four years, don't be judgmental of my mental non sequiturs.

I used this place on the rare occasions that a local job dropped into my lap. It was secluded, impossible to see from the highway, and if the planes swooping low overhead happened to notice anything, it was easily explained as a trick of the eyes. We were in the dark of the moon, too, which would add to our concealment. With a witch for a wife, I had become very aware of the moon phases, and I used them to my advantage.

Kidd climbed out and watched as I removed my armor from the duffel bag in the back. Buckling it on was a lengthy process, but I'd become quite adept at doing it without help—and in the dark. "I thought the fighting wouldn't happen tonight."

"I said 'most likely.' Never take anything for

granted." I usually left the timing of the fight to the demon's choice. When it came time for negotiating, there were other, more important things I'd want to secure first. I left the plated leg guards in the bag. I wasn't about to wear new armor without giving it a good breaking in first.

Before I could do anything else, I had to pull my hair back, but since it was shorter now, doing so was a quick process.

"Is hairdressing really necessary?"

I wound the elastic band around it to hold it in place. "Loose hair falls across the eyes and creates a vision impairment. Gives the enemy an advantage."

"Why don't you just . . . cut it all off?"

"My wife likes my hair a little longer." For centuries, men had done stupider things for worse reasons.

Though it was getting hard to see in the dark, I thought I saw him frown as I slipped the chest piece over my head. "You're not wearing a cross."

"Should I be?" Ninety percent of my clients mentioned it.

"Isn't it . . . I mean, don't you need protection?"

"The only thing that gives a cross power is the belief behind it, Mr. Kidd. It'd be useless in my hands." Not entirely true. Faith was just another tool to harness magical ability. I had a distinct lack of both.

Though the night cooled quickly, the padding beneath my armor was stifling. Hopefully, this would be a quick negotiation and I could get it off.

"You don't believe in God?" The concept obviously

baffled him. It's not an unusual reaction, but it was one that required more explanation than I usually had the patience to give.

"I suppose there's something larger than myself at work. But I've never seen him, or her, or whatever. So I tend to believe in myself. In the end, I'm the only one who can let me down."

He shook his head in amazement. "How can you see demons, believe in demons, and not believe in God?"

I had to grin. "Funny how that works, isn't it?" Even amongst the people who do what I do, I'm an anomaly. I know this. Ivan lectures me on my lack of faith. He doesn't understand that I do have faith. I have faith in myself.

Mira, on the other hand, carries more than enough faith in the unknown for both of us. The undersides of my leather bracers were carved with intricate patterns. It was Marty's craftsmanship, but Mira's precise design. As I slid them on, I swore I could feel a faint tingle, the sensation of Mira's protective spells settling into place. I consider that the power of mental suggestion. I knew she'd put them there, so I imagined I could feel it. I suppose I did have more faith than I give myself credit for. I had faith in Mira.

Full dark had fallen by the time I finished my preparations and settled my sword on my hip. I sat the squirt bottle of nastiness on the hood of the truck, then motioned for Kidd to step out into the grass. "Go ahead. Call it."

"You . . . aren't going to draw a circle or anything? To . . . confine it?"

"You can, if you think it'll work." I shrugged, the chain jingling faintly. I've never seen a circle confine a summoned demon, even if I did have the juice to lay one myself.

Think on that, kiddies. Once you say that name, you give up all kinds of rights. When you speak that name, that demon has permission to be here with very few controls on its behavior. Sure, it can't hurt you unless you let it, but you also can't just tell it to sit and stay like a good puppy. Bargains, that's all they understand. Their language is one of negotiation, tit for tat. And if they can get a bigger tit for a smaller tat, they will.

"Just call it."

With one last uncertain look in my direction, Kidd stepped out into the tall grass and took a deep breath. "＿＿＿＿＿＿＿＿!"

Not a sound meant for human mouths to utter, it should have been something impossible to pronounce. For one brief shining moment, my sanity rejected the unfathomable tangle of vowels and consonants and rage and despair and greed and . . . It's impossible to explain how all that can be rolled up into one word. Pray—if you're the type that prays—you never understand it.

I tried not to listen, tried to shut out the sound, but a demonic name is something that gets under your skin, into your skull. My ears rang, and my spine tried to crawl out of my body and run away whimpering. The logical part of my mind, the part that screamed that such a thing could *not* be, was reduced to raving gibberish, and the name lodged there, finding a home amongst others of its kind.

I willed my heart to slow, my breathing to resume a steady cadence. Releasing my grip on my sword was a concentration of effort, one joint, one finger at a time.

With the name seared permanently into my psyche, I could roll it around and compare it to the others that resided there. No, this was not one I'd tangled with before. There was always that possibility: that a demon I'd beaten could regain enough strength to come across again. It hadn't happened yet. I'm not looking forward to it if it ever does. Demons don't strike me as the kind to forgive and forget.

Nothing happened at first. Kidd shot me a puzzled look, but I kept my eyes on the edges of the dark clearing. Our bad boy wanted to make an entrance. Demons always did.

Quite often, animal vision is based on movement. You can hide in plain sight of most creatures, so long as you keep very still. In the dark, humans are reduced to animals, the shades of gray and black blending into nothing, leaving us with only our most primitive instincts to guide us. And the first flicker of movement in the trees caught my attention instantly.

An old god stepped from the trees, moonlight casting dappled shadows over a stag's haunches, though the moon should have been dark for days yet. Leaves and vines twined about the bare male chest, catching in the antlers atop a curly head. He came forward with slow, stately steps, a look of profound sadness on his aged face.

I smirked. Drawn by the feel of Mira's magic, he'd chosen his form. It was a good show, to be sure, but if he was looking to awe and impress, he'd misread his audience.

I heard Kidd gasp when he first spotted the god-demon, and wondered what he saw. Illusion was easy, even for the weakest of demons. People were inclined to see what they wanted to see. I doubted this one had the strength to take on the stag-god's form in truth, so Kidd most likely saw whatever his mind conjured when it thought the word "demon."

When it got close enough, I reached in the window of my truck and flipped on the headlights. The demon drew back with a hiss, out of character with the wise and benevolent god he tried to ape, and shielded his eyes. "Rise and shine, Sparky."

From the look on Kidd's face, I was pretty sure he was about to collapse. I shrugged at him, armor chiming. "What, you prefer something more dignified? Into the light, I command thee, foul demon?" I picked up the squirt bottle and stepped into the circle of light.

The god-demon glared at me behind the shadow of his hands, but it would not cross that barrier between light and dark. As far as I know, the light doesn't actually hurt them. But man, they don't like it.

"True form now. Please." Politeness costs nothing. Yet. To illustrate what was going to happen if it refused, I sprayed the spice mixture into the air, adding cayenne to the scents of wilderness.

The demon growled softly. "You come with threats?

Who are you to command me?" The voice slid through my mind like an oil slick, oozing taint and power.

"Pleased to meet you. Hope you guess my name." That joke never gets old. I slay me. "True form. Now." I changed the squirt bottle from mist to stream. It was like setting the phasers to kill.

It growled again, but the change was made. There was no mystic transition, no light show or swirls of smoke. One moment, he was simply one thing; the next, something else. That something prowled the edge of the light on four legs, and gleaming teeth glistened with the snarl. Hackles of ebon fur bristled in irritation.

I suppose I could call it a hellhound, but it just felt so cliché. It was definitely no Scuttle. I was dealing with a higher order denizen of Hell here, one I not so affectionately dubbed a Skin—that being what I wanted to turn it into.

The bestial demons were not the most powerful when it came to manifesting on this side of the fence, but their sheer physical prowess made them more dangerous than their humanoid brethren. In the war between good and evil, they were Hell's Abrams tanks.

"I know what you are," the beast snarled, pacing a few yards, then back again. "Slayer. Champion. Human weakling."

"Hey, careful. My ego's sensitive." Watching the thing prowl the darkness, I thought seriously about putting down the bottle. My hand itched for my sword.

The hound sniffed in my direction, muzzle wrinkling. "The wards are not yours. I smell a female. You have no power of your own, fangless pup."

To hell with it. I dropped my hand to my katana. None of them had ever sensed Mira before, and I didn't like it. "I can show you my fang, if you want. Now, are we going to wave our dicks at each other, or talk deal?" Tact wasn't my strong suit.

"I am here for a bargain, yes? For that one's soul?" The narrow muzzle sniffed toward Nelson Kidd next. "Weak, diluted . . . hardly worth holding on to."

"Then you can just give it back and we'll call it good."

The creature barked a laugh and edged into the light. With the concealing shadows stripped away, it was even bigger than I'd thought. It resembled a cross between a hyena and a wolf, with a large square head and hulking shoulders, but the size of a pony—a large, demonic pony. "I think not." Its muzzle rippled when it chuckled.

"Name your terms, then." I settled on the bumper of my truck, keeping my scabbard clear and being careful not to block the headlights. These negotiations could stretch on for hours.

"My offer is the soul of Nelson Andrew Kidd." The demon went back to pacing. "What do you offer in return?" The stakes, that was always the first thing a demon asked for. They wanted their nice, juicy, Peep-flavored souls.

"My soul. The soul of Jesse James Dawson." I swear I saw those black ears perk up at that.

The hound actually licked its chops in anticipation.

"Your name is known to us." Wonderful. My reputation preceded me. "Accepted. Name your next term."

My right hand burned suddenly, starting between my first two knuckles. The smell of seared flesh filled the clearing. In the headlights, I could see a small black curlicue, no bigger than a snail's shell, on the back of my hand. One down; who knew how many to go.

"Physical fight only. No magic powers or hocus-pocus." I couldn't compete against something that could pop in and out of existence nearly at will.

It rumbled deep in its chest as it paced, a sound I took to indicate it was thinking. "You will forfeit your mystical protection then, as well. The female's spells."

I expected it—tit for tat. Calling for no magic was a fair deal, and Mira's protection wasn't going to stop a direct blow, anyway. My agreement to forego them would negate their power, with no effort on Mira's part. No knowledge on her part, either. I wasn't lying to her, precisely. And yes, I felt like a shit every time I did it. "Accepted. Next?"

I took a deep breath and let it out slowly as another portion of the tattoo scorched itself into my skin. Never let them know it hurts.

And so it went, back and forth. Negotiating challenge terms with a demon is rather like two attorneys picking a jury—an offer, a counteroffer, a veto. I had to be careful with my vetoes, though, because every one I used was one he could use, too.

And for every term, the contract was burned into my flesh. It covered the back of my hand and would probably reach my elbow before we were done.

I usually negotiated weapons first. As in, I wanted one. I'd never stand up against the fangs and claws bare-handed, no matter what my training. Preferably, I wanted something sharp or flaming; both, if I could get it. I'd roasted only one demon, but it had been a rather satisfying experience. I ended up with a "melee weapon of my choice." ('Cause if I specified my katana, they'd find a way to break it, and then I'd be screwed. Always gotta be thinking two steps ahead.)

We addressed location, time, witnesses. I wanted secluded (less collateral damage); we settled on deserted. And while it may sound like the same thing, it most definitely is not. Semantics is everything with Hellspawn.

The demon agreed I could have a second—someone had to drive me home afterward since I'm seldom in any condition to do it myself—and waived that right for itself. Apparently, demons do not play well with others. I stipulated what was to be done with my sword, if I lost. It would be delivered to Ivan, not Mira. It was bad enough that Axel visited the house. I didn't want any of these other creatures anywhere near my family.

The demon never stopped its pacing, but its mood could be told by the lift of its tail, the tilt of its ears. It conceded to some things it didn't really like and was inordinately cheerful when I agreed to a challenge date "under the full moon." A happy demon worried me, but I couldn't think of any good reason to veto it. Nighttime was the right time, after all, with fewer witnesses and fewer chances for accidental casualties.

And the two weeks until the moon came around again would give me time to truly prepare.

I wasn't sure if it was early or late by the time we'd set all the terms we could think of. My right hand and forearm were covered in elaborate demonic art, evidence of the bargain I'd so carefully crafted. The smell had long since faded out of my awareness, and the burns had passed into a dull throbbing ache. By morning, they'd be set, and I'd feel no more pain.

Kidd watched the entire proceeding in a kind of dumb silence, finally electing to have a seat near the truck's front tire. Maybe he even dozed a bit.

The demon vanished like the Cheshire cat, its toothy white smile remaining long after the rest of it had rejoined the night. "Under the full moon . . . I will be seeing you, champion. . . ." The insidious voice drew a shudder from me, despite my resolve not to let it rattle me.

Kidd startled when I nudged him with one knee. "C'mon. You missed curfew."

The old ballplayer blinked up at me with bleary eyes. "What happens now?"

"Now you go play your ball games, Mr. Kidd." I hauled him to his feet with one hand. "Go live your life for the next two weeks. Hug your wife, call your daughter, and tell her you love her. Then, come back."

Either that answer satisfied him or he wasn't fully awake for most of the trip back to the hotel. He didn't say a lot until we pulled into the parking lot.

"I'm not the only one, right?"

"Hm?" The lights in the lot cast blue-gray shadows over everything, giving Kidd a cadaverous appearance, deep shadows hollowing out his cheeks, ringing his eyes. I'm sure I looked just as bad. It wasn't flattering lighting.

He stared at his hands in his lap. "I mean, that . . . thing . . . It has other souls, right? Other people?"

"Probably."

"So . . . what happens to them, once you beat it?"

Not many people ask. They usually didn't see beyond their own fate. It made me think better of him. "Well . . . nothing. Unless they find a champion and ask for help, they'll just go on with that thing owning their soul. If they do decide to get out of it, the next champion that comes along will have an easier time of it, with the demon being weakened."

That was, of course, a theoretical assumption. Since we'd started keeping track, none of us had fought the same demon twice. None of us had even fought a demon that someone else had encountered. It seemed their population was legion. That was a little depressing, if you stopped to think about it.

"I wish we could help them, too," Kidd murmured, echoing my own thoughts.

I'd often wished for a way to get a roster of all the souls a demon held. Ivan insisted that, if a person was interested in saving himself, he'd find a way. But I'd always wondered—what if people just didn't know they still had a choice? Maybe, if we could contact those people after a demon's defeat, they'd be more willing to seek redemption, knowing the fight would be easier. Maybe they wouldn't care at all. I was continually surprised by the foibles of human nature.

"Get some rest, Mr. Kidd. It's late." Or early, maybe. The clock in my truck said two thirty. I'd quit resetting it for daylight saving time years ago, so it was either right or an hour off. Either way, it was past time for good little boys and girls to be in bed. "Call me again in about ten days so we can make arrangements."

"Thank you, Mr. Dawson." He slid out of the truck and disappeared into the hotel. Wandering sleepily toward home, I was very pleased not to see any blue Ford Escorts in my taillights.

11

Wednesday morning dawned, not with my wife in my arms and my daughter catapulting into my bed, but with the shrill clamor of the alarm clock.

"Buh? Muh . . ." I beat on it several times before I realized I was abusing the phone by mistake and corrected myself. I blinked at the offending luminescent digits for some time before they finally obeyed and became 7:00 a.m.

Why was the alarm going off so early? Where was Mira?

It finally occurred to me that it was Wednesday— truck day at the store. Mira had gone in early and no doubt taken Hurricane Annabelle with her. So why was I getting up at seven? After how late I was out last night, why was I getting up at all? On about four hours sleep, I was not even human. Someone should know this.

Zombie-me wandered to the bathroom to do all the usual morning things, and found a note taped to the mirror. *Doc appointment, 10:30 a.m. Don't forget! Work at 3 p.m.*

Groaning, I knocked my head against the wall next to the sink. Of course I'd forgotten. I had *intended* to forget. Face it, no man wants to go to the doctor. It just isn't bred into our DNA.

I'd only just gotten up, and already my day was jam-packed with fun and frivolity. It wasn't like the night before involving mundane things such as demon challenges, snippy agents, and soulless baseball players. No, today I faced true terror—a doctor's appointment and an afternoon shift at It. I suppose it says something about me that I find the banality of real life more taxing than the really freaky stuff. I often wonder whether I could function without having an adrenaline high for more than a week or two.

I actually do my doctor an injustice. She's a really *good* doctor. She patches me up; she puts up with my crap. Most of the time, when I don't have to be hospitalized, she takes what I can pay her and doesn't fuss too much if I have to carry the bill over for a month or two. Most important, she doesn't ask too many questions. I'm pretty sure she doesn't buy the security consultant line, but she doesn't know about the demons. Maybe she thinks I'm a spy or something. That'd be cool.

Hospitals, of course, are beyond her control, and those cost an arm and a leg. You can imagine that insurance companies really don't want to take me on. Two had dropped me already, and the most recent one was charging a small fortune to insure me as a "security consultant" (I doubt they had a category for "demon slayer"). It was only a matter of time before they dumped me, too.

For the pittance they paid out on my last hospital adventure, I should have just let the docs cut the damn leg off.

Since getting up at the butt-crack of dawn meant I had some time to spare, I fumbled into my sweats and grabbed my katana. It was time for us to become reacquainted after our long separation.

As I passed the patio table, I saw that Axel had made another move, countering my knight. I paused long enough to put a rook in harm's way, then stepped into the grass.

My usual katas, performed unarmed, I did for exercise and to keep my skills sharp. My sword katas, I did for love. There was just something so *right* about feeling that weight in my hand, moving with the balance point just below the guard, feeling my own reach extend to the tip of the sharp blade.

The logical part of my mind ticked off the forms as I passed through them. Upper form was to block an overhand attack or bring the blade down with force on an opponent. Lower form was to flow into an uppercut or to block across the body. Step here, step there, move, shift, turn. But my mind's eye saw the hellhound, and each strike countered an imaginary attack or took advantage of a potential weakness.

The demon-hound outweighed me and out-massed me. I had to keep it at sword's reach and move fast—slicing wounds, not stabbing. There was too much risk of being disarmed that way. Many small wounds would bleed as much as one big one, and that was what I needed. I had to drain away the blight, the physical embodiment of the creature's will. Only its will kept it here. The thing had to bleed.

I fought my imaginary opponent for an hour and

a half, trampling patterns in the dew-soaked grass through my phantom battle. But in the end, I felt confident that I knew how to defeat it—not certain, never certain, but confident.

And you're probably thinking I should just take a gun and shoot the damn thing. It's a good idea, in theory, until you realize that when you're shooting something that doesn't have a kill point, a vital organ to hit and incapacitate or kill it, your only recourse is to cause massive amounts of damage. Most firearms don't cause enough damage, and you'll run out of bullets before you poke enough holes in it. The guns that *do* cause enough damage—the large calibers, the huge automatics—well, you can never be sure where those bullets are going to stop, after they pass through your target. And I'm not a big fan of collateral damage, so blades are best in most cases. Though, there *was* the flame-thrower incident. That was a hoot.

At the appointed hour, showered and clean-shaven in honor of spring, I appeared at the office of one Dr. Bridget Smith, who happened to be sitting at her receptionist's desk when I walked in. It was a small family practice, cozy and comfortable. The chairs, in soothing pastel colors, matched the artistic watercolor prints on the walls, which in turn complemented the delicate paisley pattern in the carpet. I had no idea why I knew what paisley was, and it vaguely disturbed me.

It was apparently my lucky day. I was the only patient there. *Oh joy, glee and rapture, even.* Even in my head, I have to be sarcastic.

"Hey, Jesse." Dr. Bridget is one of those women

who makes "heavy" look damn good. I didn't know enough about fashion to figure out why the plum-colored blouse and tailored gray skirt looked so great on her. Whatever it was, her clothes accented all the right curves. She was . . . What was the word? Voluptuous. Yeah, that's it. And if I ever said it out loud, she and Mira would both thump me right between the eyes for it. Did I mention that she's Mira's best friend from college? Yeah. Awkward much? Hell yeah. Especially when you consider that I dated Bridget first.

Realistically, I should have picked a different doctor. But as I said, Dr. Bridget cuts me lots of slack in important areas. I doubt another doc would have.

A lock of dark hair had come free from her neat bun, and she brushed it out of her eyes with a frazzled grin. Her white lab coat was tossed over an empty chair, and there were about fifteen files scattered about, presumably in some order unfathomable to the layman. "Nice shirt."

The T-shirt slogan of the day, IN TOUCH WITH MY INNER PIRATE, was emblazoned across a rustic skull and crossbones.

"Rough day already?" I found a clean, and therefore safe, place to perch and observe the chaos.

"Kim's out sick today, so I'm a little behind already." She glanced around, looking for something, then threw up her hands in exasperation when it failed to leap to her attention. "Where did I put that file? I just had it. . . ."

Yes! "We can cancel. I can come back another time." I edged toward the door, tasting freedom.

"No, no, you're a quick one. Just head on back to the grape room and get the pants off. I'll catch up in a second."

Dammit. So near, and yet so far. And for the record, there is something very wrong about your wife's best friend ordering you to get your pants off, doctor or no. "The grape room?"

She gave me a smirk. "I treat kids, too. It's to make them feel comfortable."

"I'm not saying a word." Like a good little boy, I headed back to the examination room with the very purple door and shed my boots and jeans. That left me in an icy cold office in my SpongeBob boxer shorts (a Father's Day present from Anna). Somewhere, there was a sheet thing she'd want me to wrap around myself for modesty. Now where was it?

"So, how's Annabelle doing?" I could hear her shuffle papers out front as she called back to me.

"Oh fine. Y'know—too smart for her own good."

"She excited about school this fall?"

"Oh yeah, driving us nuts about it." Sheet, sheet . . . Where would I be, if I were a sheet? *Aha!* There was a cabinet under the exam table.

Of course, as I bent over to explore the cabinet, Dr. Bridget walked in behind me. "Nice boxers."

I yelped—a manly yelp, I swear—and snatched up a sheet to hold protectively in front of me. She smirked.

"I've seen you naked, Jess."

"Unconscious and bleeding does not count as naked."

The new tattoo on my right arm caught her attention, and she turned my wrist this way and that, examining it. "New tattoo?"

"Temporary. Just trying it out to see if I like it or not before I commit."

She rolled her eyes at me with that expression of supreme female amusement. "Hop up on the table, and let me see the calf first."

I scooted my scrawny butt up on the crispy paper as instructed and arranged the sheet so she could get a good look at my right leg. The scars were almost perfect circles of shiny pink skin on either side of my calf, hairless and smooth. It looked like I'd tangled with a really big hole punch.

Bridget poked and prodded at me with cold fingers, making those "hmm" noises that doctors do. "Any tenderness?"

"Nope."

"Any muscle weakness or spasm?"

"Nope." Aside from what my workouts brought on, but she didn't need to know that.

"It doesn't look like the poison left any lingering tissue damage." She shook her head thoughtfully. "I still don't know how you managed to clear that out of your system so fast, when we couldn't even figure out what it was."

I knew how. The doctors in Bethesda ran every test they could think of to identify the toxin in my system, with no luck. In fact, more than half the samples were misplaced or destroyed. At first, the hospital staff joked that I was the unluckiest patient ever. When I kept getting worse, with no antidote in sight, it wasn't so funny anymore.

Enter Mira, her herbs, and her magic. They flew her out, quietly telling her she may need to say her good-byes to me. For three days in the ICU, she snuck me her own brand of medicine and prayed to her goddess while my right calf turned dark and sent ominous red streaks up my thigh. I don't know how high they had the morphine drip set, but I was pretty much a veg-etable for the really fun parts. All I could remember of the intense fever was being so very thirsty. And just when the doctors started mumbling about amputation, the infection receded, my skin pinked up, and I started to heal. The doctors congratulated themselves for a job well done, all the while wondering what the hell they did that finally worked.

The secret of it always made me smile. It wasn't a modern medical miracle. It was an ancient one. I al-ways wondered what the doctors would think of that if they knew.

"You still doing the exercises?" Bridget, oblivious to my wandering thoughts, continued groping my leg.

"Yep." She gave me a look that said she didn't be-lieve me. "I am, I swear! Ask Mira."

"Okay, slide down. Let me see the hip."

This was the tricky part. In order for her to see the hip to her satisfaction, the boxers had to go. It was an interesting dance to accomplish that without losing the sheet, and of course she wouldn't make it easier by leaving the room. She did turn her back, though. Hur-ray for professionalism amongst friends.

She made me do a few runway walks across the

room, and a couple deep squats, just to prove I could. "You want me to balance on one leg and juggle torches next?"

The good doctor ignored me. "Looks like your range of motion is almost back to normal. You might have some pain in cold or rainy weather, though." She leaned against the sink and gave me that thoughtful look. I hated that look. Nothing good ever followed *that* look. "That's a helluva scar collection you have going, you know." *Crap.* It was *this* conversation.

I glanced down. My legs, aside from the most recent acquisition, were unscarred. There were, of course, the lovely claw marks down my left side from armpit to hip, a constant reminder that I was most definitely human. There were also the other minor ones I'd collected over the last few years. They were nothing grossly disfiguring, but they were probably not the kind of scars a security consultant should have. Since no one was actually sure what a security consultant *did*, no one called me on it. "Chicks dig scars, right?"

Bridget shook her head, the friend gone and the doctor firmly in place. "The older you get, the more your body is going to hate you. Maybe you ought to think of slowing down some, while you're still healthy."

"I'm thirty-two, Bridge. Not a hundred thirty-two."

"You want to live to see thirty-five?"

Of course I wanted to. The odds of it, though? Not good. I accepted that a long time ago. The samurai fears not death, only a bad death. "You know, Cole's a cop, and no one gives him this shit."

"Cole doesn't have four ICU stays under his belt."

"I'm not going to argue this with you again, Bridge." She was a friend, yes. But even friends have limits.

"Mira and Anna—"

"Mira and I have talked about it," I said in my best end-of-discussion voice. In fact, we'd talked and screamed and thrown things. . . . Yeah, it had been discussed—at length. "And they will always be taken care of."

Her jaw clenched, and I could hear her teeth grinding. I have that effect on a lot of women. "Fine. But as your doctor, I'm obligated to tell you to slow down." She threw my pants at me, smacking me in the chest. Trying to catch them, I dropped the sheet, and there was a scramble to cover myself with something, anything. Bridget smirked. "And as your friend, I'm reminding you that Mira says not to forget your mom's birthday present."

"You have got to be kidding me," I muttered, dressing after the doc left the room. Was there anyone Mira *hadn't* told? This was getting ridiculous.

I wandered back out to the front to find Bridget at the receptionist's desk again and three people in the waiting room. The doc glanced up at me once. "I've got you down for another checkup in a month, Jess. Keep doing the therapy; maybe get some swimming in this summer."

That earned a grimace. I don't swim. I do sink rather well, though. "I'll see what I can manage."

She grabbed my hand when I went to leave and lowered her voice. "God watches out for you, Jess. I firmly believe that. But you can't keep testing him this way." She had that look in her gray eyes, the one that said she truly believed. How my wife the witch and this devout Catholic became best friends, I will never know.

"You worry too much, Doc." No doubt, she would spend her next visit with Mira detailing just what kind of a worthless sumbitch I was. There were times when I wondered if she was right.

The sun was bright when I walked out into the parking lot. There wasn't a cloud in the steel blue sky, and it looked as if that sky went on forever. Sometimes I wondered how the world could look so cheerful, knowing what horrible things existed there. Then I thought of people like Bridget—good people, with faith in a greater power, in absolute good. I hoped I wouldn't let them down.

12

As I was clambering into my truck, my hip buzzed. I was learning to hate my cell phone. It never brought good news. There was some wriggling involved, but I finally got it out of my pocket. "Hello?"

"Dawson." In just that single word, I could hear defeat in the old Ukrainian's gravelly voice. My stomach tied itself in knots in anticipation of bad news.

"Hey, Ivan. What's the word?" I rolled the window down and got comfortable. It wasn't like anyone needed my parking spot.

"Is there to be any chance that you are to be hearing from Archer, of late?"

I frowned at the odd question. I'd met Guy Archer only once, and we weren't what I would call close. He was a stocky man with black hair graying at the temples, stick-straight posture, a faint French accent. Stoic didn't even begin to describe his expression. Ex-military, I thought, or possibly Royal Canadian Mounted Police. In plaid shirts, blue jeans, and worn work boots, he looked like a lumberjack, and he bore that impression out when I saw him pin a playing card to a tree trunk with a thrown hatchet. Lumberjacks did that kind of thing, right?

We had exchanged nods and not much else. I stuck to the United States mostly, and Guy sat up there in

Toronto, doing his own thing. Miguel, yeah, I kept in touch with him, but Guy—not so much. "No, not for months. Why?" There was a long silence on the other end of the line. "Ivan? You still there?"

"I was to be managing to receive one message from Grapevine. Archer was to be checking in last week. He has not."

Ice ran down my spine, despite the rapidly warming day. "Maybe he just forgot."

"Maybe. But I am not believing that. Neither are you."

He was right. I didn't believe it for an instant. You *always* made your check-in call. Always. Ivan drilled it into our heads from the moment he turned up on our doorsteps. *"In this day of technology miracles, there is no reason we are to be fighting alone."* There was no acceptable excuse for missing a check-in.

Champions died. It was a fact of our existence. But in the last four years, we'd lost three total. To lose two, within weeks of each other? It was unthinkable. And these weren't rookies, either. Both men were experienced fighters. "What the hell is going on, Ivan?"

"I am not to be knowing." That baritone voice quavered. I think that was when I really knew it was bad. Ivan had seen it all. Nothing was supposed to shake him.

"Did you ever find Miguel's weapon?"

He took a deep breath, causing static on the line. It gave us both a moment to collect ourselves. I was getting more scared by the moment. Ivan was our rock. If he was crumbling, the rest of us were in deep shit.

"Ah . . . that. It is possible that mystery is to being solved. Miguel's younger brother is to also be missing."

That was supposed to solve the mystery? "And?"

"We are believing that Miguel's contract was for the machete to be delivered to the brother. If Miguel has perished, perhaps he has taken it and gone in pursuit of Miguel's soul."

That made sense, in an incredibly stupid teenager kind of way. For Miguel's family, demon hunting was in the blood. To hear Miguel tell it, they'd done it since before the Christians conquered the Aztecs.

Of course, the kid was also next in a family who had a history of getting eaten by demons. I might have bugged out, too, at that age.

"Shit, he's what, thirteen?"

"Seventeen." Easily old enough to get himself killed and have his soul stolen. Also old enough to know he didn't want to die like that.

"And you still don't know who Miguel worked for last?"

"There are leads I am to be tracing. It is being difficult, from here. Signals are bad, in the hills, and the power is not to being steady."

"You gotta find that kid, Ivan. If he *has* gone hunting, he knows who Miguel was working for." And he was about to be in way over his head.

"I am to be trying my best. I fear it is to be taking time we do not have."

"Is there anything I can do?" Please, let there be something I could do. I hated sitting here, thousands of miles away, feeling useless.

"You said you were to be having a mission?"

For me, they were paying clients. For Ivan, they were missions to save worthy souls. I won't even get into Ivan's objections to me charging money for what I do. "Yeah, here in town."

"Do not be taking it."

I sighed and resisted the urge to bang my head against my steering wheel. The black marks on my skin proved it was already too late for that. "The contract's already set. I can't back out now. But I've got two weeks until the challenge. I'm in no immediate danger."

"How powerful is it to being?"

"It's a Skin."

"A what?" Okay, so not everyone is up on my lexicon.

"A beast type. A wolf-hyena thing big enough that I could ride it to work."

He said something that was undoubtedly a Ukrainian curse. "I am to be coming there, then. As soon as I am to be finished here. Things are to being very wrong."

"Do you need me to track down any of the others, make sure they're all accounted for?" I'd met three champions, besides myself and Ivan. I had no doubt that two of those were dead now. The rest . . . their names and contact information lay within Grapevine, and though they were only pixels on a screen for me, I'd do anything in my power to protect them.

"*Tak.* That would be most helpful. Do be telling them do not take on more missions until I am giving the word."

I scratched my jaw. It itched where I'd shaved. "You think something's taking a swipe at us?" Immediately, the blue Ford Escort leapt to mind. Yeah, something was after us.

"It is not to being possible. The contracts must be followed. They cannot to be attacking without permission." He said it forcefully, as if sheer will would make it so.

In all honesty, it should have been true. Rule number one: A person had to consent to any harm a demon brought him. There was no such thing as an unwilling victim; unwitting, yes, but never unwilling. That rule was older than anyone's memory, and inviolable—until now.

"Well, 'til we figure this out, you watch your own back. Nothing would cripple us faster than losing you."

He sounded grim when he said, "*Tak*. I am to be realizing this more and more." I didn't like the sound of that. "I will to be calling you at this time tomorrow, if not to being earlier."

"If you don't, I'm hopping a plane to Mexico."

He chuckled faintly, but it was forced. "God to be watching over you, Dawson. Whichever one will to be having you."

"You, too, Ivan."

I sat in my truck for a long time after I hung up the phone. Some random, unidentifiable birds hopped around the parking lot, picking tasty tidbits out of the asphalt. There was no breeze, but the day hadn't yet hit that mugginess of which Missouri summers are capable. A multitude of cars drove up and down the busy street just beyond the parking lot, the drivers oblivious to the world changing right under them.

None of them knew two particular men were dead. Though an infinitely small drop in a huge bucket, those two men had fought all their lives to protect people they'd barely known. They had shed blood countless times for no other reason than it was the right thing to do.

Only last summer, Mira and I had gone to Mexico for Miguel's wedding, and he had presented his beautiful new bride to us. His whole face glowed when he looked at her. I felt the same way when I looked at Mira. Now Rosaline was a widow, joining the growing ranks of women who were collateral damage in the battle between good and evil. Miguel also left behind his mother, three brothers, and who knew how many nieces and nephews.

Guy . . . I didn't know Guy. Was there a Mrs. Lumberjack? Did he leave behind a family to mourn him or a child who would never know him? Or was he just one of the many nameless, faceless disappearances in the world? Would anyone have known, if Ivan didn't keep track of us all?

Fame, glory . . . A Jedi craves not these things; a samurai doesn't, either. But a part of me wanted to go grab some random person, shake him until his teeth rattled, and scream, "Don't you know, don't you care what these people have sacrificed, all for you?"

I was angry—angry at Miguel and Guy for not seeing a trap coming, because surely that's what had to have happened; angry at the forces of Hell, for taking two good men away; angry at the forces of Heaven, too, if such a thing existed, for allowing Hell to happen in the first place; furious with myself for the black brand covering my right arm. Without that, I could have gone looking myself. But no, instead my soul was in the keeping of some metaphysical escrow agent for another two weeks. Without something to bargain with, there was nothing I could do.

I gripped my steering wheel until my knuckles went white, taking breath after breath to calm myself down. It wasn't fair. The good guys were supposed to win. I punched the center of the steering wheel, and my dead horn gave a sad attempt at a chirp.

When I'm upset, there's only one place I want to be.

I slammed my poor truck through the gears faster than necessary, and she shuddered and groaned as I pulled out of the parking lot. Anything less than the speed of light was too slow to get me to my desired destination, so I'd have to be content with what I could get out of the aging vehicle.

The drive gave me time to calm down. It also gave me time to watch for a blue Ford Escort that never appeared. Great, now I was pissed off, and completely paranoid. How comforting.

The Westport district, trendy and upscale, was fairly quiet on a weekday. Dotted with small shops and galleries, it easily seemed quaint, even touristy. The bars and clubs would light the night later, of course, and hordes of on-the-prowl singles would be out exploring the wonders of the opposite sex. You could find everything from Irish pubs and classy microbreweries to sports bars and actual dives, complete with sticky seats and questionable cleaning practices. But at the moment, I had very little traffic to contend with as I skirted the outer edges.

There were no open parking spaces on the street in front of Mira's shop, so I whipped through the alley, around the back of the building, and into the tiny, oddly shaped parking lot. There was barely room back there for Mira's car and that of her coworker, let alone any customers. Parking was at a premium in Westport, where the buildings and streets had been fitted together like puzzle pieces in all shapes and sizes.

Around front, I glanced at the sign hanging over the sidewalk—proudly proclaiming SEVENTH SENSE in green vine-covered lettering—and dodged a departing customer as I came in the door. The bamboo chimes overhead clunked together softly. The aroma of some delicate incense wafted around me, and I tried to place just what fragrance it was—something light and flowery. Freesia, maybe? Yet another thing no self-respecting man should know.

The lower floor displayed an assortment of tools, artifacts, icons, and memorabilia for almost every religion found on the planet. There were pentacles, crosses of every style imaginable, Buddhas and Egyptian deities gazing down from any and all conceivable surfaces. The south wall was a fragrant cornucopia of incense and candles, herb sachets, and . . . hell, I didn't know what half of it was—smelly stuff. The north wall was devoted to an assortment of cheerfully bubbling aquatic hangings and displays, the gurgle of water a pleasant counterpoint to the faint Celtic music in the background.

A wrought-iron staircase spiraled up to the second floor, barely more than a railed walkway lined with shelf upon shelf of books. There were books on Christianity, books on paganism, books on ghosts and ghoulies, and books on pet psychiatry. If you wanted it, and it was slightly off-kilter, Mira probably had it or knew where to get it.

Mira herself was behind the counter, ringing up yet another customer. Her dark curls were a loose cloud around her shoulders, and she was wearing a lavender sweater over a silk skirt, tie-dyed in swirling shades of teal and green. When she moved, she almost floated across the floor. She offered me a smile, letting me know she'd seen me. "How was the appointment, honey?"

"Oh, fine. She wants me back in a month."

"You knew she would." She shook her head with a chuckle, returning her attention to her patron.

Annabelle was not so restrained.

"Daddy!" She came shrieking out of the back room, and I swept her into my arms, holding her tightly. "You came to see me!"

"I sure did! Are you being good for Mommy?"

She nodded solemnly, and I glanced at Mira for confirmation. Never trust a five-year-old's interpretation of "good." Mira chuckled as she joined us. "She's been fine. And you shaved!" She stroked her fingers down my cheek. "You know you *still* have to get your mother a birthday present, right? Losing the beard isn't enough."

I drew my wife close and held both my girls as tightly as I could for a moment. The scent of strawberries and Play-Doh overwhelmed the incense, and I buried my face in Anna's fiery hair, just to breathe it in. Heartbeats passed, one . . . two . . . three. . . . I held them too long, too tight.

"Daddy, you're squishing me!"

Mira leaned back and gave me a quizzical look. "Jess?"

Anna wiggled impatiently, and I stooped to set her on her feet. "Go play, kiddo." She scampered off obediently. Mira was still giving me that look.

"Is everything all right?"

"Yeah, it's fine." It wasn't, though. And in a world with so many wrongs, I just wasn't ready for things to go *more* wrong. "Can you do me a favor when you get home tonight?"

"Sure."

"Ward the house again."

She frowned at me, those little creases forming around her eyes. "Why?"

"Just . . . humor me." I couldn't be with her every moment of every day. I couldn't hire armed guards to protect her in my absence. I couldn't put her in a pretty box and keep her safe for all time. All I had were the intangible, magical protections I couldn't even touch.

Mira eyed me thoughtfully, chewing her lower lip, then craned her neck to see the upper floor. "Hey, Dee?"

Her one and only employee, Dee, glanced down from on high. The only word to describe Dee was jolly. I believe Dee was born smiling, and someday she'll die, jiggling all over from irrepressible giggles, the beads in her cornrows clattering merrily. And there was a lot of her to jiggle. I don't say that to be mean, but she was a large woman. Her dark eyes were always sparkling out of her equally dark face, and she had a heart big enough to go with the rest of her. "Yeah, Mir?"

"I'm gonna duck into the back room a second. Can you keep an eye on the door?"

"Sure thing!" Dee lumbered her way toward the spiral staircase, and for a moment, I wanted to linger just to see how she navigated it. Mira never gave me the chance, holding my hand prisoner as she dragged me into their storeroom, closing the door behind us.

It was truck day, and there were boxes stacked four high, leaving barely enough room for one person, let alone two. "You know she thinks we're ducking back here for some nookie, right?"

She was neither amused nor distracted by my crude humor. "What's wrong, Jess?" It was that "Don't give me your BS" voice.

I sighed softly. I didn't want to tell her, and yet I knew I would feel profoundly relieved once I had. "Guy Archer is missing."

She was quiet for a long time, nibbling her lower lip. "They're dead, aren't they?"

"We . . . don't know that for sure."

"But you think they are."

I ran a hand over my hair, habitually checking to see that it was still confined tightly in its usual tail. "Yeah. I think they are."

"And the others?"

"Ivan wants me to send out an all-call through Grapevine. He's gonna come up here, when he's done down in Mexico."

She sighed, shaking her head. "Goddess . . . Poor Rosaline."

"Yeah." There was no doubt in my mind that Mira would get along just fine when something happened to me. I wasn't so sure about Rosaline. "Ivan will see that she's taken care of, and she has all of Miguel's family, too."

"Is there any way to find out how it happened? To put their souls at rest?"

I shrugged. "Ivan's working on that, too. If there's a way, he'll find it."

"I could scry for Guy, too. If I had something of his."

"No." Even as I gave my flat refusal, her jaw firmed and I knew I should have chosen a different tone. "There's no reason for you to tax yourself that way. If Ivan wants him scoped out, he'll find someone to do it. Miguel's mother, maybe." Miguel's mother was a powerful *bruja* in her own right.

"Or you could just find a way to get me something of Guy's, and I could do it myself."

"I'm not going to do that."

She crossed her arms over her chest, and I did the same. Mexican standoff. Great. "We have to know, Jesse. If Guy's in trouble, if we can find him, we can't afford to wait."

I chewed on the inside of my lip for a bit, debating the different courses I could take. And in the end, I caved—sort of. "All right. I'll see if I can find something. *But*, we give Ivan a chance first. He may not even need you to do this."

A certain wariness crept into her green eyes. "And when he finds who did this?" she asked as if she already knew the answer. Maybe she did. She married me, after all.

"Then I'm going hunting." I could have told her I'd stay out of it, but she knew better. My wife is a smart woman. "I think I'm going to go in early to work. I don't really want to be alone at the house."

She nodded a bit, her eyes dark and unfathomable. "Okay. I'll work on the wards when I get home."

I reached for the door, then paused. "Hey, Mira? Keep an eye out for any blue cars cruising the neighborhood that you don't recognize, okay?"

"Blue cars?"

"Yeah, little ones. Ford Escorts." Mira wouldn't know an Escort from a Humvee, but it was worth a shot.

"Why, exactly?"

"Just because." It felt like lying, and I hated that feeling. But she didn't need any more worry. "I love you." People say you should always tell your loved ones how you feel, because you might not get another chance. I wonder if they really, truly, to the depths of their souls, understand how true that is.

She reached out to grip my hand, squeezing with all her might. "I love you, too, Jesse. Please be careful."

It occurred to me, much later, that she hadn't actually agreed to my terms on the scrying. *Dammit!*

13

Despite what I'd told Mira, I swung back past the house again. Ivan needed me to get the word out, and it was far better than just sitting and doing nothing.

I felt a prickling on my skin as I ducked through the doorway into Mira's sanctuary, no doubt crossing the boundary of some spell she'd placed there.

I didn't come in there often. I always felt as if I was intruding. But that's where the computer was, so on occasion, I dared to invade her domain. She didn't seem to mind. I fired up the machine, waiting patiently as the ancient, five-year-old contraption whined and purred in its gyrations. If we could afford it, I planned to get her a new one for Christmas.

I had to jump through three or four security hoops before I could get to the site I was actually aiming for. Ivan had named the database Grapevine. I'm not even sure why. Within, you could find the names and addresses of every champion Ivan knew. You could also find the dates of battles, identities of clients, and various and sundry other trivia. That is, if you could get in. It was hidden behind I don't know how many types of encryption and firewalls and security and . . . Well, we'll just say I consider computers right up there with magic. I don't understand them, and I don't need to, so long as they work.

The elderly computer doggedly worked at loading the site, when a window popped up with a message and a woman's electronic scream echoed from the speakers. "I see you!"

"Gah!" My heart slammed in my chest, and I heard a faint snicker coming from the earphones where they rested on the desk. After I recovered, I snatched up the headset with its handy mic and slapped it on. "Goddammit, Viljo, that's not funny!"

The man's voice on the other end chuckled. "It was from where I am sitting." It never fails to amaze me how well he speaks English, especially after dealing with Ivan's regular slaughtering of our language.

A Finnish native now residing somewhere near Pikes Peak, Viljo is our pet computer geek. By "our," I mean Ivan and his champions. As far as I know, Ivan is all that stands between Viljo and extradition back to Finland to face charges for computer crimes.

Once upon a time, dear Viljo bargained his soul away. I'm not sure who fought for him, but as repayment for being freed, he kept Grapevine functional and tightly locked down as only a hacker can.

You might ask what a computer genius sells his soul for? (Well, I wanted to know, at least, so I asked.) The answer is the world's greatest hack, of course. Ever hear of the Great Firewall of China? Yeah, that thing that pretty much edits whatever the Chinese folk get to access on the Internet? A couple years ago, a hacker with the handle GMontag brought it crashing down to the point where it took the Chinese government three months to get it functional again. GMontag was a legend amongst hackers, their very own cyber-messiah (or so I'm told). And GMontag was none other than our very own Viljo.

I asked him once if it was worth it. He said, "If I had been thinking clearly, I would have arranged to bring it down forever, not just for three months." Ah, the clarity of hindsight.

"What brings you to my neck of the cyber world? You are not due to check in for another two weeks." Another window popped up, this one with a choppy video feed of Viljo's face. Our poor computer could barely handle it, and the resulting image was grainy and barely recognizable. It didn't help that he was sitting in a dimly lit room, surrounded by at least seven computer monitors (that I could see). All I could make out was the dark outline of his glasses and the dyed matte black of his long hair. And was that a tiny scraggly attempt at a mustache? Ye gods.

He frowned at the screen in disgust. "You still do not have a camera? Or even an adequate operating system?" I watched him for a few moments as his attention focused on the three keyboards he kept within easy reach, the image jerking like bad stop-action animation. I knew he was poking around inside Mira's computer as easily as he did his own.

Some ungodly wail came over the headset, and it took me a few moments to realize Viljo was listening to music. "Are you listening to Björk?"

He made a quick motion with his hands, and the song cut off in midhowl. "No." Even over a crappy webcam feed, he looked sheepish, and I laughed. "Do you know what I could do to your computer from here? And still you mock me."

I snorted. "You won't do anything to it. You're afraid of Mira."

"That is not true." Yes it was. Anyone in his right mind would be. My wife is a formidable woman. I guess it's true that we look for wives just like our mothers.

"Even if I did not plant a virus here, anyone else could." The flustered little geek gave me a stern look. It might have had a better effect if I had never heard him scream like a girl at the sight of a spider. "You realize that even the manufacturer says this operating system should not be connected to the Internet, yes? Do you even listen when I tell you these things?" The stuttering picture shook its finger at me, glowering behind the thick lenses. Nerd rage is an amusing thing to see.

"Ivan wanted me to check in. He has no Net access where he is."

"Is he still in Mexico?"

"As of this morning, yeah. He's still trying to find out what happened to Miguel."

Viljo sighed and shook his head, his pixelated image taking a few seconds to catch up with his words. "I do not like it. It feels all wrong."

I agreed wholeheartedly. "Can you send out an all-call to everyone, and have them all check in early? Ivan wants a head count."

"Even the Knights Stuck-up-idus?" The Ordo Sancti Silvii, the Order of St. Silvius, was a small band of champions attached to the Catholic Church. They considered themselves separate and apart from (and snidely superior to) our loose organization. Personally, I thought they were a bunch of elitist snobs, but Ivan claimed responsibility for them, anyway, and expected us to defend them just as we would anyone else.

"Yeah. I doubt they'll answer, but we can try." I rocked in Mira's chair, noting absently that it was nice to have a chair with both arms firmly attached. "Can you check and see when Miguel and Guy logged in last?"

"Yeah, sure, easily done." I could see the frown, even in the grainy image. "But it is funny you ask. They both e-mailed me, saying they were having problems connecting to the site."

"When was that?"

"Oh . . . three weeks ago, for Miguel. Guy was longer than that. Five weeks? Of course, I do not hear from Miguel that often. He must go into the city to get a connection as it is. But Guy, he has never missed a check-in, until now."

Shortly before Miguel disappeared, then. And, if Guy was truly gone, then shortly before his disappearance as well. "You figure out what the problem was?"

"No. I needed to be on at the same time they were to see what was happening, and we never got the chance. Why? You think it is connected somehow?"

"Viljo, in the three years you've been doing this, the site has never gone down or had any access or security issues. Not once. And suddenly two people have problems, and then disappear? Yeah, it's hinky."

"I did not think of that." He sounded ashamed.

"Listen, why don't you flex those hacker skills of yours. See if you can find anything in their phone records that match up, or any registered travel plans or anything."

He grinned at the webcam. "You are asking me to hack across international lines, you know."

"That a problem?"

"Not as long as the old man has bribe money for immigration."

I snorted. "If you get caught, you deserve to get deported. You're better than that."

He flexed for the camera. "I know. I just wanted to hear you say it. Anything else?" I hesitated long enough that he asked, "Jesse?"

"I'm here." I so did not want to do this. "Do you have anything of Guy's? A personal item?"

"Um . . . I have the card he sent me for Christmas last year." That made me feel bad. I'd never sent Viljo a card.

"That might work." I'd be happier if it didn't. "Could you send me that, or anything else of his you have?"

"Mira working some mojo?"

"Maybe."

"Yeah, I can overnight it. You'll have it tomorrow."

"Thanks, Viljo. Nice mustache." I shut down the window before he could retort, then sighed, finding myself alone in the quiet house.

Part of me hoped that Viljo didn't find anything on Miguel and Guy. I wanted this to be a horrible, tragic coincidence, even though the churning in my gut was telling me otherwise. I wanted to laugh with Miguel and Guy about it, a week from now. Most especially, I did not want Mira trying to scry for Guy's location—not this close to the last attempt; not at all, really.

While normally I enjoyed peace and quiet as much as the next guy, today the house was eerie without Mira's bustling and Anna's usual chatter. Even the creaking and groaning of the building itself seemed ominous, a warning of impending collapse or something. I didn't want to be there.

Had I remembered that Rookie Paulo would be at work, I don't think I'd have been in such a rush to get there, either.

Señor Sulk was slouched against the wall behind the register, where someone had apparently left him on his own. Thankfully, there were no customers. His sullen gaze followed me all the way to the back as I dumped my stuff in my locker, then back out to the front.

"Hey, Paulo." I glanced up to find Sarah on a ladder above me, rearranging the T-shirts on the wall. "Hey, Sarah." Realizing what she was wearing, I averted my eyes quickly. Please, someone tell the girl *not* to wear skirts when she's climbing ladders. *Kids.*

"Hey, old dude. You wanna hand me that?" Her hand fluttered in the air until I blindly slapped a T-shirt board into it. If she was surprised to see me start my shift early, she didn't say so. "Kristyn says we're moving the clearance shelves to the other side, if you wanna start on that. Paulo's got the register, and I'm right here to keep an eye on him."

If I hadn't been in such a grim mood already, I might have danced. Okay, maybe not danced, but I could have twitched a little or something. Training Paulo was not high on my list of life's enjoyable events. "So who else is coming in today?"

"Um . . . Chris, I think, and Kristyn's coming in at five to close."

"Cool." I liked closing with Chris and Kristyn; we always had fun. Granted, I wasn't technically supposed to close tonight, but if Kristyn needed the help, of course I'd stay.

The clearance shelves were a disaster. The shirts were scattered every which way, with nonclearance merchandise stuffed in between. "Damn savages." I mentally cursed whoever closed the night before, and set about getting things organized before I could even start trying to move the fixture. The best therapy is often mindless menial labor.

I know I worked on it for a good hour before I felt that heavy gaze on me again. Standing up, I found Paulo on the other side of the fixture, sneer firmly in place. "Hey, Paulo. Something you need?"

"So . . . what does a security consultant do, exactly?"

That made me blink. I didn't realize he'd paid that much attention to Kristyn's introduction upon our last meeting. "Depends on the client. Sometimes I just test security systems. Sometimes I do actual bodyguard work." *Please don't let him ask me anything about computers.*

His dark eyes ran up and down as if he could actually see me through the shelving. "You don't look like much. You're skinny."

"Looks can be deceiving. And I'm wiry." I bent to my work again. I didn't need to get into a dominance struggle with a kid who obviously thought I was the big dog he had to take down. Though, I have to admit, sometimes it's hard to remember I'm supposed to be the adult.

" 'Course, all you have to do as a bodyguard is get shot instead of the other guy, right? I could do that." In some way I couldn't figure out, I'd made him mad. His accent was stronger. "A mannequin could do that."

"Yeah, but mannequins have a union. It's a bitch to get around the paperwork." I stood again and folded my arms on the top shelf, giving him the eye. "You know, I'm not having the best day of my life right now, so I'm just gonna ask. Did I do something to you I'm not aware of, Paulo? Or are you just a pissy little bastard in general?" Okay, it was not my most adult moment. I admit that.

Hatred flared in those dark eyes. Not just anger, but deep-seated, depths-of-the-soul hatred. No one that young should be capable of that much rage. "You don't know me. Don't think you get to judge me." His accent grew thicker with every word. In another moment, he'd start spitting Spanish at me, and I'd be lost. Languages are Mira's strong suit, not mine.

"Look, you're right; I don't know you. So I don't know what your problem is. But if you can't get a grip, one of us is gonna get canned, and I can guarantee you it won't be me. You want this job, you cool it." *Whee, lookit me be adult again!*

Maybe Sarah saw a problem brewing. The doorbell sounded its cheery "bing-bong," announcing a customer, and she said, "Hey, old dude, you take this one, I need Paulo's help on the ladder."

Paulo gave me a look that could have melted titanium, but he went back to work under Sarah's direction. What *is* it with kids these days? In my day, the worst we had to worry about was somebody keying a car. (Yes, saying "in my day" officially makes me old.) These days, I thought kids were scarier than any demon I'd ever stared down. I hoped Annabelle wouldn't grow up to be one of those angsty teens.

The customer turned out to be an angsty teen himself, sporting a blond Mohawk and enough metal in his ears to make drowning a risk if he fell in a pool. I noted his clothing as I approached, trying to guess what I might be able to sell him. With his white T-shirt, low-slung jeans, and pair of scuffed boots, he looked more like he belonged in a fifties greaser movie than our usual goth customer base.

"Hey, welcome to It. Is there something I can help you find?"

Mohawk looked up at me with a sly grin, and I felt ice run down my spine. His eyes flashed red, and I heard my own voice drip from his lips. "Is there something I can help *you* find?"

"What the hell are you doing here?" I grabbed Axel's arm and dragged him to a convenient corner.

"Hands off the threads—these were expensive." He frowned and pretended to dust my touch off his bare arms.

Looking over his current form of choice, I felt sick. "Tell me you didn't possess some idiot kid."

"Nah, humans are too much work. This is all me, baby."

It wasn't an illusion. His arm felt all too real under my hand. In the future, I would have to rethink my opinion on just how dangerous Axel was. "You're not welcome here."

He grinned lazily, perusing the shelves with half interest. "Public place, Jesse—you can't keep me out." His eyes roamed over the store. "Cute place. You sell men's clothes here?"

"What do you want?"

Axel shrugged his shoulders. "Just shopping. Trying to expand my social horizons, that sort of thing."

"Get out." A glance around revealed that Sarah and Paulo weren't paying attention to us—yet. I needed to keep it that way.

"Nah." True to his word, he started browsing, picking things up, and letting them fall to the floor. "You don't really want me to go, anyway—not until you find out why I've bothered to get all gussied up and come a-callin'."

"Hey! I have to pick all that up!" I followed along behind him, scooping up the mess he was making.

Axel snorted. "Demon . . . Hello . . ."

I dumped the armload of baby tees on a rack and moved to get in front of him again. "I don't want you here. Nothing you have could be that vital."

There was a chorus of noise from the back as Chris arrived for his shift. He was easily visible over the racks, towering above most other folk in his bright SUPERHERO T-shirt. His shaggy brown hair hung in his eyes, a futile effort to avoid notice.

"Oh, I know your soul's in hock at the moment,

Jesse . . . but I'd be willing to take one of theirs." For the first time, Axel's voice took on that quality that screams "demon." It was an oil slick in my head, a taint at the back of my tongue. To hear my own voice echoing in the recesses of my skull was disconcerting at best; nauseating at worst. "Take that one, for instance." He nodded toward Chris, a dark smile on his otherwise handsome face, and pointed a finger at the kids.

Atop the ladder, Sarah toppled with a startled squeal when her foot slipped on a rung. Chris, moving faster than I ever thought him capable of, caught her at the bottom.

"How horrible life must be for him," Axel almost purred. "Freakishly tall. Too awkward for sports. Hopelessly in love with that girl but terrified to speak to her . . . What do you think he'd give me, for just one night? Just one kind word from her?" The two teens stared at each other for a moment before Chris set Sarah on her feet and retreated, blushing to the roots of his limp hair.

"Or the girl." He tsked softly, shaking his head. "So terrified that no one loves her. That she's not good enough, that someone will find out she throws up every single day. What would it be worth to her if I could promise her eternal beauty, unconditional love?" As if his words had conjured it, I could feel the despair settling into my bones; the loneliness, the choking uncertainty, the weight of a terrible secret. Despite knowing it was an illusion, I found it hard to shake it off.

"Or maybe they're too close to home. Maybe . . . someone you don't know." He put his hands on my shoulders and turned me toward the windows, pursing his lips thoughtfully. "That one there, the girl in the pink shirt? She's trying to get into Yale, but she plagiarized her last paper." He smirked as he murmured into my ear. "You'd be amazed what she'd give to have that go unnoticed. Oh! And the tall man just past her, he's pretty sure he has an STD, and he's in deep shit if his wife finds out." Axel snickered, and I felt my stomach do sick somersaults with someone else's dread. "They're not even *good* people, so what would it hurt?"

"Don't." Through sheer willpower, I relaxed my muscles and blocked out his voice. I concentrated instead on my own heartbeat, a bit elevated but still steady. It grounded me, and the heaviness of other people's feelings faded—for the most part.

"What do you care? You don't even know them. And I'm not hurting them. I'm offering them their dreams, Jesse, in exchange for something they wouldn't even miss. . . . Generous creature that I am, I am willing to throw in a bonus for you, too, something you so desperately need to know." He shrugged and released my shoulders, his predatory gaze returning to my teenage coworkers. "I don't think you'll find a better deal, but I am nothing if not negotiable."

"It doesn't matter if they're strangers, or if they're not lily white in the deeds area. They're not for sale."

Behind the counter, a shaken Sarah refused to go back up the ladder, so Paulo took her place. He almost attacked the T-shirt wall, yanking things into position with a screech of tortured plastic.

The demon smiled. There was something ravenous in his eyes, a starving man eyeing a feast. "Ah, now that one. You wouldn't believe the secrets I could tell you about him. So angry. So betrayed . . . An emo-rock song, just waiting to happen. What would he be willing to give up to have one chance to *just get even*?" Axel's eyes glowed, more than the mere flash he usually let slip.

I grabbed his hoop earring and yanked his head around to look me in the eyes, all but growling in his face. "These people are off-limits. Get out now." I could have escorted any human Axel's size out the door with no problems. But Axel wasn't human, and I had no idea how to get him out of the store if he wouldn't leave voluntarily. My keys with the small canister of demon Mace were in my locker. No way was I leaving him alone with the kids long enough to get it.

He chuckled, calmly extracting his earring from my grip. "Ah, Jesse, ever the honorable warrior. It's going to get you killed." He patted my cheek, just short of a slap, then wandered toward the entrance. At the door, he paused to give me a sorrowful glance over his shoulder. "And there're so few of you left as it is."

Mentally, I said every four-letter word I knew, and a few I made up for the occasion. "What do you know, Axel?"

He shot me that thousand-watt grin. "I know someone's not playing by the rules. Shame shame, I know his name. But I'm not telling you without something in return."

The bell chimed as he let himself out. A pack of kids

passed by outside the plate glass window, and when they were gone, so was the demon. Only then did I think to unclench my fists, useless gesture though it was.

I felt a presence behind me, and nearly turned to swing before Paulo spoke. "Friend of yours?" Apparently, he'd taken more notice of our "customer" than I'd thought.

"No. No, that was definitely *not* my friend."

"He comes back, you want me to throw him out?"

I only shook my head to the negative, and I found reasons to stay near the door for the rest of the night. If Axel came back, I wanted these kids to run away screaming, but I didn't think they'd believe me if I told them.

As a precaution, I grabbed my key chain out of my locker and stuffed it in my pocket. My assorted anti-demon trinkets made for uncomfortable bulk, but I'd rather be safe than sorry.

Kristyn arrived on schedule at five, and Paulo and Sarah left at seven. I should have gone with them, but I just couldn't bring myself to leave Chris and Kristyn unprotected. The logical part of my brain knew he could still get to the kids outside work, but the totally irrational part was quite certain my mere presence would ward Axel off. It wasn't unusual for me to stay well past my shift, and since we were busy, no one thought anything of it.

As the evening wore on, I felt increasingly stupid. Axel was obviously not coming back. He'd accomplished what he'd intended by sowing doubt and temptation in my mind—the big jerk. And if he wasn't here hassling me and threatening my coworkers, where was he? My first thought was for Mira, of course, but I knew she was safely behind the house wards.

Still, what if he'd only avoided the wards because he had no reason to go inside until now? What if he himself was the one breaking the rules? I wouldn't put it past him to bargain a soul for a confession. What if . . . ? It occurred to me, when I noticed Kristyn staring at me, that she'd been trying to talk to me for several minutes. "Huh?"

"I said, Chris and I are gonna haul the trash out to the Dumpster; we'll be back in a bit. You okay, old dude?"

"Yeah. I'm fine." I forced a smile for her. "I'll hold down the fort." Once they were out the door and out of sight, I dropped my head to the glass counter with a sigh. I wasn't sure I was fine at all. My stomach was in seven different kinds of knots, and I couldn't seem to shake the goose bumps along my arms. Maybe I was getting sick.

I crouched to fish under the counter, looking for any Tylenol left behind. I had no luck, of course, but as I closed the sliding door, something caught my eye in the reflection. It was no more than a flicker of movement, somewhere behind and to my left, a black blur darting out of sight.

Whirling, I reached for the volume on the stereo, plunging the store into eerie silence. Nothing moved. "Who's there?" Why do people always ask that? I mean, if something's hiding from you, you really think they're just going to pop up and say, "Oh, it's me!"

I stepped out from behind the counter, glancing beneath the clothing racks and even the shelves, though something would have to be the size of a rat to fit under there. Nothing. *Ok, maybe you're taking paranoia to an extreme, old boy.* You know . . . maybe I *was* taking paranoia to an extreme. And that wasn't usually like me.

I fished my key chain out of my pocket, singling out the tiny mirror dangling on its chain. On the surface, it was the kind of compact mirror any girl might carry to check her makeup. But on the back, out of sight, Mira had scratched some runes that turned it into something more. It would take only a moment to see if my new suspicion was true.

I held the mirror up so that I could see over my right shoulder, turning slowly to scan the back of the store. Something twitched in the shadows under the clearance rack. I turned to look without the help of the mirror, and sure enough, that darker spot wasn't there. "Tricky little bastard, aren't you?"

Using the mirror again, I watched beneath the rack. Slowly, the culprit emerged to sit in the middle of the aisle.

It would have been easily mistaken for an extra-filthy dust mop, black coils of fur sticking out all over, except, y'know, for the four vaguely insectoid legs protruding from the scruffy mass, each ending in three grasping fingers. There were no eyes that I could see, but as I watched, the thing opened its massive mouth and started to groom its fur with its creepy little hands. The mouth took up nearly half its bulk, and I could see row upon row of sharp white teeth within—like a shark, and venomous to boot.

It was a Scrap demon, one of the parasites of Hell. I'm not even sure it should properly be called a demon. They had very little intelligence and normally existed by draining the life force out of unsuspecting humans. Like all true parasites, they weren't strong enough to kill their host, but the intense feelings of despair and paranoia they exuded generally made for short life spans in their humans.

In rare circumstances, a stronger demon would use them to soften up his prey, and I had to wonder, "Who sent you, Creepy?" It almost had to be Axel. Dog Boy already had my soul under wraps; he'd gain nothing by this little guy's sucking me dry. But Axel had reason to push me, to beat me down.

It obviously wasn't smart enough to realize it had been seen. The Scrap demons hovered just on the other side of the veil, invisible to the naked eye or seen only in peripheral vision. Most of the time, they were explained away as a trick of the light or the neighbor's cat. Only with something like Mira's mirror could I get a decent look.

It appeared to be bored. It spidered its way around the floor, idly exploring this and that as it scuttled from shadow to shadow. Its legs bent at impossible angles with more joints than should have been necessary, and it opened its mouth on occasion as if making a cry I could not hear.

I couldn't just leave it running loose. It was obviously sucking on me, and if I let it alone, it might attach to one of the kids. I just needed to get it into the physical where I could deal with it. Luckily, I had my handy-dandy magic mirror for that.

We sold novelty letter openers in the shape of swords, and I slowly slipped one from the counter. It'd do well enough. I followed the parasite's reflection in the mirror, waiting to catch the whole thing in the glass. "Come on . . . just a bit farther . . ." As if it heard me, it paused with one foot poised, hesitating as I framed its image fully within the mirror. "Gotcha."

With a quick clench of my hand, I snapped the mirror in half.

The screech behind me was almost deafening. I turned in time to see the nasty thing scuttle under the CD tower. "Come here, you little bastard!" I dove after it.

The mirror trick would work for only so long, and when the Scrap was done being startled, it'd fade back across again. I had to kill it before it got away . . . and before my coworkers got back.

It scurried out the back of the tower as I reached in from the front, and it made a break for the front of the store. I scrambled after it, throwing a novelty pillow ahead of it to startle it back away from the door. The cushion knocked an earring display off a shelf with a crash, and the demonic dust mop reversed direction in midscuttle, darting beneath a rack of T-shirts.

I slid to my knees to reach under there, only to find it gone. *Dammit!* Had it already faded back across? At the last possible second, I heard a low rattle above me. I jerked my head back as the Scrap dropped down from its hiding place in the shirts, jaws clacking viciously.

As ridiculous as the thing looked, the poison in its teeth wasn't anything to laugh at. The venom splattered across the back of my hand and instantly burned like all holy hell. I backpedaled fast, scrubbing my hand on my jeans and upending the rack. The vermin charged at me for all of about two feet, screeching at the top of its demonic little lungs, then ducked away under another shelf again.

"Okay, that's it!" I grabbed a shirt hook off the wall and went fishing. Lying on my stomach on the floor, I could just see the light reflected off its knobby legs, and I poked and prodded with the long hook until I hit something squishy. The thing came boiling out of its hiding place like a little hair ball of fury, snapping and snarling at my face. I don't think I've ever jumped to my feet so fast in my life.

I managed to stomp down on one spindly leg, but before I could feel any kind of triumph, it just snapped the appendage off and limped for the door on three clawed hands. "No you don't!" Heedless of the venomous bite, I flung myself on it, pinning it under my chest. The thing squirmed and howled through clenched fangs, unable to open its mouth with me on top of it. "Now you're mine, Creepy."

Careful to keep the body pinned, I got to my knees. The fur was bristly and greasy under my hands, and I felt my stomach churn. "Done with you now." The squealing was cut off as I plunged the letter opener through the body with a sickening crunch. The remaining legs twitched and spasmed before finally succumbing.

The door binged cheerfully, marking the return of my coworkers. Kristyn stared at me, and I realized belatedly how it probably looked. The rack of shirts was overturned, the earrings were scattered all over the floor, and one of the CD towers was on its side. And there I was, with a letter opener driven an inch into the linoleum, the telltale remains of the demon parasite already dissolved into nothingness.

The question was plain on her face, and I finally just had to shrug. "Cockroach. Really big cockroach."

I'm not sure whether she believed me.

14

Around eleven, no doubt still a bit worried about my destructive jaunt through the store, Kristyn strongly suggested that I get myself home to my wife, although her language was slightly more colorful.

"You sure? I can stay, walk you to your car." It was dark, but the nightlife at Sierra Vista was in full swing. She wouldn't be alone, and that's what bothered me. Even though I'd disposed of the little parasite, there was worse out there.

"Chris can walk me out. Go home." She tucked a lock of purple-pink hair behind her ear and gave me *that* look. "What'd you get your mom for her birthday?"

Oh crap. I hadn't even thought of that, today. It must have shown on my face, because she laughed at me. "Wal-Mart's open. Go across the street and buy something. Perfume or a pretty necklace or something."

The Wal-Mart was a garish beacon of light, its own little island of fluorescent-lit commerce in the night. You find the weirdest people shopping in the middle of the night—people like me.

It seemed wrong to be shopping for a birthday present when the world around me was going nuts. Still, it wasn't my mom's fault I was up to my eyeballs in insanity.

I wandered into the perfume aisle and was immediately flabbergasted. I had no idea what kind of perfume my mother liked. I couldn't even tell you what Mira wore, only that she always smelled like strawberries. There were boxes with movie stars' faces on them, things with names I couldn't pronounce, and something I was almost positive belonged in the smelling salts family of aromas. And why on earth did some of the tiniest bottles cost like fifty bucks? I beat a hasty retreat.

You might think, charging the fees I do, that a fifty-dollar bottle of perfume wouldn't be so intimidating. But when you figure I spent two weeks in the hospital after my last gig for the president, a week of that in ICU, and the insurance company was still rejecting my claims, you see how that fee disappears pretty quick. That's why I work at It between clients. Those paychecks help us scrape by.

The jewelry counter was no better. I couldn't tell you the difference between a diamond and a piece of cut glass.

I must have been making security nervous, because two uniformed guards found a place near me to stop and have a rather loud conversation. That, I'm used to. In the heart of the Midwest, anyone the least bit different is always the first suspect.

The appliance section boggled my mind. There were things to dice, gadgets to juice, doohickeys to puree. I just shook my head and moved on. I firmly believe that our ancestors got by with fire and a stick. It's good enough for me.

When in doubt, hit electronics. At least there, I was

more in my element. Was there a movie she might like? She had a camera, so how about a new case for it? Twice, I started to dial Mira, then snapped my phone shut. If I woke her up this late for shopping advice, I'd be sleeping on the couch for a month.

I found about twenty things I wanted for myself, but nothing for my mother. And I was running out of time. There were only two shopping days left before the party.

A small part of me was absolutely incredulous that I was still thinking of going to a party at a time like this. Men were dead. Something could be stalking me, or someone like me, at this very moment. The thought made the skin crawl across my shoulders as it tried to creep away from the imaginary eyes boring into my back.

No . . . wait. I *could* feel eyes on me. No doubt, the security guards were just waiting for me to stuff a big-screen television into my pants and walk out. A cautious glance around revealed no brown uniforms in sight. Then I wondered why in the hell I was being so careful. I wasn't actually doing anything wrong.

Turning to scan the area around me, I saw no one. *Wonderful. Next, the nice young men in clean white coats will come to take me away.* Unless you counted the store security cameras, no one was watching me. Sadly, the itch between my shoulders refused to acknowledge my superior logic. I was getting damn tired of this continual and irrational certainty that I was not alone in the universe.

Maybe shopping tonight was a bad idea. I'd come

back tomorrow when the sun was shining brightly. (No, I am not afraid of the dark. I'm afraid of the things *in* the dark.)

I meandered my way out through the various aisles, still halfheartedly hoping that something would jump off the shelves with the tag MOM'S PRESENT already attached. No such luck, but as I rounded the corner to head toward the front, I caught sight of someone dark ducking into another aisle. There is a distinct difference between someone walking down an aisle and someone trying not to be seen, and that was it right there.

Three long strides took me to that aisle, but there was no one there. *Deep breath, Jess. Your imagination is getting the better of you.* My hand clenched at my hip where my sword should be, and I muttered unpleasant things to myself. Right now, if I had another Scrap demon on me, I was screwed. My mirror was spent, and there was no way I was asking Mira to craft another—not this week, and maybe not ever. She was spending too much of herself, casting spells on my behalf. My only defense would be getting into the house, safe behind Mira's wards.

You know the old saying, right? Just because you're paranoid doesn't mean they're not out to get you. At the other end of the walkway, out of sight, something toppled over with a crash. I darted to the end to see a pile of metal cake pans rolling drunkenly around the floor. One of them wobbled to a stop against my boot. Running footsteps echoed down the linoleum aisle to my left, and I was off in pursuit.

My mysterious stalker rounded another end cap in

time for me to see the back of a black hooded sweat-shirt and one fleeing sneaker. It was a tall figure, lean and moving quickly. The chase took us down the pic-ture frame aisle, and there were footsteps behind us now.

"You there, stop!" Security didn't like our playing tag through the store, evidently.

Normally, I am a law-abiding citizen, but at that exact moment, I was more interested in who had been following me than in stopping. And face it—rent-a-cops don't exactly count as the law. At least, that's what I'd say when I felt guilty later.

A walkie-talkie tweeted, and I heard a panting voice say, "I need backup in housewares!" *Backup? Are you kidding me?* A tinny announcement blared from the in-tercom overhead. "Code forty-seven in housewares. Code forty-seven in housewares." Well, now I knew what a code 47 was.

We didn't stay in housewares long. He was leading me out toward lawn and garden, and since I didn't think he had a sudden urge to fertilize his lawn, there was probably a rear exit there. In and out of aisles and clothing racks we ran, my stalker toppling displays into my path to slow me down. I hurdled a tower of scat-tered DVDs easily, but the security guards were having a harder time of it. I could hear them huffing and puff-ing behind me as several more joined the chase.

It occurred to me in a moment of perfect absurdity that this was the second retail establishment I'd de-stroyed in as many hours. If I hadn't been running so hard, I might have spared the breath to laugh.

I probably could have outrun security indefinitely, except for one thing. I rounded the office supplies end cap and saw the WET FLOOR sign a split second before I hit the damp linoleum. I went skidding, arms pinwheeling for balance. Yeah, it wasn't my most graceful moment. We'll just pretend that didn't happen, all right?

Ahead of me, my quarry met the same fate and crashed into a rack of greeting cards. Wrapping paper and ribbons went flying in a colorful explosion, and a piñata shaped like an ogre bounced off my head with a soft crunch. One trampled card played a garbled version of "Happy Birthday" as it died.

Time froze in that funny way it does, and the two of us stopped there amidst the wreckage and stared at each other. I knew those wide black eyes. "Paulo?"

With a scramble and the chirp of wet sneakers, he was up and gone. Before I could follow, meaty hands laid hold of both arms. "All right, buddy, you're outta here."

As they "helped" me to my feet (and I use the word loosely), I eyed both rent-a-cops. It would be so easy to make them release me, especially with the adrenaline pumping through my body. Both were middle-aged and out of shape. One was red faced and gasping for air after the short run, dark sweat stains marring his shirt. A quick twist, and my arms would be freed. Maybe jab the breathless one in the gut, really take him out of the race. But they'd gathered two more friends during the chase, and the extra security guards crossed their arms over their chests as they glowered. Boy, they sure thought they looked intimidating in their rented brown uniforms.

I wasn't intimidated, but I was practical. Four-to-one was a bad fight no matter how I looked at it. And it wasn't as if they were bad guys. *They're just doing their job, Jesse.* Yeah, dammit, I knew that. It didn't mean I was happy about it.

I grudgingly allowed myself to be escorted from the store, and the guards waited at the door to be sure I was leaving. No doubt, the news tomorrow would say Wal-Mart security foiled some nefarious terrorist plot.

The parking lot was a ghost town, with only twenty or so cars under the humming lights. Moths and other flying critters darted around the pools of light like little biting fairies, shadowed by the bats that preyed on them.

I accosted the single poor soul who happened to be walking into the store at that moment. "Hey, did you see a Hispanic kid, about my height, come running out this way? Or a blue Ford Escort?" The man shook his head and made haste to put distance between us.

I stood in the parking lot for a long time, watching the darkness beyond the sickly yellow light. Nothing stirred, save the gnats and the bats. And there was no sign of a little blue Ford Escort, though, somehow, I didn't think Paulo was the type to try and kill me, no matter what tough-guy front he wanted to put up.

Whatever Paulo had been up to, he was gone now. I didn't know what the hell was going on, but the next time I saw him, he and I were going to have a long and heartfelt discussion in the back room. First and foremost on the topic list was the proper way to tail someone. I never would have spotted the little idiot if he hadn't run in the first place.

Only when I got into my truck did I realize how badly my right leg was throbbing. A wince escaped as I reached down to examine it. Nothing seemed to be grossly out of place (I'm not a doctor, but I visit them a lot!), but the calf muscle was extremely tender to the touch. The fall had done more damage than I'd thought. Maybe I was getting old after all.

Driving a stick shift was going to be interesting. I put the truck in gear and coasted out toward the highway, experimenting with hitting the clutch and accelerator all with my left foot. *Damn, damn, damn!* My kingdom for cruise control.

It occurred to me, once I was already on the highway, of course, that I still hadn't gotten my mother a present. I used the opportunity to truly exercise my creativity at cursing. That entertained me for a good ten minutes.

Thankfully, traffic was light at nearly midnight, and there was minimal shifting involved. I started to think I was going to make it home without any undue stress. I should have known better.

I only vaguely noticed the dark car parked on the emergency access road in the median. People left disabled vehicles all over the road all the time, and cops liked to lurk there, waiting for hapless speeders.

The headlights flicked on as I passed, though, and the car pulled onto the highway. *That* I noticed. "Oh, do not do this now." The last thing I needed was a ticket. Out of habit, I checked the speedometer, and I was going a nice and sane sixty-five, under the seventy speed limit. I broke out in sudden goose bumps, shivering in a nonexistent chill. That, as well as the car's never flipping on its cherries and berries, made me certain this was not a cop.

As a test, I stepped into the gas, but all it did was make him work a bit harder to catch me. *Paulo, if that's you, I'm going to pinch your head off.* As I watched those headlights loom larger and larger in my rearview mirror, there was no doubt in my mind that this was my mysterious vehicular stalker and he was going to hit me again.

Not if I hit you first. I had had it with being a victim.

The highway ahead of me was a long straight stretch across acres of flat grassland. There were no bridges to fall off; no hills to plow into. Even more important than all that, it was completely empty except for me and my new best friend—just what I needed. I apologized profusely to my soon-to-be-abused truck and took a good grip of the wheel.

(Later, we'll talk about why this is actually *not* the stupidest thing I've ever done.)

I waited until I could no longer see the headlights over the tailgate of my truck. I braced myself for the coming impact, gritted my teeth against the pain in my leg, and hit the brakes.

I felt the crunch of metal before I heard it. The jarring impact seemed to travel through my steering wheel, up my arms, and into my shoulders, slamming me against my seat belt. The back end of my truck swung around, no matter how I tried to steer out of it, and next thing I knew I was careening into the grassy median. Somewhere in all the bouncing and jouncing, my head met my window with a smack and a spider-web of shattered glass. Stars burst behind my eyes, and I blacked out.

My own voice woke me, which is a really weird sensation even without having just taken a blow to the head.

"Jesse! Jesse, open your damn eyes! You have to wake up!" Someone was pounding on my pillow, which turned out to be the cracked glass of my side window.

I blinked my eyes open, and for a brief moment, I saw a face outside. A blond, with a Mohawk and piercings, staring anxiously through the shattered glass. *Axel?* The moment I thought it, the face was gone.

My truck wasn't running, and I hoped she had just stalled out when my foot came off the clutch. Fighting against the grogginess in my head, I threw the door open and stumbled out into the grass. Somehow, I'd wound up facing back in the wrong direction, but at least the truck hadn't crossed into the oncoming lanes.

Across the southbound lanes, I could see the dark Escort crumpled against the guardrail, steam from the engine billowing through the beam from the one remaining headlight. The night reeked of boiling antifreeze where it spewed all over the asphalt, and the driver's door was hanging open. I managed to limp across the dark highway, only realizing halfway there that I was unarmed. Oh well. Hopefully, he was in worse shape than I was. "Time to find out who you are, buddy."

No such luck. The mangled car proved to be totally and completely devoid of life. Sometime during my brief bout with unconsciousness, the bastard got out and ran off. He obviously knew how to bleed, though. The spiderwebbed windshield was smeared with red. It wasn't enough to be fatal, but he'd have a helluva headache for a week or two.

"God-fucking-dammit!" For good measure, I caved in the back fender with a well-placed kick. Unfortunately, that's when I remembered that my leg wasn't even close to sound. What followed was the most colorful one-sided exchange of cursing I'd ever heard, and I'm still proud of what small bits I can remember.

I was still ranting and raving by the side of the road when the highway patrol car pulled up. The trooper got out, training his flashlight right in my eyes. "Sir, is this your vehicle?"

I spent the next hour standing on the side of the highway while two more units showed up to check out the wreck. The Escort had been stolen from Utah two months earlier. That much I got from eavesdropping on the radio chatter. The cops noticed the blood trail, too, following it a few yards down the road where it ended abruptly. It seemed that Evel Knievel had another ride.

I got near the car only once and managed to snatch a crumpled bit of paper from the console before I was shooed away. Sitting on my own tailgate, I inspected it by the flickering blue and red lights.

It was a fast-food receipt, dated a month ago. Not a big deal, except that my home address was scribbled on the back of it. I stuffed it into my pocket before the cops got too curious.

How long had they had that address? And why hadn't they used it? Something between cold-sweat nausea and immeasurable rage brewed in my gut. If this lunatic had gone anywhere near my family . . . I had to get home.

It took even longer to convince the highway patrol that no, I had not been drinking; no, I did not see where the other driver went; and no, I did not need a hospital. It was the last one that took some fast talking on my part, but finally Officer Allen resigned himself to writing "Refused medical treatment" in his report and let me drive my poor abused baby home. The truck, for her part, still ran like a champ, and as far as I could see the damage to the rear end seemed strictly cosmetic. That's my girl.

"Don't worry, baby. I'll get you fixed up, I promise."

Pretty sure I broke a land speed record getting home, all the while watching every car that came up behind me with a healthy dose of suspicion. Who knew what kind of car he would be driving next?

At home, Mira was blissfully asleep and didn't see me limp in. If she even suspected I was hurt, I'd be on my way back to Dr. Bridget faster than I could blink, and I didn't want that. I settled on a plan of distract and evade, if the subject came up. I'd explain the damage to the truck later—somehow.

I knocked back two aspirin, swallowing them dry, and stuck a bag of frozen peas on the giant lump on my head. While I waited for the painkillers to kick in, I hobbled into Mira's little sanctuary to boot up her computer.

I sank gratefully into Mira's comfortable desk chair. The room glowed a flickering blue from the monitor, casting bizarre shapes over the walls. I watched the shadows dance, a tiny part of me quite certain that something horrifying lurked in the darkness. Even when you get old enough to know there's no monster under the bed, there's always that little voice that asks what if you were wrong. I debated long and hard about flipping on a light, even if I risked waking the family up.

There was nothing in my e-mail, so I logged on to Grapevine. (Well, there was nothing from Viljo, but I did have one advertisement for a dating service and two offers to greatly enlarge my penis. How does any self-respecting person actually hit Send on an e-mail like that?)

Too late, I realized I hadn't turned the volume down. The same woman's voice screamed, "I see you!" and I nearly knocked everything off the desk in an attempt to hit the MUTE button in time. Snatching the tumbling speakers before they hit the floor, I froze, waiting to hear Mira get out of bed. I counted five long breaths in silence before I finally concluded she'd slept through it.

Carefully replacing the speakers, I put on the headset, muttering, "Viljo, I am going to strangle you."

Almost immediately, the webcam window sprang

up, the geek in question waving a cheery hello. No one should be that cheery this late at night, even counting the time difference.

"Dude, do you ever sleep?"

"I can sleep when I am dead. And if there is coffee and Red Bull wherever I end up, maybe not even then."

Even the thought of it made my stomach churn. "How your head has not exploded by now, I will never know."

"Your words wound me. Right here, in my heart." He smirked; I could see that much over the grainy feed. "But I, most magnanimous and brilliant Viljo, will ignore your insults and produce the information requested of me."

He'd found something. He only strutted and preened like that when he was proud of himself. "It's only been a few hours!"

"More than ample time."

I had to grin as he flexed his thin arms for the camera. He made me look muscular. "Well, spill it, oh guru of the perpetual signal."

"Checking Miguel's phone was easy. I should see if the phone company down there needs a Net security consultant." He did something with his keyboard, and a window popped up on my screen—a call history, apparently. "Guy's was a little harder, but really, their 'secure' site is laughable." Another window popped up, and I adjusted them so I could see both at once.

"Okay, what am I looking for here?"

"On Miguel's, three weeks ago, there is a number with a California area code, 714. See it?"

I located the number in question. Miguel had talked to that number five times in the week leading up to his disappearance. The calls were always inbound, though Miguel never called the number back. "Okay."

"Now look at Guy's record, for five weeks ago. The same number is there."

Sure enough, it was repeated quite a few times there, too, but again, only inbound. "Well, whose number is it?"

Fuzzy Viljo frowned in choppy stages. "That is where things get tricky. I have more digging to do, but right now, it is looking like a prepaid cellular phone."

"Maybe it's nothing. Maybe . . . it's another champion's number. Who's the guy out of San Fran. Avery?"

"That is not Avery's number, nor is it any number that Ivan has used. I have a few more places to poke around before I will know for certain."

"Well, don't forget to sleep, man. You're no good to me passed out over the keyboard."

His snort came through the headset loud and clear. "As if."

"G'night, man."

"Hey! I am not done!"

I halted in the middle of shutting the window down. "What else do you have?"

Viljo's image held up one finger, indicating for me to wait, and in another moment, more windows popped up on my monitor. "Miguel and Guy have both tried to sign onto the system in the last week. Unsuccessfully."

"Are you sure?"

"Do you think I would make a mistake like that?"

He frowned at me. Great, now I'd offended the little geek. "Both attempts were made within hours. They did not gain access because they failed the security checks. Things Miguel and Guy would not have forgotten. Someone is trying to get in."

"You've had hack attempts before. Amateur stuff, you said."

"Not like this. It gets weirder. I cannot get an IP address on it."

We were rapidly descending into that realm of mumbo jumbo where I was definitely out of my element. "And that is . . . not normal?"

"No. All Internet presence has an IP address. You can mask it, or confuse it, but you still have one. This is just . . . vapor. A ghost in the machine."

"So it's someone better than you."

He snorted. "There *is* no one better than me. I am telling you, something is fucked up here."

"Well . . . batten down the hatches or whatever it is you do. I'll let Ivan know." And, as an afterthought, I asked, "Have you heard from the others?"

"Everyone has checked in except Sveta and the Knights Stuck-up-idus."

Sveta was in Eastern Europe somewhere. At least, I thought she was. She was the only female champion I was aware of, and that is where my knowledge ended. "I'll let Ivan know that, too. Get some sleep, Viljo."

"You, too."

Two tries to call Ivan resulted in a "Customer has gone beyond the service area" message, and I almost threw my cell across the room in frustration. Dammit.

Of all times for the phone service to go down. Why couldn't Miguel's family live in a real city, instead of some hole in the mountains?

I did my usual house walk, checking for open locks and windows and rogue Ford Escorts, then crawled into bed beside Mira with a (manly) whimper and did my best to sleep. In my dreams, the Yeti was there, gnawing at my right leg like a starving terrier. It wasn't the most pleasant of nights.

15

"Jess."

"Jesse."

"Jesse!" Although my head was buried under my pillow, Mira's voice wouldn't let me sleep in peace. Then, to make it worse, she started shaking my shoulder.

"Wha mrrmfh? G'way." I swatted blindly at her, connecting with nothing.

"Wake up. Ivan's on the phone."

That at least penetrated the foggy haze in my head. I fumbled my hand free of the tangled sheets to take the cell phone and tried not to groan as every muscle in my body protested. It was official. I was way too old to be water-skiing across linoleum floors. "H'lo?"

"Dawson! I am to be waking you. Much to be apologizing." A deep voice thundered in my ear, sounding totally unapologetic despite words to the contrary.

Oh hey . . . It was Ivan. Dimly, I knew Mira had told me that already. "Ivan. Um yeah, hi . . . Hang on, I gotta jump-start my brain." Coffee—I could smell coffee. Like a zombie, I shuffled out into the hallway in only my plaid pajama pants, searching for the source of that divine smell. I don't drink it often, but when I need it, I *need* it.

It didn't take me long to realize that my right leg was still rather annoyed with me for last night's escapades.

It reinforced this message with a sharp pain every time I stepped down—not a good start to the day.

"I am not to be knowing what this 'jump-starting' means." He didn't wait to find out, either. "What news are you to be having from Grapevine?"

"Everyone has checked in but Sveta and the Order."

"This is not to be surprising. Svetlana is to being difficult in the best of times. You will to be having Viljo contact her again, until she is to being responding." Ivan sighed, and I could picture him running a hand through his snow-white hair. "And the priests . . . Well, they are to being warned, and this is the most we can do for them. At least, they are not alone." There were never fewer than five of the Knights Stuck-up-idus, and I was inclined to agree with Ivan. Right now there was strength in numbers.

"I'll pass the message on to Viljo." Limp, step . . . limp, step . . . It was going to be a very long day at this rate. "I had him do some digging, too. He looked through Guy and Miguel's phone records and found one number in common."

There was a long silence on the other end of the line, and for a moment, I thought I'd lost the connection. Finally, Ivan's gravelly voice came again. "It could to be a coincidence. Archer declined a contract, so they were to be contacting Miguel instead."

"It's possible, yeah. And we don't know just when Guy vanished. But it doesn't look good."

"Is Viljo to be having a name to go with this number?"

Shambling into the kitchen, I had my eyes on the prize—nice hot coffee, in the biggest mug I could find. No sugar, no cream, just as black as black gets—it was slap-you-in-the-face kinda coffee. The first sip touched my lips, and I almost disgraced myself by whimpering. "No. He's working on it, but he says it may be a prepaid cell out of California somewhere. Could belong to anyone by now."

"You Americans and your disposable society." I could hear the growl in the old man's voice, and my inner child flinched. I never wanted Ivan mad at me, at least not without a *really* good reason.

"Have faith in Viljo. If it's there to be found, he'll find it, and we can put a contract ban on whoever it is." Rule number two: You only get one shot at redemption. If it fails, you're done. No other champion will take up your cause. In the days before long-distance communications, it was easier for someone to try and pull a fast one. In these modern times, thanks to Ivan and the network he'd created, no one coughed without all the champions knowing—that is, usually.

"This number is to being from California. Who is this person you are to be aiding?"

"Nelson Kidd, baseball player. He's always called me from the local hotel, though, so I don't have his personal number to compare." In the era of prepaid cellular phones, it certainly wasn't impossible for someone in Arizona to have an out-of-state cell number. That thought made me frown as I savored my coffee. Was I being played? Had Guy and Miguel already tried to help Kidd out? No . . . Walter Brandt vouched for him, and he knew the rules. "I think he's on the up-and-up."

"He is what?"

"I think he is a legitimate client."

"All the same, I will to be coming there next. I am preferring the contract be voided, if possible."

My stomach knotted at the thought. True, contracts could be voided under certain circumstances, such as deception on the part of either party or violation of the terms. But it left me feeling clammy. When you start looking for loopholes, it's too easy to hang yourself with one. That's how most of the people who came to me wound up in a jam in the first place.

And on top of that . . . "I can't back out, Ivan. I gave my word." My honor was all I had, when you got down to the nitty-gritty. I couldn't just go back on an oath.

Ivan cursed, using words and terms I didn't want to understand. "You and this honor of yours. Sometimes, honor must be put aside!"

"And that's usually when you need it the most." Guess we were gonna find out what happened when Ivan's unstoppable force met my immovable object. I always kinda wondered how that would turn out. Ivan's gruff voice spat out a string of words that were definitely not complimentary. It was time to distract and evade. "Hey, Viljo had some other info, too."

"Well, to being out with it," he snapped, obviously not pleased with me.

I gave him the non-computer-genius version of events in cyberspace, concluding, "Viljo says he's going to lock the system down, then see if he can't catch this mysterious ghost." Okay, so he didn't say that, but I assumed that was what he'd do. It's what I'd do.

"Then that will to being that, until Viljo has more information, I suppose." He sighed, sounding weary. "I am liking this less and less, Dawson. Every day is to be bringing worse news and more questions than answers."

I was inclined to agree with him, but at this exact moment, there was nothing I could do about it. I hated that feeling. "So, um . . . did you ever locate Miguel's little brother?" Smoothly change the subject; that's the ticket.

"No. The people at the village are to be saying that he took a bus into Mexico City some weeks ago."

"How in the world do you misplace a seventeen-year-old for two weeks before someone questions it?" Maybe it would make sense after the caffeine kicked in; coffee, sweet nectar of the gods.

"This is not unusual for him, they are saying. He is to be going to the city often, without word."

"Well, let's hope he's just off on one of those trips, and he hasn't done something stupid." I knew better, deep down. Somewhere, there was a seventeen-year-old kid wandering around with a machete or who knew what, trying to avenge his brother. I would have done the same for Cole at that age. Hell, I still would.

"We are to be praying to God for that."

Laughter from the backyard drew me to the window, and I stood in the patch of bright sunlight on the kitchen floor, watching Mira and Anna play some approximation of baseball.

My daughter was not what one would call athletically inclined, and they were chasing the errant ball more than anything. The light gleamed through her red hair, making it look like spun copper. Her laugh was one of pure delight, that laugh that only young kids have.

The sun cast golden spirals through Mira's chestnut curls, too. Maybe she felt me watching her. She looked up and smiled at me through the window, pointing me out to Anna. They mouthed, "Hi, Daddy!" and waved happily. I waved back, fingertips brushing the glass between us.

Mira's color looked better than the day before. The dark circles under her eyes had faded, and only someone who knew her like I did would see that she was paler than usual.

"Dawson? Are you being all right?"

It looked so peaceful, out there; so tranquil in the early-morning sunlight. "Yeah, I'm fine. Just watching Anna play."

Ivan chuckled. "She is to being so precious. I will to be bringing her something special, when I visit."

"You don't have to do that." What I meant was, *please* don't do that. Ivan was worse than my dad about spoiling her. He'd show up with a pony or something equally labor intensive.

"I am to be putting Rosaline on the line now, to be speaking to Mira. You go. Hug your daughter for me."

"I can do that."

There was static on the line as Ivan's phone was

passed to Rosaline. "Jesse?" Her voice was high and clear, a girl's voice with a lilting Mexican accent. At twenty, she could barely be called a woman. "How are you?"

"Doing all right, I suppose. Is Ivan behaving himself down there?" What do you say to a woman, when you know her husband is dead and his soul imprisoned by the forces of darkness?

"Oh *sí*. Señor Ivan has been very helpful." The silence stretched out for long uncomfortable moments.

"I'll get Mira for you." I'm not good at this comfort thing. That's why I have Mira.

"Wait, Jesse. I have something to ask of you."

Obediently, I waited.

"If . . . if Señor Ivan can find who . . . can find the thing that . . . can find out what happened to Miguel, can you . . . can you send his soul on to Heaven?" I wasn't sure she was going to finish her sentence, by the end. She was so choked up, near tears. It made me squirm uncomfortably. I can't handle crying women.

"Rosaline, I . . ."

"*Por favor*, Jesse. If anyone can defeat this thing that has taken my Miguel, it is you. Miguel always said this." That was rather high praise, but it made my stomach sink to somewhere around my ankles.

What could I say? That anything that could take out two experienced champions was probably out of my league? That the odds of getting it to offer Miguel's soul up were about a million to one? That even *finding* one particular demon, in the entire underworld, without knowing its name was . . . impossible? "I will do everything I can. I promise." *Sucker*. I hated myself for promising her even that much, knowing that I'd likely never fulfill it.

The sound of sniffling almost muffled the fervent "God bless you, Jesse." What was it with everyone God-blessing me lately? I couldn't help but think if God was going to bless me, it would have happened already.

Walking out onto the patio, I realized, if he existed, he'd already given me all the blessings I could ever want. My two girls glanced up at the sound of the door and treated me to identical smiles. Annabelle looked so much like her mother, except for her coloring, which came from my Scottish roots. They had the same cute nose, the same willowy build. Maybe Anna would have my height, but other than that, she was her mommy through and through. They were like a pair of angels alighting on the grass.

"Daddy!" Annabelle launched herself at my knees, and I bit back a wince. I was *not* limping, dammit. And if I said it enough times, it would come true. While I'm at it, I would like five million dollars, the new video game console, and a Harley.

Mira had that speculative look on her face as she watched me, so when she got within arm's reach, I grabbed her around the waist to pull her close and kiss her soundly. "Jesse . . ." She chuckled softly as she pulled away, giving me a smile that promised "later." She didn't, however, ask me anything about my leg. Mission accomplished.

"Rosaline wants to talk to you." I handed the phone

off and snatched Anna up when she started her chant, "I wanna talk on the phone; I wanna talk on the phone!"

"Nope, button, you stay with me. Mommy wants to talk on the phone in peace." Mira gave me a grateful look as she disappeared inside. "So, what were you and Mommy playing?"

"Baseball!" Annabelle wriggled to get down and was off like a shot the moment her sneakered feet touched the grass. "You throw the ball!"

With visions of funniest home video clips running through my head, I was relieved to find they were using a sponge ball and bat instead of something that could do actual damage.

I tossed it to Anna a few times, and she nearly spun herself dizzy trying to whack at it with the oversized bat. She didn't care if she hit the ball. Chasing it when she missed was just as much fun. Her giggle floated in the air, bright as the sun as she romped around the yard in the cool spring dew.

This was what baseball was supposed to be, I thought; playing for the fun of it, for the thrill of the game. It shouldn't be about the money, about the endorsement deals, and the multimillion-dollar contracts. Seeing the current state of the game I adored made me sad. I had to wonder, if Nelson Kidd had been in his prime sixty years ago, when baseball was played just because it was baseball, would he have sold his soul to gain a few more years of playtime?

"Daddy, chase me!" The redheaded little imp abandoned her baseball game with the fickleness of childhood, and I grudgingly gave chase, gratified to feel my sore muscles loosen up under the exercise. My right leg, though . . . I'd pulled something, or twisted the wrong thingy or . . . something. It hurt—a lot.

Finally, I flopped onto the warm bricks of the patio with a groan. "That's it, button, you defeated Daddy." Her little face fell. "Hey, why don't you practice that kata I taught you? Let me see how well you remember it."

She perked up immediately and took a few moments to find just the right place in the yard to perform. Her face solemn with concentration, she bowed from the waist and I returned the gesture.

At five, her movements lacked grace, and maybe she didn't flow from stance to stance as I did, but darned if she didn't get every movement just as I'd taught her. It was a dance to her, something fun she did with her daddy. I'd wait until she was older to show her how to use each movement to defend herself. What, you think any daughter of mine wouldn't know how to knock a boy on his ass? Yeah right.

She ended the series with a punch and her sharp little "Kyai!" yell, then bowed to me again. I applauded loudly. "Well done, button! You looked real good out there!"

With a running leap, she landed with both knees in the middle of my stomach, and only my expecting it saved me from injury. "Oof! What'd I tell you about jumping on people?"

"You said it was funny when I did it to Uncle Will."

Oops. Speaking of which, I needed to call him and reserve his services for two weeks from now. "Here, lemme up, button. I need to call Uncle Will, now that you mention it."

"Can I talk on the phone?" She followed me inside, jumping at my hip like a miniature kangaroo.

"Maybe in a minute, okay?" Mira's voice was soft and muffled in the rear of the house, and I heard her shut the door to her little sanctuary. Mira had tried to explain to me once that being the wives of men in dangerous professions—policemen, soldiers, demon hunters—created a unique bond amongst women. I hoped whatever she was saying was some comfort to Rosaline.

Anna tugged on my pants. "Can I have a peanut butter sandwich for breakfast?" The innocence shining from my daughter's tiny face was picturesque. And I guarantee you she wouldn't have asked her mother. That's my girl.

I thought for a moment (and it was a short moment), weighing the pros of indulging my daughter against the cons of getting scolded by my wife. Finally, I shrugged. "Yeah, why not." It was always much easier to ask forgiveness than permission.

So, as I dialed the phone to call my best friend, I, Jesse Dawson, samurai, demon slayer, and champion of lost souls, made two of the world's best peanut butter and jelly sandwiches.

16

"**D**ude! I was just about to call you! It's like ESPN!"

"ESP, you dork. And, creepy."

"Like, totally."

I had to chuckle around my mouthful of peanut butter sandwich. Will always made me laugh. Despite having grown up in rural Missouri like the rest of us, he still managed to sound like a born-and-bred Californian surfer. You'd never guess he was a bespectacled gaming nut, and like me, part of the long-haired club. The man was also a trained EMT and brilliant in his own right. "So, what did you want?"

"Dude . . . you called me."

Sometimes, it's like trying to talk to Ivan. "Yes . . . but you said you were going to call me, so what did you want?"

"Oh . . . um . . ." He whispered to someone in the background. "What did I want?"

Anna wandered off into the house with her sandwich, cheerfully dripping a trail of grape jelly behind her. I wet a rag down and started mopping the purple spots off the kitchen floor while I waited for Will's brain to catch up with the rest of him.

"Oh! I remember!" *Congratulations, Will.* "Marty and I both got the day off, and we wanted to see if you wanted to hit the ball game today. Arizona's in town. We could see Nelson Kidd pitch."

My stomach roiled unhappily at the thought of watching Nelson Kidd pitch. "I don't know. . . . I'm supposed to be shopping for my mom's birthday, and Mira's had Annabelle at the shop every day this week, and she's not feeling real good."

"Dude . . . come on. . . . It's Nelson Kidd. You have those tickets just sitting around. You may as well use them."

The hazard of having season tickets is that everyone knows you have them and wants to use them. Granted, they're not the greatest seats. I don't rate a skybox or anything, but seats are seats.

"Let me ask Mira, and I'll call you back." I heard a chorus of "whipped" in the background as I tossed the rag into the sink. I'd have to pummel Marty later. He was married, too. He of all people should appreciate the things it took to keep a household peaceful. "Shut up, asshole. I'll call you back." I hung up on Will's laughter.

"Mommy, Daddy said a bad word!"

Aw crap. Never underestimate the range of hearing on the modern child. "Tattletale!" I followed Anna's shrieking giggles to the bathroom, where Mira patiently scrubbed her breakfast off her face.

My wife raised one brow at me. "Peanut butter and jelly?"

"Pure protein. And I used the whole wheat bread!" I leaned against the doorjamb, watching them.

"Who was on the phone?"

"It was nothing important. Will and Marty wanted to know if I wanted to go to the ball game this afternoon."

"You should go. Have a bit of fun." She thought I didn't see the slight grimace as she stood up straight.

"Mir . . ." She gave me a blank look. Apparently, I need to work on my chiding tone. "You need to rest. You can't be chasing Anna again all day."

She waved her hand dismissively. "I'm fine. You should go." When I just continued to look at her, she sighed. "If it makes you feel better, you can take Anna all next week. I'm behind on inventory as it is, and that would give me a chance to catch up."

"You're sure?" I reached to brush her cheek with my fingers. Her skin was so incredibly soft.

She caught my hand, kissing my fingers. "I'm sure. Go."

"Yes, ma'am."

"And you still have to go shopping for your mother."

"I'm off tomorrow. Anna and I can spend all day finding a birthday present for Grandma."

"If those storms move in as they're predicting . . ."

"Then we'll improvise." I kissed her nose when she stood up. "Thanks."

She smiled and shook her head at me. "If I ever collect on all the things you owe me . . ."

"I looooove you," I called down the hallway, heading to call the guys back.

"I love you, too, Jess. Goddess only knows why."

Amidst making arrangements to meet Marty and Will, Mira and Anna slipped out the door and headed to the shop. I was a little hurt that they didn't even tell me good-bye, but it kept me from having to distract Mira from my limping again.

Once I was sure they weren't coming back for any forgotten items, I dialed the phone again, flopping onto the couch to get the weight off my sore leg.

"Dr. Smith's office, how can I help you?"

"That you, Bridget?"

The doc sighed. "Yeah, Kim's still out sick. That's what happens when you have children in daycare, you know."

"If you're busy, I can call back."

"Nah, you caught me before my first appointment. What's up?"

"Well, what if . . . and this is hypothetical, mind you. . . . What if some guy slipped and fell on a wet floor, and then his leg hurt really bad? What might that be?"

I could picture the incredulous look on her face. "You slipped and fell? I just saw you yesterday!"

"No no! Just . . . hypothetically." There was no way I was going to see her again, barring visible bone or spurting blood.

"Well . . . it could be a sprain. Is there swelling at the knee or ankle?"

I eyed my offending appendage thoughtfully. "No, no swelling. And it would be mostly the calf that hurt, not the joints."

"Your right calf, Jess? You need to come in and let me have a look at it."

"Hey, I didn't say it was me. I said hypothetically."

"Yes, and you're a shitty liar." There it was, that gritting-the-teeth voice. "It sounds as if it could be something as simple as a badly pulled muscle. Or you—no, no, your hypothetical klutz—could have torn a muscle, or a ligament, or something else that may require surgery. Only a doctor's examination could tell for sure."

"So what treatment do you recommend for a pulled calf muscle?"

"Well, rest of course. Occasional ice packs for the first forty-eight hours. Then you can start trying moist heat and gentle exercise. The key is to *stop* if it hurts."

I made agreeing noises as if I were taking careful notes.

"Hey, Jess? Did you happen to send a new patient my way?" Papers shuffled in the background, the good doctor multitasking up a storm.

"Um . . . no?"

"I didn't think so." There was a definite grumble in her voice.

"Why, what's up?" I eyed my offending leg, idly wondering if I should skip the ice packs and go straight to moist heat. I was a fast healer, usually. That should count for something, right?

"Had a guy in here yesterday afternoon. Said he was new in town and that you'd recommended me as a doc. He started off asking questions about the practice and all, but it turned into asking more questions about you. I finally got pissed and threw him out."

She had my total attention, suddenly, leg be damned. "Let me guess. Young looking, suit and tie, clean-cut, slimy?"

"Yeah, that's him. Did I do wrong?" She suddenly sounded uncertain.

"Oh hell no. He comes back, you call Cole and get his ass arrested for trespassing. He's just . . . a jerk giving me some trouble."

"Oh good. I didn't think he seemed like the kinda guy you'd be friends with."

"As usual, your instincts are spot-on, Doc." I managed a smile, hoping Bridget wouldn't hear the barely contained anger in my voice. Verelli had officially stepped over the line. "Did you tell him anything? About me?"

She snorted into the phone. "What do you take me for, Jess, a rookie? Patient information is privileged."

There was a small bit of relief there. I don't know what Skippy the Chihuahua could have learned from her, but I didn't want to chance it. He was being a bit too persistent.

"Jesse, you know I'm going to tell Mira about your leg, right?"

Aw crap. Distract and evade. "No, you're not. Doctor-patient privilege, remember?"

"I hate you sometimes."

"You love me; you know it."

"Please come in and see me?"

I shook my head. "Nope. I'm not hurt."

"Argh! You're impossible."

"No, I'm incredible." I grinned as I hung up the

phone. Bridget was so going to make me suffer at my next appointment. The smile faded, though, as I pondered the latest developments.

Verelli had to have followed me. I wondered briefly if he was the culprit in the blue Escort, but I dismissed that quickly. Men like Verelli didn't drive Escorts, and even if he was going to kill me, he'd hire someone professional to do it. I'd worked with professionals, and the guy in the car wasn't one.

Dear God and Buddha, how many people did I have tailing me? I was going to need a parade permit if this kept up.

And if Verelli had followed me to my doctor's appointment, had he also followed me to Seventh Sense? I toyed with the phone, debating whether or not to call Mira and warn her. I finally decided against it. Mira was a she-wolf in a den, fierce when provoked, and Dee . . . Well, rumor had it that Dee had played middle linebacker on her high school football team. I don't know if it was true, but I believe she could have if she wanted. The ladies could take care of themselves. If I hadn't been so pissed, I might have even felt sorry for Verelli.

In fact, I had gone past mildly annoyed and straight into freaking livid. It was one thing to be a pain in my ass, but it was entirely another to start accosting my friends and associates—especially those who had no idea what I did in my secret life. Mr. Verelli and I were going to have a long and intimate conversation about boundaries and personal space.

The only outlet for my anger at the moment was exercise, and I headed out to the backyard for my usual morning workout. I wasn't sure if my katas counted as "gentle exercise," and you will notice that I didn't ask the good doctor. Ignorance is bliss. I went through them as best I could while favoring my right leg, and I convinced myself it did feel a bit better. I just needed to limber up some. That was it.

I attempted to meditate afterward, but my mind kept wandering in other directions. I lingered under the nagging suspicion that I was in the doghouse with Mira, and even if I wasn't, I probably ought to be. She should be home resting, not chasing Anna around the store. Not for the first time, I wondered if I should so easily take her at her word.

Maybe I'd get her something, too, while I was out shopping tomorrow. I had no idea what, though, and asking her seemed counter to my purpose. The puzzle of that, on top of my sheer pissed-off-edness at Verelli, kept me from concentrating, and in the end I gave up, frustrated.

Thankfully, Axel was a no-show for our usual morning discussion. I didn't think I could stand his smug jibes, and I'd probably end up doing or saying something rash. I wasn't sure if I was more pissed at him for . . . well, for being himself . . . or at myself, for being surprised by it.

I burned off the last of my anger in a rather enthusiastic mopping of the kitchen floor, erasing the last traces of grape jelly, and I even hummed a little as I made my way toward Marty's house to meet the guys at the agreed-upon hour.

As much as I love my truck, she's only a two-seater, and until I could get the rear-end damage assessed, I didn't want to drive her too much, anyway. So we piled into Will's brand-new cherry red PT Cruiser for the ride to the ball game. Being the shortest, Marty got stuffed into the back and didn't even complain.

The highway was jammed with carloads of fans, and I had to wonder that none of those people had to be at work on a weekday afternoon. Somewhere, there were a lot of businesses with employees playing hooky. But that was the great thing about summer; the great thing about baseball. Everyone was a kid again, and it was okay.

The parking lot shimmered with reflected heat, and the truly hot days wouldn't even hit for months yet. The smell of baked asphalt mingled with the aroma of grease from the deep fryers, and I inhaled deeply, grinning ear to ear despite myself.

A few years ago, someone had come up with the brilliant idea of making ballpark food healthier. They tried offering veggie burgers, salads, and fresh fruit. It was a spectacular failure. People came to ball games for the hot dogs, the cotton candy, the popcorn, grease-coated French fries and nachos with reconstituted cheese, huge cups of lukewarm beer—sweet bliss. I was a firm believer that all food consumed inside a stadium was automatically absolved of all caloric sin.

My buddies and I made an interesting trio: short, stocky Marty with his shaved head and ragged jean shorts (no kilt today) and the white tank top that displayed his fully tattooed arms; lanky me in my cargo shorts and a T-shirt (witty saying of the day: IF YOU WERE ME, YOU'D BE THIS COOL, TOO), ponytail hanging out from under my ball cap; Will, whose brown hair was as thick and curly as Mira's and twice as long, slightly overweight and squinting at the world behind his glasses.

If we looked strange, no one noticed. We walked into the stadium next to men and women in business suits who had obviously come straight from their nine-to-five office jobs. There were families with kids, couples on dates, and elderly men with a Little Leaguer in their hearts. Variety was the spice of life, and the game was the great unifier.

It didn't matter that none of us knew any of the others. It wasn't important that our hometown boys had a really poor showing last year. We were here to cheer them on regardless. That's baseball.

Although it was early, and a weekday, the stadium filled up nicely. I waved and grinned to a few people I knew in our section, fellow season-ticket holders. After a while, you got to know the people in your section, like neighbors from down the block. You may not know their names, but their faces were familiar and welcome sights, friendships renewed each spring and missed come fall.

I flopped into my seat and propped my sore leg up on the one in front of me. If someone came to sit there, I'd take it down, of course, but until then it felt better up. If the guys noticed I'd been limping my way up the concourse, they hadn't said anything. That meant they either hadn't noticed at all, or they had, and they were worried. I wasn't sure which I preferred.

Kansas City was just heading back to the dugout after their warm-up, and the buzz in the crowd escalated when Arizona took the field. I could see people craning their necks to see if Nelson Kidd was in the bull pen. He would be, of course. Any coach would be insane not to play him when he was so hot.

It was almost physically painful to watch the excited faces around me. If they only knew what their hero had done. Ah well, it wasn't their fault, and even if anyone would have believed me, I wouldn't have told them. Sometimes, people just need heroes.

"Dude, you okay?" Will nudged my arm, frowning. "You look constipated."

"Shut up, asshole." I swatted him and did my best to drag my brain out of work thoughts. "Get me a beer."

"On it." Yeah, they'd noticed my leg. There was no way Will would have agreed to fetch if they thought I was fully functional. For a few brief moments, I debated going to get my own beer, just for pride's sake, but good sense won out for a change.

We settled with beers and some nachos of dubious quality right as the game started. I managed not to grimace when I stood up for the national anthem. As the innings started ticking by, I completely forgot my sore leg, and demon contracts, and soulless pitchers.

By some miracle, we were winning in the fifth inning (3–2) with runners on first and second when the hot dog vendor wandered through the section, giving the usual "Hot dogs, getchyer hot dogs here!" chant. I'm not sure what made me look over, seeing as how I didn't want a hot dog. But look I did, and the vendor met my eyes.

He looked to be fiftyish, potbellied, with dark hair and a spindly mustache. The deep tan of his skin spoke of something exotic in his heritage, be it Hispanic or something else. He grinned at me, flashing a gold front tooth, and his eyes gleamed red for a split second.

My stomach dropped to somewhere around my feet. "Oh hell."

17

The hot dog vendor ambled up the stairs, carefree as all get out, still hawking his wares. I scrambled over Marty to follow him, committing alcohol abuse in the process.

"Dude, my beer!" Marty gave me a dripping wet glare, but I hardly noticed.

I made up something about using the john and buying a new beer and hurried up the cement stairs as fast as my leg would allow. The vendor got to the top of the stairs without pausing to make a single sale, then made a left toward the next aisle.

"Hey, watch it, buddy!" A businesswoman in a pin-striped suit gave me a glare when I lurched into her, my leg betraying me with every step. She muttered curses after me as I mumbled an apology and kept climbing. I didn't remember our seats' being so far down the section before, but the top seemed impossibly far away.

When I reached the peak, the man-demon was gone. I turned in a slow circle, eyes searching the aisles for the dark-haired hot dog vendor, but he had vanished into thin air. Had it been Axel, causing his usual trouble, or someone else? Given Axel's little display of shape-shifting earlier, I had no doubt he could take on any form he wanted. If I stopped to think about it, that was a little scary—okay, a lot scary.

The river of baseball fans parted to pass around me, the crazy man standing in the middle of the walkway. I thought about asking if they'd seen a hot dog vendor, but on some level I knew they hadn't. I limped over to lean against a concrete pillar near the men's bathroom, intending to rest my leg for a moment before I began the trek back down to my seat.

"Hide-and-seek, peekaboo." Warm breath wafted over my left ear, and I swung before I thought. It was a rather pretty backhand sweep, technically perfect in every way, but I sensed my target duck before I ever laid eyes on him. I pulled the blow a hairbreadth from slamming my hand into the pillar.

Axel, in his blond Mohawk punker guise again, stood up from a low crouch, whistling. "A swing and a miss!" He grinned, lounging against a trash can. "Scared ya?"

My heart thundered in my ears, and the adrenaline washed away all traces of pain in my right leg. I held the loose fighting stance for long moments, until it became clear Axel wasn't moving. *Idiot.* Of course he wasn't moving. He couldn't hurt me unless I gave permission. I forced my hands to relax at my sides, just another guy standing near the bathrooms at a baseball game.

"What do you want?" Man, I was sick of hearing myself say those words.

"You were thinking about me. I came to see why."

For a moment, I felt cold. Then reality slapped me in the face, and I gave him a disgusted look. "You can't read minds."

Axel snickered. "Well, no, but you should have seen the look on your face."

"Was that you? The hot dog guy?"

His eyes, blue as any normal human's when he wasn't being all demonic, roamed the crowd around us. His nonchalance didn't fool me for a moment. "Maybe I just like baseball. Did you ever think of that?"

"Not for a moment." I still didn't believe it, and it didn't escape me that he hadn't answered my question. "I don't want you here."

"Public place, Jesse. I'm a free-range demon here."

I glanced around quickly to see if anyone had heard him. Of course, what would they think? A couple of loonies having a talk over a trash can? Had one too many brews, maybe? "Leave these people alone."

He laughed. It was a joyful, rich sound. It was my laugh. Shouldn't demons have nasty, evil laughs? "What, you're going to take responsibility for the entire stadium? I indulge you too much by letting you extend your protection to your coworkers as it is. Even you aren't worth giving up all of this." His sweeping gesture took in the whole stadium, and maybe the world beyond. "You're good, Jesse. You're not that good."

"So . . . what? You're here hunting souls?"

The demon shrugged his lanky shoulders and sighed. "Nah, one of the others pretty much has the baseball market sewed up tight. I think you've met him." I hated that grin; that smug I-know-more-than-you smirk. "I just came out to annoy you, taunt you, generally make myself a pest."

"Mission accomplished. You can go now." Dammit,

I spilled Marty's beer for this? I knew I was glaring when I turned to walk away, and I didn't care who saw it.

"Whoa, hold on! I've done the annoying bit, but I still have some taunting to get in." He grabbed my elbow, and something snapped between us like a bad static shock. With a hiss, Axel snatched his hand back, shaking it. "Damn protection spells . . ."

Mira. All her gods bless her. I did my best to look as if I knew that was going to happen. "You know, those only work against people who mean me harm. You got something you wanna tell me, Axel?"

The blond man snorted, flexing his fingers one at a time to see if they still worked. "I want your soul. It doesn't get much more harmful than that." He cradled his hand close to him now. It may have felt like a static shock to me, but he was hurt—interesting. "And yes, there's a lot I want to tell you, but I can't just blurt it out. There are rules, Jesse, and I'm as bound by them as you are. I shouldn't even be doing this much, but there are certain things you *need* to know!"

Across the concrete walkway, two small boys started tussling in the popcorn line. The noise drew my attention long enough to be sure the parents were going to separate them, and then I looked back to my pet demon. Axel's gaze came back to my face. He'd been watching the kids fight, too.

"If this is so against the rules, why would you risk so much to help me?"

"Maybe I like you." I rolled my eyes, and he smirked. "Maybe, if I can't have you, nobody can. I've put a lot of work into you, Jesse James Dawson. I'll be damned again if I let one of the others get you."

I was more inclined to believe that.

"And just what do you want from me? Nothing you know is worth my soul." I immediately wanted to kick my own ass. Never enter negotiations with a demon. Don't even give them two fives for a ten. It starts bad habits, like a gateway drug.

"Not your soul . . . maybe something smaller, something you can bear to part with. Harmless really." His smile was oh so charming. If the goose bumps on my arms got any bigger, I was going to sprout feathers.

Voices rose in anger behind me. The parents of the brawling children had apparently taken exception to each other's existence, and the fathers were shouting obscenities at each other. One of them had on a #1 DAD T-shirt. Two security guards, in their neat blue pseudo-cop uniforms, hustled over to take control of the situation.

"Maybe . . . a name. Your daughter's name. Give me that, and I'll tell you what you need to know."

I couldn't keep my eye on the fight and Axel both, and it was making me edgy. My hand flexed at my hip where my sword should be. "You know her name already."

"Exactly! No harm in it . . . Just . . . give me her name, and I can tell you the things you need to know."

I may not be a religious man. I may not even be widely educated in the ways of magic. But even I know that the giving of a name, known or not, can have power. Every culture that is or ever was has agreed on that. "No deal. And stay the hell away from my daughter."

Not ten feet from us, a blonde in line for the women's restroom drew back her hand and slapped the brunette next to her with a resounding crack. The two went down with shrill screams and the flailing of tanned arms and legs.

"Okay, one of your companions, then. The blacksmith . . . He'll never miss it. You have to give me something! You need what I know!" The blond man-demon was all but wringing his good hand in frustration and dancing from foot to foot.

In disbelief, I watched one of the security guards draw a Taser from his belt and jab it into #1 Dad's ribs. The combative man dropped like a stone, shrieking. The odor of urine wafted over the crowd as he wet himself.

Angry murmurs grew louder all around me, and three large men detached themselves from the swelling throng to descend on the hapless security guards. The women, meanwhile, had rolled into the legs of their line-mates, adding at least three more thrashing, pummeling figures to the chaos. The two conflicts slowly oozed toward each other, a blob that sought to be whole again.

I jerked my head back to the demon in time to see Axel lick his lips in satisfaction. "Such anger . . . so delicious . . ."

Realization hit me, as usual, a bit late. "It's you. You're doing this."

"Give me something, and I'll go away. . . ." The red

glow sprang into his eyes again, and I was certain no one would ever notice in the chaos.

A third fight sprang up at the top of the stairs, the combatants tumbling down the concrete walkway into the seats before I could even see if they were male or female. Shouts from below told the tale of the spreading conflict. *Dear God and merciful Buddha all in one . . .* It leapt from person to person like a grass fire. And like a grass fire, it would burn as long as it had fuel—an entire baseball stadium full of fuel.

"Are you insane? You'll start a riot!" I made a grab for Axel's shirt, and he darted out of my reach faster than humanly possible. We played ring-around-the-rosy around the pillar for a few moments.

"Just a name, one name in exchange for all these people, and information you need . . . a bargain, really . . ." He poked his head around the pillar and grinned, caught somewhere between pleading and threatening. "You may as well give me the name. You can't make me leave. . . ."

"Yes, I can." My keys had been in my pocket. I didn't remember getting them out, but they were in my hand now. I thumbed the cap off my mini Mace key chain and took a deep breath. The next time he peered around the column, I depressed the trigger.

I heard Axel shriek once, but with my eyes clenched tight shut I missed his actual exit. There was a faint pop as air rushed in to fill the space he abruptly vacated, and I knew he was gone. The angry shouts around me became startled exclamations, ending up as desperate coughing and gagging. The cloud of cayenne and cumin spread through the violent crowd, turning rage into an instinctive scramble for air and self-preservation.

I held my breath as long as I could, and even then I choked on a cloud of pepper when my body finally demanded oxygen. Eyes watering fiercely, I watched as the remnants of the crowd fled, leaving behind the wounded.

The blonde lay on the cement floor, a trickle of blood at the corner of her mouth as she gagged and coughed, too dazed to get out of the demon Mace spray. Her opponent was nowhere to be seen. Leaning against one of the massive support pillars was #1 Dad, keening like a wounded rabbit, cuffed and forgotten in the upheaval. Someone nearby was making horrible retching noises.

I wondered where the security guards went, until a strong hand grabbed my arm. "Sir, you'll have to come with me." Well, that's what he tried to say, under the coughing and choking. I got the gist of it.

Twice in as many days, I had run afoul of security guards. Oh sure. I use a little Mace, banish a demon, break up a potential riot, and I'm the one who gets arrested. Mira was going to kill me. Somewhere, someone was finding this hilarious.

18

As it turned out, I was not arrested. Given that the fortuitous "breaking" of my Mace canister happened to end a rather ugly situation, the stadium authorities were willing to forgive and forget. I was, however, strongly encouraged to wait for my friends in the holding cell in the bowels of the stadium, and not to come back for the rest of the season. That one hurt. It hurt a lot.

From the conversations I overheard down there, the security guard with the Taser was in deep kimchi, too. Poor guy. I would try to explain to his bosses that he was under demonic influence, but I was pretty sure he wouldn't appreciate the help.

Marty and Will, bastards that they were, watched the entire game before they came down to retrieve my scrawny ass. It gave me a lot of time to brood, while pretending to meditate.

Axel had been part of my life for the last two years, give or take. I couldn't remember exactly when he'd turned up, inhabiting random local fauna, exchanging witty pleasantries over breakfast. But he'd resisted my best efforts to get rid of him. Once his continued presence was established, we'd set limits, laid down ground rules, and I thought no more on it. Not once had I seen him act . . . well . . . like a demon. Maybe I'd become complacent, forgetting that there was a fiend of Hell wrapped in whatever little furry body he'd chosen to possess for the day.

The thought chilled me to my very core. That thing had been in my yard. Hell, before Mira warded the entrances, he'd been in my house! He'd been around my family, my friends, my neighbors. What had he whispered to them, in weak moments? What seeds had he planted when I wasn't looking?

You can't save the entire world, Jesse. No, dammit, but I could try to save my little part of it.

While my brain slowly worked itself into a short circuit pondering all the what-ifs and mighta-couldas, I was forced to admit that there were worse physical ways to spend an evening. The "cell" was really just a corner of one of the offices, isolated and quiet. There was a cot to lounge or sit on as I chose, and a convenient soda machine. I could hear the game on the radio in the security office, and every so often, one of the guards wandered by to check on me.

One of them even tossed me a book to read, some action adventure spy epic by some author I'd never heard of. It was full of explosive action scenes and heroes walking away from easily lethal injuries—complete and utter fiction. I guess people found it entertaining. It was a bit ridiculous, by my tastes.

I should have known my pseudo-incarceration was going too well. Normally, I operate on the assumption that at any given moment, someone is going to walk up and kick me in the nuts. When Travis Verelli walked through the door smiling, I knew I was right.

"Mr. Dawson, I can't possibly tell you how good it

is to see you." The little weasel beamed at me as he set his briefcase on the desk to open it. I would almost call him giddy. He did own some casual clothes, apparently, having donned a pair of khakis and a preppy-looking sweater for the ball game. The loafers were still there, though. Guess he still hadn't learned to tie his shoes.

"I'm glad I could make you happy." I laid the book aside and stood up. This was an enemy. You don't face an enemy lying down. That's not *bushido*; that's just common sense.

"I mean really, inciting a riot? Dispersing a toxic chemical? I couldn't have planned this better myself." He produced a form from the case and handed it to me. "I was going to surprise you with this, but since you're here . . ."

Warily, I looked it over, then looked up at him in amazement. "A restraining order? Does Kidd know you're doing this?"

"Well, technically, that's just the paperwork requesting one. The judge is still reviewing it. But I expect he'll finalize it tomorrow, especially in light of tonight's little . . . incident." He perched himself on the corner of the desk, looking like the cat that ate an entire flock of canaries. "And no, Mr. Kidd is unaware of my actions. The beauty of it is, he'll never be asked to make a statement of his own. Famous people slide through the cracks that way."

"You're requesting it on what grounds? I haven't *done* anything!"

He held up one finger. "Technically, you just haven't done anything I can *prove*. We'll call this a preemptive strike. I can attest that I am in fear for my client's safety.

Might even throw my own safety in there, too, given that you're a violent man, and all."

"I've never threatened you harm." I wanted to, though. Oh how I wanted to.

He shrugged, picking some lint off his sweater. "That's your word against mine. And I'm fairly certain when I show off the black eye I got in my altercation with you, the judge will be most obliging."

I was floored. Yeah, Axel was evil, but he kinda couldn't help it. This guy . . . He was in a class by himself. "You're going to get someone to punch you, and claim that I did it."

"A crude tactic, I agree, but most effective." He stood up, snapping his briefcase shut. "You can keep that, by the way. I have another copy."

I tore the paper into tiny bits just to be petty, letting them flutter to the cement floor. "You know what? I hate getting in trouble for something I didn't do."

He barely had time to blink before the punch landed, sprawling him on the ground in a tangle of gangly limbs and office chairs. He flailed about in total shock for a few moments, one hand clapped to his face.

I eyed my bruised knuckles with a grimace. "Oh, come on, I didn't even hit you that hard."

"You broke my node, you don of a bitch!" His voice came out nasal, and blood trickled between his fingers. He fumbled a handkerchief out of his pocket.

"Did I? Damn. I was going for a black eye." Yeah, it wasn't my smartest moment. Not the best example of *bushido*, either. I should never have attacked a weaker man. There's no honor in that.

Verelli finally clambered to his feet, red-spotted handkerchief clutched to his abused proboscis. "I'll have you up on charges. I'll—"

"Get a restraining order? Do that. Now you need one." Later, I'd regret it. Later, I'd kick myself all over for being so impulsive. But just now, it felt really damn good. "And if you come anywhere near my friends and family again, a broken nose will be the least of your worries."

The agent made a scurrying retreat, briefcase clutched to his chest, and I slumped on the cot. *Way to go, Jess.* I was so screwed. Verelli would most definitely bring assault charges against me, and not even Cole was going to be able to keep me out of jail this time. I banged my head against the wall a few times.

Somehow, the game ended without the police coming to clap me in irons. My friends—and I used the term loosely, at this point—came to get me somewhere around eight o'clock, and awarded me the Great Foam Finger Award for "sticking it to the man." While security was willing to buy that my little toxic vapor incident was an accident, my buddies were not. They'd have just shit if they knew about my decking Verelli. I elected not to mention it, and I ushered them out of the stadium as quickly as possible.

"Dude, you made the news! There were camera crews all over the place for the rest of the game!" Will, in particular, seemed rather jubilant over events. "There were chicks fighting, and shirts ripped off and boobs everywhere. It was great!"

I cringed. "Mira's going to kill me."

Marty was perhaps a bit more sympathetic, being the other married man of the group. "They didn't use your name, as far as I know. You should be in the clear."

Oh, if only he knew. I might have been off the hook for the riot, but there was one very disgruntled sports agent out there with an ax to grind. And Mira was not going to be amused when the cops showed up at the house to arrest me. In fact, I'd probably be safer with them than with her. Being bashed in the skull with a cast-iron skillet is *not* a noble death. And I had at least a good hour to ponder my bleak fate as we sat in the parking lot, waiting to get out.

Marty, having been up for nearly twenty-four hours, crashed in the backseat and began snoring almost immediately. If you've ever seen the backseat of a PT Cruiser, you will appreciate it when I say that Marty is a musician. It means he can sleep anywhere.

Will and I sat in the front, illuminated by the green glow of his dash lights, listening to the sound track from some anime movie. The taillights of the car in front of us strobed red every time the line inched forward another few feet.

Finally—and I knew it had to be driving him nuts to wait even that long—Will asked, "So . . . you saw one, didn't you? I mean, that's why you went tearing up the stairs?"

I glanced back to be certain Marty was still sleeping. Yeah, Marty knew, but . . . I'm not sure he really believed. That was okay with me. At least one of us ought to sleep well at night. "Yeah, I saw one."

"Aw, man!" Will pounded on the steering wheel once with his fist. "I wish I could see one."

"No. You don't."

Will drove for me. He flew to all areas of the country with me. He patched me up with his EMT training, even going so far as to duct tape my insides to my insides once, to get me to the hospital. That was how I justified asking for his help. But I kept him at a distance, for the challenges. He didn't need to have demon names flitting around inside his skull. He didn't need to see the horrors that existed just outside human perception. It was the only way I could repay him, really.

"So did you do some of that kung fu shit and kick his ass?" Despite the injuries he'd helped repair, Will still had some grand Hollywood vision of what being a champion entailed. No doubt, he dreamed of epic battles across rooftops with me dodging bullets and flinging ninja stars.

"No. Just sprayed him with Mace. He left." The line of cars in front of us seemed impossibly long. I suddenly didn't want to be in the car, discussing my altercation with Axel. Would Will even know if he'd met Axel? Would he recognize the danger?

"Well, that's kinda anticlimactic. I heard there was a big brawl and stuff." The doofus actually looked disappointed.

"Other people were fighting. We were just talking." Other people would have taken the "I don't really wanna talk about it" hint. But not Will.

He gave me an odd look. "What do you talk to demons about?"

I shrugged. "Souls. Hell. Stuff like that." Not entirely true. I don't think Axel and I had ever talked about Hell. And we talked about way more than souls.

He'd been almost frantic—Axel, I mean, not Will—wanting to tell me something. *"What is it, Lassie? Timmy fell in the well?"* I doubt Axel would appreciate the similarity. What did he know that was so damn important? It had to be about Miguel and Guy. Axel knew what had happened to them, which meant it was more than just an unfortunate coincidence. And that, sadly, was what I had believed all along. Sometimes, I hate being right.

"Dude! You talk about Hell? What's it like? Have you seen it?"

I blinked at him, then reached over and smacked him lightly upside the back of the head. "Are you nuts?"

"Ow." He rubbed his head and glared at me, pushing his glasses back up his nose. "I was just askin'. . . ."

To our right, horns blared and voices shouted. I wondered if it was some of the earlier combatants, meeting for round two. Axel may have nudged them over the edge, but he couldn't create such rage out of nothing. At least, I didn't think he could. I hadn't thought he could assume human form, either, and we'd seen where that had gotten me. I hate being wrong, too.

"So . . . you need me to drive for you?"

"Yeah. How'd you know?"

"I didn't think you sat around talking to demons for fun, dude." He pointed to my tattooed right hand. "And that usually means you got work to do. And then, I got work to do."

Will has always been strangely pragmatic about the oddities in my life. "Two weeks from now. Night of the full moon."

He nodded and finally got the car pulled out onto the street, where a traffic cop waved us on through the red light. If Will noticed that I ducked down in the seat, he didn't mention it. "That'll give me time to stock up on supplies. You're not expecting any burns this time, are you?"

"No, not this time." In all fairness, the fire fight—in the most literal sense—had gone heavily in my favor. I barely got singed, that time. Well, and lost my eyebrows. And burned my knuckles. And lost maybe two inches of my hair. It was a good day!

"Just a normal hack 'n' slash, hmm?" He nodded his head in time to the music as we pulled out onto the highway and headed north.

"Yeah. For whatever 'normal' is."

"Truth, dude."

We rode in silence for several miles before he spoke again. "So, can you beat him? The one you were talking to?"

Now that was an interesting thought. If it ever came down to it, could I beat Axel? I was never cocky enough to answer with a "Sure thing!" about any of my challenges. But once, I might have been more confident where Axel was concerned. Now . . . I wasn't sure.

What I said was, "Yeah. I can beat him." Explaining the difference between the demon following me around and the demon I was contracted to fight was more than I was willing to go through tonight.

"Cool." Will fell silent. Maybe he finally figured out that I wasn't really up for witty repartee.

I stared out at the city lights whizzing by, my own reflection glaring back at me from the dark window. Somewhere in this whole situation, I was getting screwed. I knew this as surely as I knew the sun would come up in the morning. Even worse, my options weren't looking good. I was stuck between a very nasty demon and a very hot place.

On one hand, I could bargain with Axel. I could sacrifice something of mine or betray someone I cared about, in order to get some unknown information that may or may not have any practical value. For all I knew, I could give him what he wanted, and he could tell me the sky was blue and water was wet. Dealing with Axel was the same as dealing with the devil, and the first rule there is "Don't."

On the other hand, Miguel and Guy were dead, and I was sure someone had worked damn hard to make them so. Neither of them would go down peacefully. Given my recent road-rage incidents, I was fairly certain I was next. Maybe the bull's-eye was on a champion I had never met. It didn't matter. If Axel was willing to give up the murderer, was the exchange worth it? He wasn't asking for a soul, only a name. I wasn't even sure what he could do with that kind of information. Could I justify betraying a friend, if it saved a life and soul of someone I didn't even know?

There was no way out that didn't make my stomach pitch and roll, and the little voice in my head called me eighty kinds of a moron for not figuring something out. And to top it all off, I was pretty sure I was going to be in jail in the next few days. *Think, asshole! Think harder!* The highway signs whipped past with a rhythmic whooshing noise that sounded suspiciously like "Loser! Loser!"

The mocking silence stretched on, broken only by the music and Marty's soft snores, until Will took the exit toward Liberty. "Hey, Jess?"

I turned back toward my best friend. "Yeah?"

"If you die, can I put the moves on your wife?"

I drilled him hard in the shoulder and his yelp of pain woke Marty. Any serious thoughts I might have been having were lost in the good-natured roughhousing that followed. It's a wonder we made it back to Marty's in one piece, and it was another two hours before I trundled on home.

There was a package on the table when I got home, with a Pikes Peak return address on it. *Thank you, Viljo.*

While I had intended to creep into the house quietly, the bedroom light was on as I tried to tiptoe my way down the hall, proving that my ninja skills were sorely lacking. Mira was dressed in her usual tank top and pajama shorts, her curly hair piled atop her head in an artfully disheveled mop. She laid her book aside and shook her head at my weak attempt at stealth.

"How was the game?"

"It was okay. We lost." I sat on the bed to pull my boots off and tossed them into the corner with a thump. With my back to her as I undressed, maybe she wouldn't see the telltale guilt on my face. If I was any sort of lucky, she hadn't heard about the brawl.

I should know that luck is not my strong suit. "They said on the news there was trouble out there. Something about a big fight."

"Yeah, I heard that, too." While it wasn't a lie exactly, it felt like one, and that made me feel like shit. I was developing a nasty omission habit where my wife was concerned, and I made a silent promise to rectify that. "I kinda punched a guy in the face and got banned from the stadium for the rest of the season." I pulled my shirt off over my head and almost missed her quiet sigh.

"You don't start fights without a good reason. Was it important?"

"Technically, I didn't start it. I finished it." And the fact that the punch and the banning were totally separate incidents didn't bear mentioning. "But yeah, it was important." The sheets rustled as she reached for me, and her hand felt cool on my bare back. I turned to find her giving me that serious look.

"Just be careful that you pick the right battles, Jess. I don't want to lose you over something stupid." Those lines were there again, around her eyes, making her look older than her thirty years.

I'm sure she wouldn't appreciate my mentioning it. It was bad enough that I knew they were my fault. How many nights had she walked the floors, waiting to find out if I was alive or dead? How many hospital meals had she eaten, and how many crappy fold-out chairs had she slept on? I will never understand why she stays with me, but I'm so grateful she does. My life would be a lot darker without her. Hers would be a lot safer without me.

"Do you think what I do is stupid?"

She frowned at me, clearly offended, and withdrew her hand. "Of course not. I believe you're doing the right thing."

"Even if I wind up leaving you and Anna alone?"

"Jesse, if everyone in the world stood by and did nothing, think what a horrible place it would be. Someone has to take a stand. And if I say 'not my husband,' I'm just as bad as those people who turn a blind eye. Worse, maybe." She bit her lower lip, trying to find the words.

"That first time, when Nicky was suddenly healthy and Cole and Steph were so happy, all I could think was, was it such a bad thing? If it had been Anna so sick, I'd have done the same thing. I'd have done anything to save her. How many other people like that are there, Jess? Good people, trying to do good things the only way they can find. I don't believe that no good deed goes unpunished. Someone has to help them, when they don't deserve to suffer for eternity." Her hand found mine again, squeezing hard. "I can't fight like you do. The best I can do is use my own power to keep you safe, and to simply allow you to fight. Am I always happy about it? No. It scares me to death every single time, knowing that it might be the last. That doesn't mean it's not worthwhile."

"You shouldn't have to do . . . this. Any of it." If I had even an ounce of magical ability, she'd be safely out of that much of it. We both knew it.

"I don't *have* to. I want to."

I had to do something to take that great and terrible determination out of her eyes. I traced her smooth cheek with one finger. "You're sexy when you're all serious, you know that?"

It worked. She rolled her eyes at me and caught my hand. "You're a pervert."

"No, come on, I'm serious." I scooted over until I could pull her into my arms. "You're the most beautiful woman in the whole world, and I don't deserve you."

"You got that right, buster." She poked one finger playfully into my chest. "And don't you ever forget it."

"Oh yeah?"

"Yeah!"

The teasing turned into wrestling and that turned into . . . Well, never you mind what it turned into. If you can't figure out what married people do when they're alone, then you're probably too young to know, anyway.

Later (much later), I drifted to sleep with the scent of strawberries all around me, and Mira's head pillowed on my shoulder. Her breath was warm across my skin, and she clung to me as if she could keep me safe by sheer force of will. Who knows, maybe she could.

If I dreamed, I didn't remember it. If I had, I might have woken up sooner.

I think it was the smell from the spent matches that first invaded my rather nice nap. "Mmrf?" One arm flung across the bed found Mira's side empty, and my eyes snapped open. My internal clock told me dawn was still a long way off. There was no reason for her to be up.

"Mira?" Maybe Anna had had a nightmare. Or maybe it was just a nighttime bathroom trip. Or maybe she'd gotten into that FedEx box on the kitchen table and was trying to scry for Guy's location.

I was out of the bed and struggling into my pajama pants as fast as my gimpy leg would let me. "Mira! Don't!" But I smelled the matches, the lit candles. I knew I was already too late to stop her.

She didn't even look up from the basin when I stumbled into her room. The air was thick with candle smoke and something else indefinable—the taste of magic. It was like cloves on the back of my throat.

"Mir, please don't do this."

"Shh." Watching her hands weave invisible sigils in the air was rather like being hypnotized. I could almost see tracers following her fingers, like the glare left behind by Fourth of July sparklers.

"I'll break the circle, Mir."

"No you won't." Damn her for being right. I didn't know if crossing that line would hurt her in some way, and she knew it. I made a mental vow to get someone to teach me magic, even if I could only learn the theory of it. "Watch . . . It's coming together."

The salt swirled in the bowl, drawn into coherent images by my wife's will. I could see the white of Guy's hair and beard—dark in actuality—and even catch some of the pattern in his plaid shirt. The plaid was broken by something dark across his chest, and at first I thought it was armor. But I could see the shirt flap with every movement, and I finally realized that it was hanging open, unbuttoned. Guy wore no protective gear, and the dark shape was his bare chest in negative. He was armed—I could see the hatchet in his right hand—but where the hell was his armor?

As we watched, he fought a losing battle against an unseen opponent just like Miguel. Whatever it was, it was something big. Guy's blows were aimed at something chest-height on him. And it was fast. He never had time to turn. The invisible thing latched onto the back of his thigh, flinging him through the air to collide with a solid barrier of some sort. Even downed, the lumberjack champion tried to fight until his arm was literally ripped off at the shoulder and tossed away. Dark blood flowed in negative, white salt taking the place of vibrant red in the reversed image.

Mira moaned softly at that, and I pressed as close to the circle as I dared. "Stop it. Turn it off and let me in there. Mira, dammit, I mean it!" Even in the dim light, I could see the color leaching out of her skin, the trembling in her hands.

"I can hold it . . . a little longer. . . ." She spoke through clenched teeth, the cords in her neck standing out with the strain of it. "We have to see. . . ."

"Mir, he's dead." The words felt like the tolling of some great bell, a final nail in a coffin. "There's nothing more to see." Her green eyes looked up at me for long moments, stubbornness and vain hope vying against the finality of truth.

Finally, her shoulders sagged and she dropped her hands. The salt dispersed, making the water milky once more, and Mira scuffed the circle into nonexistence with one bare foot. I somehow managed to catch her as she slumped toward the floor. Her skin was blazing hot this time, and already as dry as parchment. I fully expected blisters to rise on my bare chest as I scooped her into my arms and stood.

"Wh-what are you doing?"

"You're going in the tub, for starters."

It was hard as hell to carry her down the hallway on my bad leg, but I was determined to do it regardless. I got her into the bathtub and turned the shower on as cold as it would go, holding her upright as best I could from outside. The spray steamed when it hit her at first, but I could tell it was bringing her temperature down quickly. Maybe we wouldn't need the ice packs from the freezer after all.

"Why the hell did you do that? Dammit, Mir!" I tipped her chin up so I could look into her eyes, thumbing her eyelids open until she swatted weakly at me. I grabbed a washcloth and soaked it through, bathing her forehead.

"We had to know. . . ." She rested her head against the tile wall, ignoring my ministrations, arms wrapped around her knees.

"Not that way, we didn't. Twice in one week? Are you nuts?" Okay, it was my worry talking. Normally, I wouldn't dream of speaking to my wife like that. But . . . dammit! "And why didn't you wake me up?"

"Because you would have told me not to do it." The thin tank top and shorts were nearly transparent under the steady stream of water. Her dark curls hung limp and heavy around her face, and as the moments went by, her lips started to turn faintly blue. Examination found her skin properly chilled.

The cruel hand of fear slowly eased its grip on my heart as Mira seemed to be cooling down quickly. We got lucky. I think I preferred the cold reactions to the hot ones. High fevers could do all kinds of damage.

I leaned my head against the shower door, trying not to shiver myself where I was seated on the linoleum floor. "What am I going to do with you?"

"Love me?" She reached to take my hand, and I threaded my fingers through hers.

"Isn't that my line?"

"Usually."

We sat there for a long time, holding hands in the cold shower. Neither of us said much. I honestly didn't know what to say that wouldn't make me look like a big insensitive jerk.

Yes, I appreciated her efforts. And I knew that her ability to help me meant a lot to her. I just couldn't seem to get it through her head that nothing in the world was worth her risking herself like that—absolutely nothing, and especially not me.

Somewhere around butt-crack-of-dawn o'clock, I bundled us both into bed to get what little sleep we could.

19

The promised high pressure (or low pressure? I can never keep that straight) front moved in overnight, and Friday didn't so much dawn as slink in with promises of tantrums forthcoming. It reminded me a bit of Paulo. The thought amused me, but Mira didn't get the joke when I told her. Oh well.

I slipped out of bed and dressed quietly with the intention of letting Mira sleep as long as possible. She didn't even stir, which attested to her exhaustion.

I went through my morning katas in near darkness. Though the sun remained firmly imprisoned behind gathering clouds, it wasn't cold. The presummer warmth lingered, and the air tingled with electricity. I could smell rain on the faint breeze. The world seemed to be waiting on the verge of something momentous. Even without seeing a weather broadcast, I knew we were in for some nastiness.

My right leg hated me. I wasn't sure if it was the changing weather or still the strain from my spill on the wet linoleum, but the muscles twitched and spasmed despite my considerable warm-up. I pushed myself to overcome the hesitancy in my movements, and in retrospect, it was probably not my smartest decision. By the time I finished, my calf was on fire. As much as I hated to admit it, I was going to have to curtail the physical exercise for the next two weeks, or I'd never be in shape to fight for Kidd's soul—if I wasn't in jail by then. How the hell do I get myself into these messes?

Thankfully, Axel didn't make his usual morning appearance. The chess set hadn't been touched since the last time I looked at it, so he hadn't even dared to come by when I wasn't looking. I wasn't sure what to say to him, anyway. *"You're a demon!"* Well duh, genius. I was the only person shocked by that little revelation. And the worst part was, at one point, I had honestly thought we were friends—in a semihostile, wary sort of way.

I pondered having Mira ward the boundaries of our yard, but if he could find me anywhere, anytime, what was the point? I'd never been a man to hide safely behind walls, even magical ones. I believed in me, above all else. I would protect the people I cared about.

I took some time to tend to my garden before I went back inside. That usually consisted of raking my rock path and straining the algae out of the little pond. The pond itself was the easier of the two tasks. There hadn't been enough sun and warmth to truly turn it into the swamp it could be, if I didn't stay ahead of it. The rock garden, however, was a larger project.

Even with my leg gimped, I found the process soothing. I changed the patterns occasionally, altering the design to fit my mood and meditations. The smooth river stones made pleasant little clicks and clacks as I raked them into order, the tan pebbles forming a sinuous stone stream through the creamy white. The black ones I scooped into tiny mounds, obstacles for my river to flow around. I thought it fitting.

My little bonsai shrubs were still recovering from their winter indoors, but I retrieved the clippers to nip off a few stray growths that didn't fit with the shape I was cultivating. I took the new greenery as a sign that they were still healthy plants.

The house smelled like bacon, and Mira was cleaning up the breakfast dishes when I came back inside. She paused to catch her breath every few moments, but had that stubborn set to her jaw that said her mind was made up.

"I would have done that, baby."

She just shrugged, her back to me. "You were busy. I'm fine."

I snagged a piece of bacon off Anna's plate, earning the five-year-old's lecture. "That was mine, Daddy!"

I winked at her but watched concerned as Mira fumbled with the flatware. "You're not going to the shop today, are you?"

A handful of silverware jangled as it slipped from her hands onto the floor. She sighed, hanging her head in resignation. "No. I will not be heading to the shop today. I will be staying home to watch Anna, while Dee watches the shop for me."

"I was gonna take Anna with me when I went shopping today. You can get some rest." I was, really. I even remembered promising to do that.

"No, you're not. Because Kristyn just called, and she had a no-call, so she needs you to come in."

My heart sank. "You have got to be kidding. I'll just tell her no."

"You can't do that, Jess. She wouldn't call if she

didn't need you. You know that." Mira raked her wet fingers through her hair with a frustrated sigh.

"I'm sorry, baby." I slipped my arms around her waist. "I'm a screwup."

"Sometimes." She sighed and leaned her head against my shoulder.

"I wanna hug, too!" Anna squirmed between us, and there was nothing to do but let her. I gathered my girls close for a group hug.

"I'll get my mom a present when I'm on break from work today. You and Anna just have a play day together, okay?"

Mira nodded, withdrawing from the embrace to turn back to the dishes. "If it storms like they say, we'll probably go to Dixie's."

"Yay, cookies!" My daughter was off like a shot, no doubt to pack her bags for the big move across the street.

Mira sighed, trying to find the humor in the situation. "Great, she'll be bouncing off the walls on a sugar high."

"She'll sleep well tonight, at least." I traced her cheek with one finger, marveling at how soft her skin felt against my calloused hands. "I really am sorry, baby."

"I know. It can't be helped." She caught my hand and kissed the scarred knuckles. "You'd better take a shower before you go in to work."

"Are you saying I stink?"

She smirked at me, a trace of her usual fire underneath all the weariness. "You'll be lucky if that's all I say about you. Git."

I got. Or gat? I don't know. I'm not a linguist.

On the way to the shower, I made a detour into Mira's room to fire up the ancient computer. Part of me wished the thing had a couple of Tesla coils and a big rusted power switch so I could cackle and say, "It's alive!" I've always wanted to do that.

Clever me, I muted the speakers before Viljo's WatchBot could announce to the world that I'd logged on. *Ha, take that!* I slipped the headphones on as the webcam window popped up.

"That you, Jesse?"

"Who else would it be?"

Viljo chuckled. "I do not know. I have nightmares of your beautiful wife logging on by mistake, and me saying something highly inappropriate to her."

"I'd kill you, you know."

"Not if she killed me first." He stretched in the grainy window and shook his head. "So, I have learned some strangeness, if you are interested."

"Hit me." I cringed as windows started appearing on the screen. "Just tell me, okay? I don't need a full-color presentation."

Viljo just chuckled. "Ivan pays me to be the best. Enjoy the show."

More windows popped up on the screen, and the computer took on a labored wheeze. "Hey, Vil? Remind me to have you look at this thing later, okay? It doesn't sound so good."

"Shoot it. Bury it. Let me build you a new one. In the meantime, I have messages from Sveta, and Father Gregory, and all is well with them."

"Father Gregory?"

"The senior member of the Ordo Sancti Silvii. It turns out, he is a very pleasant man, and he said to thank Ivan for the consideration."

"Well, that's good." Yay for diplomacy, I guess?

"And in the bad news, I did confirm that the phone number is a prepaid cell phone. Nothing useful there."

"Dammit."

"Indeed." Windows vanished, others reappeared, and the computer whined plaintively.

"Seriously, Viljo, stop with the windows. I don't think this thing's gonna handle it much longer."

He frowned at the camera. "That bad? Strange . . ." Still, the windows shut down immediately, and the noise in the tower subsided a bit. "I was very disappointed about the phone, as you may guess, but I have discovered something else that may redeem me."

The image on the webcam got choppier, and I couldn't even make his mouth match up with the words I was hearing. I frowned, fiddling with the buttons on the monitor in the vain hope that it would help. It didn't. "Well, what is it?"

"Miguel's credit card was used, one week ago, in Del Rio, Texas."

"Say again?"

"Miguel, or someone with his credit card, used his card in Texas." Even his voice over the headset was starting to hitch. "They booted me out once. I am still looking for another back door so I can get more specifics."

"Viljo, man, you sound like a drive-through intercom. What's up with the connection today?"

He peered into the camera, giving me a close-up of his nose for a second, as if he could see across the distance between KC and Colorado. "Did you get a second computer?"

"No . . . why?"

His frown was very clear, even in the grainy feed. "Because . . . there is something. . . ." I could hear his keyboards rat-a-tat-tatting as his fingers flew over them, and Mira's computer gave a strained whine.

"What are you doing, Viljo?" I'm not even sure he heard me the first time. "Viljo? What's up, man?"

"Shit!" He vanished from the webcam's view for a few frames, but I could still hear him. "He's . . . in your . . . -chine!"

Who was what? I watched in fascination as the geek's choppy image flitted around his little control room frantically. "What the hell is going on?"

"Hack- . . . in . . . machine. Catch this . . . -ther fucker . . ."

Meanwhile, the computer was making a horrible roaring noise, like a jet engine about to take off. I eyed it warily, wondering if something evil was going to jump out of it at me. Stranger things had happened. "What do you need me to do?"

"Nothing . . . -got it . . ." There was a pause, and then he added, "I think."

I could only watch, and I had a crappy view as it was. Viljo seemed to be teleporting around the room, so badly did the image jump. One moment he was at his usual keyboards, the next he was in the back of the room fiddling with something, and then he was front and center again, a snarl on his geeky little face.

Though I had no idea what he was doing, I saw the moment it all went wrong. There was a look of absolute horror on Viljo's face. "Shit shit shit!" He vanished again; then his silhouette appeared in the rear, yanking cords out of equipment willy-nilly.

I lost the visual feed and the sound at the same moment, Viljo blipping out of existence. Then my monitor went black, and Mira's computer gave one last ominous pop and was silent. Blue smoke trickled from the tower in a stench of burned electronics. "Oh shit." *What the hell just happened?*

The phone's ringing nearly jarred me out of my seat, and I snatched the cordless before anyone else in the house could get to it. "Hello?"

"Jesse?"

"Viljo?" He sounded different on the phone. Younger, maybe. "What the hell?"

"Shut your machine down. They were hacking through your security clearance."

I eyed the now-smoking ruin. "I don't think that's going to be a problem. Did you get him?"

"No, dammit. I threw everything I had at him, and he walked through it like nothing. I had to use the air firewall."

"The what?"

"You know—yank the cords out of the walls. No Net connection, no hack."

"You're sure he didn't get anything?" I could hear

Mira coming down the hallway, no doubt drawn by the aroma of charred motherboard. I was doomed.

"I do not think he did. It is going to take me a bit to be sure. Tell Ivan, until further notice, Grapevine is off-line."

I groaned. Ivan was going to chew me a new asshole, as soon as Mira was done throttling me for nuking her computer. "I'm a dead man."

"What?"

"Nothing. You gotta get it up and functional again, Viljo. We need a way to keep an eye on everyone, and you're it right now."

I could almost see him straighten up, emboldened by his sworn duty. "I will. A day, maybe two. I need to put some extra security in place. It will take equipment I cannot get easily."

"While you're at it, order the stuff to build Mira a new computer." I sighed, shaking my head. "This one is toast."

"Ouch. You *are* a dead man. I will call when things are up again."

"Take care of yourself, Viljo. And here, talk to Mira about her new computer." I tossed the phone at my startled wife as she entered the room, then fled toward the safety of the shower.

I stayed under the running water until I was certain that Viljo had time to talk Mira out of any retaliatory rages. I also ran out of hot water.

The shower eased my aching muscles, but the right calf still wasn't sound. Testing it as I moved around the bathroom, I kept thinking that they used to shoot lame horses. The thought of *two weeks, two weeks* beat inside my skull like a bass drum. I had two weeks to get better again. Two weeks to keep Mira from ending up a widow, and Annabelle from going fatherless.

As I limped out of the bathroom, I could hear my cell phone ringing in the den. "I got it!" I did my best to run down the hall with a towel draped around my hips, grabbing the phone just before it went to voice mail. "H'lo?".

There was a puzzled pause, then, "Dawson?"

"Ivan!"

"I am to be interrupting? You are to be sounding out of breath."

I flopped into my chair, keeping my weight off the right arm lest I wind up sprawled on the floor. "Nah, you caught me in the shower is all. What's the word?" Water dripped from my hair to puddle around the castors of my chair as I talked.

"I was wishing to ask you the same question. What news are you to be having?"

Well, let's see, I had a Mohawked demon stalking me, a blue car tried to run me off the road a couple times, someone just blew up Mira's computer, there was probably a warrant out for my arrest, and I was gimpy as hell in one leg with a fight coming up. I told him none of these things.

"We have a problem with Grapevine. Someone tried to get in again today, and Viljo had to take the whole system off-line to keep them out."

A string of Ukrainian curses flowed from my phone, and I waited patiently for the flood to subside. "Was any information to being compromised?"

Viljo hadn't really said, but I was willing to elaborate on his behalf. "No. Viljo shut it down before they got to anything." I hoped.

"Is there any news that is *not* to being bad?"

"Well . . . the phone number was a prepaid cell, as he thought. But right before the system went down, he said that Miguel's credit card was used a week ago in Del Rio, Texas." I mentally cursed the mysterious hacker who had interrupted that conversation. "If he found anything else, he didn't get a chance to tell me before everything went haywire."

"Then we are to be having two choices. Either Miguel's brother has taken the card or . . ."

"Or? Miguel was dead a week ago. It has to be the brother. He either grabbed the machete and went demon hunting or . . ."

"Or?"

"Or he's running, Ivan. I mean, he's seventeen, and his family expects him to take up the mantle next. I wouldn't have wanted that job at seventeen." I still didn't want it.

"We are only guessing that the boy has taken Miguel's weapons and armor. What if Miguel has them still? What if he is traveling . . . somewhere?"

Hope is a cruel, cruel thing. I ruthlessly crushed even the first glimmer. "Without calling Rosaline or checking in?" He was grasping at straws. Calling him on it probably made me a bastard, but it was easier to believe that Miguel was dead. It was better than having the hope crushed later, when the worst was confirmed.

"*Tak.* You are right, of course. Most likely, it is Estéban." The old man sighed wearily. This thing was really getting to him. "I am to be taking an airplane to Kansas City in two days, to be dealing with your contract. I will continue investigating once I am to be releasing you from that."

"I told you no."

"I am to be ignoring you."

Ugh, the man was infuriating. I wanted to bang my head on my desk. "Ivan, I really don't like the idea. . . ." There were too many ways to screw up, too many ways to hang yourself. There was too much at stake.

"I am not to be asking permission." Yeah, he'd definitely been military at some point. It never occurred to him to expect anything other than absolute obedience.

And really, what was I going to say? "*Sorry, Ivan, I'm just gonna go get my ass killed on my own, thanks.*" "Yessir." The champions were loosely associated at best, but when Ivan snapped, we all jumped.

"God to be blessing you, Dawson. I will be there soon." He hung up in my ear. Once again, I mentally vowed to stop doing that to people.

Much to my own annoyance and despite my misgivings, I felt better knowing that Ivan would be on the scene relatively soon. It was much akin to the relief felt when, though you knew you were in deep crap, your father showed up to talk to the angry man whose window you just broke.

I had my own little lake pooling on the floor when I stood up. It was amazing how much water my hair could hold even as short as it was now. After fetching another towel to mop that up, I went to get dressed. The T-shirt of the day read IT'S ALWAYS FUN UNTIL SOMEONE LOSES AN EYE. THEN IT'S FREAKIN' HILARIOUS! Mira hated that shirt, but it always got rave reviews at It.

"Gimme hugs, button. Daddy's gotta go to work!" The redheaded imp came barreling down the hallway to squeeze my knees tightly, and I bit back a wince. "Be extra good for Mommy, okay?"

Anna nodded solemnly. "I will, Daddy. I promise."

Passing through the kitchen, I gave Mira a quick kiss. "You gonna be okay today?" She nodded. "Did Viljo get the computer issue worked out?"

"He says he's going to put green lights all over it. Why do I need green lights on it?"

I had to chuckle. "Honey, by the time he's done, you'll be able to pilot the Space Shuttle from it."

She rolled her eyes at me. "We need to ship him the dead one. He's going to see if he can recover anything off the drive."

"Can do." I slipped my cell phone into her hand. "Answer it, just in case it's Ivan, okay?"

She nodded, then threw her arms around me, nearly squeezing my breath from my lungs.

"Oof!" I leaned back to look down at her. "Hey, what's wrong?"

She bit her lip, the familiar gesture meaning she was trying to put whatever it was into words. "Something feels wrong today. Everything's unsettled." Her eyes were troubled, but finally, she just shook her head. "It's probably just the storm making me all jittery. Or

PMS or something." I wasn't about to touch that one. There's no right answer to that.

"You sure?" She nodded after a short hesitation. I kissed her forehead. "Okay, I'm gonna head out. Call me at work if you need anything. You guys have fun at Dixie's."

A feeling I could only describe as lingering ickiness stayed with me as I climbed into my truck. Mira was right. Something felt off about the day. The goose bumps on my arms refused to go away, and I felt as if I had swallowed a fifty-pound lead weight. Neither of those signs ever heralded anything good.

I sat for long moments, weighing the pros and cons of taking my katana with me. The cons won out, knowing that I couldn't afford to repair a broken window when some jerk broke into my truck to steal the sword. And really, what was I going to do with it, besides stand out in the storm and do my lightning rod impression?

As I pulled onto the highway and headed north, I kept waiting for flashing blue lights in my rearview mirror, but they never came. Twice, I saw cop cars cruising up on my tail, but while I held my breath and kept both hands at ten and two, they sped on by, intent on some other miscreant. I couldn't believe that Verelli hadn't gone to the police, but why weren't they coming after me? I wasn't exactly hard to find.

What the hell was I going to do if they arrested me? Mira was going to be so pissed, not to mention how much work I'd be missing. My income from It wasn't much, but those paychecks made the difference between scraping by and breathing a bit easier. There were bills that still needed paying, and her car needed new tires and . . .

Worry settled between my shoulders and got quite comfortable, the muscles there knotting up painfully. I forced my hands to relax on the wheel and tried to meditate, the low hum of tires on pavement as soothing as any mantra. My thoughts refused to be soothed, and instead they took a forced march through some of the darker parts of my life.

The first line of the *Hagakure* says that the way of the samurai is found in death. It goes on to say that you should instantly choose death if it benefits your cause, because integrity is more important than life.

That was the part I had a hard time with. Sure, I was accepting of death. I mean, no one escapes it in the end, so why be afraid of it? And living honorably is very important to me. Sometimes, honor is all you have.

Bushido says that to lay down your life for your beliefs is a noble death that few can understand. It is the way of the warrior. But when it comes down to it, if I ever truly have to make the choice between dying to achieve my goal, and living on to fight another day . . . I wonder if I could really do it. I wonder if I really believe it.

They had a lot of absolutes, those ancient samurai, and they never talked about having multiple goals. My short-term goal may be saving the next guy's soul, but what about my long-term goals? What about growing old with Mira, or seeing my daughter graduate from college? What about being a grandpa someday? If I succeeded in one but failed in the others, did I come out on the losing end, anyway?

Sometimes—a lot of the time, really—I'm a pretty lousy samurai.

Pondering death on a day like today just had to be a bad omen. I turned up the radio to drown out the gloom and watched the sky.

The low-hanging clouds were dark with unshed rain, and the wind came in fits and gusts, threatening to goose the unwary right off the road. There was no thunder yet, but I could feel it coming, down in that deep primeval instinctive place all humans still have. You know, that place where you are secretly still afraid of the dark no matter how old you get.

Yes, we were definitely in for some bad weather.

20

I wanted it to rain. Maybe if it rained the tension in the air would snap and we could all breathe again.

There were no theme songs for the day. Instead, Kristyn and I kept the radio tuned to a local station for weather updates. The store was nearly deserted. In the three hours I'd been at work, we'd seen two customers. Perhaps two dozen people had walked past the door in total. Sierra Vista looked like a ghost town. No one was willing to brave the ominous clouds, even though no actual precipitation seemed forthcoming.

My punk-haired boss grumbled. "I feel bad calling you in. If I'da known we'd be this dead . . ."

"You're not supposed to be here alone. You know that." We were victims of corporate policy. No one worked the store solo. I think it was supposed to cut down on employee theft or something.

"I shoulda known he was too good to be true." All morning, she'd been beating herself up for hiring Paulo, our no-show of the day. "He was probably illegal—I never could get him to put his social on the paperwork."

I had other reasons for cursing Paulo. If fleeing from me in the Wal-Mart hadn't made him look guilty of *something*, refusing to show up and face me again certainly did. I had a lot of questions, and very few available answers. Therefore, it was with a heavy heart that I decided to commit that greatest of mortal sins, nosiness.

Under the pretense of reworking next week's schedule for Kristyn, I set up camp in the small closet that served as her office. Flipping on the turquoise lava lamp for light, I began rifling through the employee files. Later, I would have to point out to her that she should really lock that cabinet, but for the moment it worked to my advantage.

My own file was in the folder marked *O*—for "old dude," I presume. Paulo's was under *T* for "temporary." In our high-turnover world, no one counted as a permanent employee until they lasted through two paychecks. "Well well, Señor Riaz. Let's see what I can find out about you." I kept an ear out for the thud of Kristyn's boots as I perused his paperwork.

There wasn't much to know. The application was filled out in neat block lettering with a sketchy ballpoint pen. Paulo listed no social security number, as Kristyn said, and when I tried the phone number, it went to the car dealership across the highway. The only address was a street name, no number, and he hadn't even bothered to write down the zip code. And she hired him with only this information? Kristyn baffled me—often.

My superior's hiring ethics aside, there was no doubt in my mind that Paulo had been hiding something. Sure, all the omissions could have been explained as laziness or maybe even a language barrier (though I'd rate that as a stretch), but when the gut tells you it's hinky, it usually is. Without Paulo there to interrogate, I wondered if I would ever find out the truth.

Putting the paperwork neatly back in place, I shut the cabinet up tight and scribbled down a rough draft of the schedule for Kristyn's approval. I even remembered to pencil myself in for some time off in two weeks.

Once I returned to the front, Kristyn and I busied ourselves with putting out new stock, and when that was done, we shot paperclips at each other in a running rubber-band fight through the store. She called an end to it after the third time she scored a hit on me because I was staring out the plate glass window into the growing darkness.

"It's no fun playing with you if you're not paying attention."

"Sorry."

She came to stand next to me, tugging on a lock of violently purple hair. "It looks nasty out there."

"Yeah. We're gonna get nailed." I hoped Mira and Anna had gone to Dixie's. The lack of a basement was the one thing I hated about our house. In this area of the country, a basement is almost a necessity.

The wind whipped up a small dust devil amidst the construction debris. I watched it dance across the open grassy courtyard and bend the new saplings nearly in half. Just as abruptly, it spent itself in a fit of dusty pique and vanished.

"You can go home if you want. Go make sure Mira and Annabelle are okay."

"Then you'd be alone. Mira's tough. She can take

care of anything. I'll stay here with you." In the distance to the northwest, I could see flickers of light in the towering clouds. "Lightning's coming."

The phone rang, a jarring sound misplaced against the low throb of the punk music currently playing. We both jumped, then exchanged sheepish chuckles.

Kristyn hung headfirst over the counter to answer it, her plaid hind end aimed skyward. I swear I didn't look. "It is where it's at. This is Kristyn. How can I help you?" Her business voice changed quickly to her friendly voice. "Oh, hey, Mira! We were just talking about you! Yeah, he's right here."

She launched the cordless phone at me, and I caught it with a minimum of fumbling, thankfully. "Hey, baby."

"Hey. How's work going?"

"Super slow. You guys at Dixie's?"

"Yeah, Anna's finger painting with banana pudding." Now there was an image. I had to chuckle. "Um . . . your phone keeps ringing."

"Did you answer it?"

"Yeah. It's some guy, not Ivan. He won't give me his name, but he insists that you know him, and that he needs to talk to you immediately. He's called about four times now." And she'd probably started giving him nasty answers after the first two. My wife wasn't one to play coy with. I'd seen her reduce telemarketers to tears in a matter of moments.

It had to be Kidd. "Give me the number. I'll call him back from here." Grabbing an ink pen shaped like a famous wizard's magic wand, I scrawled down the digits. Yup. That was the hotel number. "You guys had better get your heads down. It looks like this thing's about to open up and blast us to Oz."

"We'll be okay. You be careful, all right? Please?" There was no hiding the worry in her voice.

"I will. Promise. I'll call you as soon as it passes, so you know we're not marching on the Emerald City." After mutual I-love-yous, I hung up the phone. "I'm gonna go in the back for a minute and make a call, Kristyn."

"Make it quick. I need help with all these customers." She smirked, gesturing at the empty store.

Our employee break room consisted of a wall of basket lockers, a soda machine, and the hot-water heater for the three tenants around us. Yeah, someone didn't think that design out real well. I found a free spot leaning against the bulletin board—between the year-old ROCKFEST TICKETS NOW ON SALE! sign and the reminder to clock in and out for breaks—and called Kidd's hotel room.

He answered almost immediately. "Hello?"

"Mr. Kidd, I understand you've been annoying the hell out of my wife." I wasn't nearly as irritated as I sounded, but he didn't need to know that.

"Oh . . . yes . . . that . . . I'm sorry. I just . . . I needed to speak to you, and that's the only number I have for you and—" I don't know how much longer he might have babbled on, because I interrupted him.

"What did you *want*, Mr. Kidd?"

"I—I wondered if perhaps we couldn't speed up the process and everything. I mean, two weeks is a long time. A lot can happen in two weeks. What if something were to happen to me in the meantime? I don't want to die, with this still hanging over me."

"I didn't set the time, Mr. Kidd; your 'friend' did." And yeah, with my leg hurt, I wasn't going to rush into the fray by any means. "Nothing is going to happen to you."

"Things happen, Mr. Dawson. All the time. Car accidents, plane wrecks." There was very real fear in his voice. He truly thought he'd never live to see his soul returned. Just because you're paranoid doesn't mean they're not out to get you, but there is such a thing as taking it too far.

"I can't speed up the cycle of the moon. Two weeks. Less than that, even."

"Could I come talk to you in person? Where are you?"

"No, you may not." Never mix work with . . . other work. Just safer for everyone involved that way. "I'm at my other job, and they don't know about things like—" Realizing at the last second that to say "things like you" would not be a good idea, I finished instead, "Like what we're dealing with. I intend to keep it that way."

"But I really think—"

In the background, I heard the unmistakable and imperious sound of Travis Verelli's voice. "Is that him? You're talking to him, aren't you? Put down the phone, Nelson! We discussed this!"

Kidd tried to get his plea out in a rush. "Please, Mr. Dawson, I really need to . . . Ack!"

I listened in amazement as the two grown men proceeded to tussle over the phone. I couldn't even tell who was winning, but there were many grunts and half-muffled expletives. In all honesty, I didn't hold much hope for Verelli in a physical scuffle, especially not against a professional athlete—even an old one.

The phone crashed to the floor with a jarring clatter and I winced, holding it at arm's length. When I finally put it back to my ear, I heard nothing but silence beyond. What the hell happened?

"Um, Mr. Kidd? Hello?" I got no answer; not even the sound of heavy breathing. "Uh, listen, you work things out with your agent, and I'll see you in two weeks, okay?" I hung up on dead silence, unsure what else to do. *Weird.*

Sure, Kidd's pleas made sense. I am not a man without sympathy. The thought of dying while the minions of Hell owned my soul was not pleasant; I admit this. But I couldn't speed up time, or protect him from the random acts of nature, or God, or even his well-meaning agent. And considering that I was most likely facing jail time in the near future, Nelson Kidd, for good or ill, was on his own.

Something low and mournful, fitting to the darkness outside, wailed from the radio as I walked back to the front. I flicked it quickly to a bouncier station. We didn't need to add to the oppressive atmosphere.

Kristyn stood at the windows, watching the wind whip the leaves from the tiny trees. "Ellen came over. She says they're closing up shop and going home." She nodded toward the jewelry shop across the street.

"You wanna go home?" It wasn't my first Missouri storm. It wouldn't be my last. But even I could tell that this was going to be one for the record books.

"Jesus, if corporate found out I'd shut the place down during business hours, they'd burn me at the stake." Kristyn chewed on her lower lip, though, watching the lightning strobe through the darkened sky. It was closer now. "I'm gonna call Chris and Leanne and tell them to stay home, though. No reason to drag them out in this mess."

"Good idea." The shopping center was deserted, from what I could see. Nothing stirred, save the billows of yellow construction dirt on the far side of the courtyard, churned up by the sporadic wind gusts. The shop lights opposite us gleamed weakly through the clay dust fog. Something white and plastic went bumping down the street and out of sight—a bucket, maybe. "Come on. If stuff gets nasty, we don't want to be standing by these windows."

I put my arm around her shoulder—normally a no-no with our strict corporate stance on sexual harassment, but damn the Man—and led her to the back of the store where we could hover over the radio and pretend we were contributing to the greater good. It was going to be a long damn day.

21

My day got significantly worse when the doorbell chimed, announcing someone's arrival. Believing that no human would be insane enough to go shopping on a day like this, I fully expected it to be Axel.

As it turned out, I was wrong about Axel, and the sanity of our visitor was definitely in question.

Nelson Kidd struggled to get his umbrella down, but the wind had warped it beyond salvation, and he finally flung it to the floor to watch it spin in drunken circles. Even at a distance, I could see the staring, glazed expression in his blue eyes. I'd seen that look before, in victims of sudden catastrophe. It was the look they had right after they went numb and just before they started screaming.

Kristyn rounded the counter to greet him with her retail-brilliant smile, but I grabbed her arm and shook my head at her. I'd handle this one.

"Welcome to It. Is there something I can help you find?" Out of Kristyn's view, I gave Kidd a warning look. He'd better be damn careful what he said here. Pretending he'd answered me, I grabbed his elbow, squeezing just the right place to make his fingers go numb, and dragged him into the racks of assorted hoodies. "How the hell did you find this place?" I hissed.

The old man winced and extracted his arm from my

grip. "Caller ID on the phone. I did a reverse lookup on the Internet."

Damn the Internet. "Well, in case you're wondering, coming out in *this* is what is going to get you killed. Are you insane?"

He ignored my question and clutched at my shirt like a drowning man. "You have to help me. Look, I wired the funds like you told me. Twice your asking price." He waved a crumpled piece of paper in front of my eyes. "He doesn't want to give up my soul. He's going to kill me before you can help me. . . ."

"No. He's not." I snatched the paper from him, mostly to get it out of my face, then carefully extracted myself from his fevered grip. "They can't hurt you, unless you allow it." But oh, if the demon could find a loophole, trust me, he would. I firmly believe that the very first lawyer was a demon. I didn't tell Nelson Kidd that. The man was an inch away from snapping as it was. "Where's Verelli?" As much as I didn't like the slimy agent, I thought he could at least corral his client until this bout of paranoia had passed.

"He's . . . tied up. Agent stuff, I dunno." Kidd's eyes darted nervously, but before I could question him further, thunder boomed directly overhead and the lights, giving one flicker, went out. A few tense heartbeats passed before the generators kicked in and the emergency lights hummed to life. In the sickly green lighting, I could see the whites of Kidd's eyes, wide with panic. "He's going to kill me. . . ."

"No one's going to kill you." I grabbed his arm again, just to keep track of him. "Kristyn? Let's go ahead and hit the storm shelter, 'kay? I'll lock the doors." Well, I'd lock them once I could get Kidd confined. It was rather like dragging Annabelle when she was in one of her obstinate moods. Every step toward the back was an exercise in pitting my weight against his.

I almost made it.

Outside, a low whine began and quickly swelled into a strident wail. The early-warning system, tornado sirens, shrilled their warning for blocks around.

"No!" With a strength born of sheer terror, Kidd wrenched free of my grasp and bolted for the door. It binged cheerfully as he disappeared into the storm.

"Fuck!" Kristyn stared at me wide-eyed as I grabbed one of the hoodies from the rack and pulled it on. "I'll get him. You get to shelter."

I don't know whether she locked the doors behind me as I ran out. The rain had just started to fall, large drops the size of fifty-cent pieces, big enough to sting against bare skin. The wind whipped my hair around my face until I pulled up my hood, scanning the area. Only our side of the shopping center had lost power. On the lighted side, the neon storefronts threw rivulets of colored light across the rain-slicked pavement.

Down the block, I watched Kidd's fleeing figure disappear just past the Starbucks. Where the hell did he think he was going? The parking lot was in the other direction. "Hey! Get back here!" Although my right leg reminded me I was a bastard, I ran after him anyway, calling Kidd every nasty name I could think of— you know, the really good ones I can't say in front of Annabelle.

Lightning struck close enough for me to smell the ozone, and the thunder made my teeth rattle. I rounded the corner past Starbucks and caught a glimpse of Kidd headed toward the opposite side of the empty grandstand. No bands were playing today. No one was around at all, except me and the lunatic I was chasing through the rain.

"Kidd!" My voice was lost to the grumbling clouds above us and the wail of the tornado sirens.

In all fairness, I was hurt, and he was a professional athlete. It didn't matter that he was twenty years older than I. He ran like a damn jackrabbit. I even lost sight of him once, darting between the Thai place and some expensive perfume shop.

Soaked to the skin already, I came around the corner to find him stopped in the middle of the sidewalk. Rivers of yellow mud ran from the construction site across the street, marring the cheerful neon reflections from the shop windows. I slowed to a walk, afraid to startle him into bolting again. "Kidd?"

His eyes fixed on something above us, he never seemed to notice the rain pouring down his face. I followed his gaze to the sign for the newest restaurant on the block. It was the garish marquee for Moonlight & Roses. The neon full moon shone like a beacon in the darkness, the purple roses casting everything in a mauve sheen.

Kidd looked at me, finally, and I realized that tears mingled with the rain on his weathered cheeks. "I'm sorry."

Wanting to ask what he was sorry for, I started to

form the words, but then, seeing a sick determination settle into his eyes, I realized his intention. We were in a deserted place, and that sign was there above us— the one with the full moon, shining down. *Under the full moon* . . . I couldn't move fast enough to stop him.

"_____!" The hound-demon's name screeched through my skull, drowning even the tornado sirens for a moment.

"You son of a bitch!" I hit him square in the jaw, but it was too late. The damage was done. It was here, under the full moon, as agreed.

"I had to. Please believe me. I had to!" Kidd rubbed his jaw, cowering against the restaurant wall. "He said he'd release me. . . ."

The darkness gathered, solidified, and the pony-sized hellhound padded out of the black nothingness with a growling chuckle. "I never said when." Kidd moaned and sank into a shivering, sodden heap.

Lightning flashed, throwing the demon into sharp relief, a mountain of black fur seemingly untouched by the downpour. My hood had long since fallen down, my mop of wet hair hanging around my face. I looked like a drowned rat or maybe something skinnier—a weasel or a ferret, maybe. I'm sure I was the scariest rodent in the county.

The demon smiled, long canines gleaming white in its muzzle. "I have come at the appointed time, champion. Let the battle commence."

"I don't have my equipment; we can't fight now."

"I agreed only to *allow* the armor. You did not say it was a requirement."

Fuck! The demon was right. I hadn't been careful enough in my wording. Dammit, I knew better! "I don't have a weapon. The terms said a melee weapon of my choice." *Shoulda grabbed my sword. Knew I shoulda grabbed it. This is why we listen to the voices, Jesse.*

My katana was at home. Sure, I could stall long enough to go get it, but I knew the moment I laid my hands on it, the demon would be there. And there was no way I could put Mira and Anna in danger like that. My mind raced for other choices.

Even if I could get to my truck, I had only my small skinning knife in the door. That wasn't going to do much against this behemoth. Hair spray and a lighter? Not in this rain. Kitchen knives from a restaurant? Not much better than my own blade.

"Do I understand that you choose to fight with only your hands?"

"Don't rush me!" Did that thing look bigger than just a moment ago? I was so screwed.

"I am at the end of my patience. Choose now, or fight as you are!" It rocked back on its massive haunches, prepared to spring.

I did the only thing I could. I ran.

My leg burned, but I ran as if the hounds of Hell were on my heels. Oh wait—they were. Somehow, despite the constant thunder and wailing of the sirens, I could hear the demon's claws on the sidewalk and its panting breath as it loped behind me, expending only minimal effort in catching me. It would wait until I tired, then run me to ground. I had to find a weapon before then.

Part of me knew there were still people behind those darkened storefronts, innocent bystanders who could easily become casualties. I ran the other way, into the construction site. Maybe someone had left something I could use—a claw hammer, a crowbar. Hell, I'd take a forklift at this point, and I didn't even know how to drive one.

The yellow mud slithered under my feet, making running precarious at best. I crested the first mound of dirt and slid down the opposite side on my rump, covering myself in good Missouri clay. I heard the thing slip and slide down the same hill behind me, the sludge giving way under its heavier weight. I glanced back long enough to see it sprawled in the muck, struggling to get to its feet again. I savored the petty pleasure as I gained distance on it.

Angry now, the demon raised a low howl, baying in counterpoint to the incessant sirens. I fought the despair that tried to settle into my guts and just kept moving, telling myself that I refused to die wearing a sparkly vampire hoodie.

The skeleton of the unfinished parking garage loomed in the strobing light, and I darted for a gaping hole in the wall. Fido came galloping after me, snarling when it could only get its massive head through the opening. For a heartbeat, it tried to force the hulking shoulders through, then abandoned the effort. *One point for scrawny guys everywhere.* I lost track of it as it circled around to find a larger door.

There was no roof to stop the rain, and the partial walls did very little to deflect some of the wind. The strident wail of the tornado sirens reminded me that somewhere nearby, something very big and nasty was on the way. They didn't sound unless there was a funnel on the ground. *What a time to be playing hide-and-seek.*

The hellhound bayed, proving that it had my scent again, and I stumbled on my bad leg, scrabbling a few feet on hands and knees before I could regain my footing. Great, now I was gonna die embarrassed, too. Dammit, I needed more time!

The lightning showed me the shell of an empty elevator shaft ahead, and I ducked into it. There was no car there, no cables, just the concrete tower stretching three floors above me. *Think quick, Jess.* It was coming. It bellowed again, closing in on me.

My hands found rungs built into the wall, and I was climbing before I'd formed a conscious plan. The wall shuddered under my hands as the hellhound barreled in headfirst, slamming its massive bulk into the wall. Jaws snapped inches below my heel. A split second before it leapt again, I flopped out onto the second level, and I kicked at those enormous paws as it tried to scrabble up after me. "Down, boy! Bad dog!" It hit the ground hard, and I heard it snarl in irritation. It would have to find yet another way to get to me. I'd bought myself a few extra moments.

The second floor wasn't finished, and at the far end, the mud formed a ramp for the machines that hadn't been there in months. There were tools there, and I slid to my knees, frantically sorting through the discarded implements. In the yellow muck, my hand landed on something cold and metal. I didn't care what it was anymore. I grabbed it.

It was only a piece of one-inch pipe, maybe two feet long, bent at a right angle at one end. But it was heavy, and it would serve as a makeshift *tonfa* until I could find something better. A brief search found another of similar shape, and now I had a pair. It was better than nothing.

I put my back against a concrete wall and waited, my new weapons resting against my forearms. Against a sword or knife, I could parry with them, disarm with them, snap bone. Against that maw full of fangs, I could maybe break a few teeth before it crushed my arm to jelly. *Wonderful.*

The corner I sheltered in would be good to protect my flanks, but I was also pinned with nowhere to retreat. I couldn't stay here.

"Come out, come out, little slayer."

I resented that. "I'm just wiry!" Never let it be said that I didn't go down a smart-ass to the end.

The hound padded around a column, every muscle illuminated by the flashes of lightning. It was smiling. Splattered all over with yellow mud, it looked even more like some giant dire hyena from prehistoric times. Were there dire hyenas? I guess I'd never know.

I dropped into a fighting stance, hoping the thing hadn't seen me favoring my right leg. If I could dodge left the first time, I was good. If it forced me right, onto my bad leg . . . Oh, who was I kidding? I was puppy chow.

It came fast, faster than anything that size had a

right to be. I ducked left, improvised *tonfas* guarding my right side, and I was running again. The hound hit the concrete wall with all four feet and bounced off in pursuit. This was no leisurely chase now. I was armed, the contract fulfilled. Now the demon meant to kill.

The tingle down my spine told me there was a snap coming at my hamstring, and I jinked hard right. My leg screamed in pain, but held, and the vicious teeth snapped loudly on empty air. I wasn't so lucky next time, and something sharp raked down my left thigh. I was never sure if it was claws or teeth.

There was no electric pop, no shock from my wife's warding spells. I'd forfeited that protection when I had negotiated for a strictly physical fight. At the time, it had seemed a fair trade, but now I frantically wished for something, *any*thing more between my skin and those wicked teeth.

The demon's massive paws threatened to tangle with my own feet as we ran, and it threw its shoulder into my hip. I let the fall take me, rolling through it and back to my feet. I swung into that mass of solid fur and muscle with one pipe, and connected hard with something that sounded like it hurt. Blight wafted off into the air and the thing snarled, but it kept coming.

I could feel my blood soaking through my torn jeans only because it was warm against the rain-soaked chill. There would be no finding a better place to fight. I was done running, and the demon knew it. It held me at bay and circled, trying to find an opening. One lunge met with my makeshift *tonfa*, metal against muzzle,

and I heard a crack as one of the sharp canines shattered. The white bone chips evaporated into black mist,
flitting away to join with the rest of the demon's spent
energy. It backed away, shaking its head and growling.
Man, did that thing look pissed off.

They say, when you're about to die, your life flashes
before you. People talk about seeing loved ones gone
before, or forgotten things from childhood. Maybe I
should have been thinking of my wife and daughter,
soon to be without husband and father. I wasn't. My
only thought, which I voiced crystal clear above the
pain and pounding adrenaline, was, "Hotel phones
don't have caller ID."

The demon actually paused at that, head tilted com-
ically to the side.

"Hotel phones don't have caller ID. He said that's
how he found where I worked." A rumble started
somewhere in the demon's chest, and it gathered itself
to spring again. "How did he know where I worked?"

Thunder crashed, deafening both of us, and in the
flashing light, I spied another figure standing behind
the demon. The demon followed my gaze, and I was
too surprised to even take advantage of its distraction.

I thought at first it was Kidd, until I realized it was
too tall, too skinny. Then hope flared irrationally, and
for one interminable heartbeat, I thought it was Miguel.
The stranger walked forward, and a flash of lightning
illuminated his face.

"He made it his business to know." Paulo appeared
from the depths of the parking garage. His usual

T-shirt and jeans had been exchanged for ill-fitting studded leather armor. A machete, the blade so old it was nearly black, dangled from one hand.

The demon backed away to put both of us in its sight. "Treachery . . . fouled contract . . ." I swear, it lisped around its broken teeth, and it made even that sound purely evil.

The dark teen kept his eyes on the demon as he spoke. "They stalked you, Jesse Dawson, as they stalked *mi hermano* and Señor Archer." He pointed the stained blade at the hellhound. "So now I stalk them."

22

The storm itself seemed to grow quiet to listen to Paulo—or, not Paulo apparently, but Estéban, Miguel's younger brother. I know, I probably should have seen that coming. What can I say? I'm a bit dense at times.

The rain stopped as if a faucet had been turned, and the swirling wind died. In its place, the air grew heavy and still, and I struggled to breathe through the pea soup atmosphere. The immense pressure of some great and invisible hand pushed down on us. Only the wail of the storm sirens remained, strident and ululating. Maybe you've never been through a tornadic storm. Trust me when I tell you, all of the above are *bad* things. We were running out of time.

The thunder in the distance was a quiet rumble, barely distinguishable from the demon's throaty growl. "Deceit, treachery. To bring another to fight your battle. The bargain is broken, Jesse James Dawson. Your soul is forfeit."

I laughed, leaning against the wall to get what rest I could. My right leg was throbbing, and the cuts down my left thigh stung fiercely. Any moment I could use to collect myself was vital. "The deal is broken, you're right, but you don't get my soul. The deceit was yours, and Kidd's. His soul is yours to keep." In case you're wondering, that makes me a hard-hearted bastard. But the man had gotten two good men killed.

To prove me right, the tattoo on my right arm abruptly crackled and flaked away, leaving unmarred pink skin beneath. I was free.

I could see now how it had played out. "Mascareña. It's just over the border from Arizona, isn't it." The baseball schedule, dammit. I'm so fucking stupid! "Kidd just drove down from spring training. And he had an exhibition match in Toronto. That's how he found them. And how the boy found us."

I'm sure Kidd's demon promised him all kinds of things if the man would help lure champions into combat. They set seemingly innocuous terms, then sprang them when Guy and Miguel were unprepared. "Under the full moon" my ass. Good men, good fighters, and they never had a chance.

The hellhound snarled, but it knew I was right. Blight dribbled from its mouth, no doubt from the stump of broken fang. Its concentration was wavering. "Then our business is concluded."

"No!" We yelled in unison, Paulo and I. Estéban! *Dammit.* The boy tried to open his mouth, and I silenced him with a glare. He was a child, comparatively. He had no place here. "You have something I want. I propose a new bargain." I had no time for this. The air was hot and muggy beneath the low-hanging clouds, and no rain fell. No wind stirred. We were in deep shit. But I couldn't let it get away. I couldn't let it lie in wait for me again, springing when I wasn't ready. This had to end now.

"I listen." The hound's eyes flashed red, reminding me of Axel. If I lived through this, I was going to throttle him. *Damn you, Axel, why couldn't you just tell me?*

"I offer you the soul of Jesse James Dawson, in exchange for the souls of Miguel Alejandro Cristobal Perez and Guy Thomas Archer." Full names have power. They'd known mine as well, just in case. Ivan planned for everything.

The demon barked a laugh, and more blackness escaped its maw to wind away through the concrete columns. Somewhere out of sight, a portal was forming. "One soul for two? Even yours is not worth so much, Jesse James Dawson."

"Then add mine. I offer my soul." Paulo-Estéban needed to learn to keep his mouth shut. "I offer the soul of Estéban Paulo Juan-Carlos Perez." Man, I bet he hated learning to write all that as a child.

Before I could come up with a suitable objection, the demon nodded. "Done! Name your terms!"

Fuck fuck fuck. I didn't want to be responsible for the kid's soul, too, but it was too late to quibble now—too late in more than one way. "We fight here and now, as we are. We finish this now."

In a perfect world, I would have named some time in the future. I would have let myself heal, found my sword, something. The odds weren't in my favor, in the rain-slicked mud, armed as I was with pipes, and already gimped in both legs. But I stood a better chance, fully aware and as prepared as I was going to get, than letting this thing get the drop on me again. *Guy, Miguel . . . I hope I'm doing right by you guys.* I couldn't afford to be wrong.

That hellish muzzle wrinkled in a grin. "Done."

The contract mark burned bright and fast across the

back of my hand. No elaborate tattoo, this, but an ugly black slash of burned flesh. I heard Estéban gasp when his own seared in, but I didn't even notice the pain.

I pushed off the wall, my improvised *tonfas* held at the ready. This was going to hurt. Paulo-Estéban stepped up beside me, worn machete still leveled at the hound.

"What are you doing, kid?" I didn't dare take my eyes off the hound to ask.

"You said 'we' fight here and now. I am part of 'we.'" He was pale under his dark skin; he was terrified. His brother's armor was too big on him, a boy who hadn't yet seen his full growth. Had he watched Miguel fall? I wondered. Had he seen his brother's soul ripped from his body? I had to give the kid credit, though. No matter his age, or experience, his hand was steady on his brother's weapon. I felt bad for ever thinking he'd run away.

And damn, I was proud of the boy. He was right. At that moment, I could have called in an army to send the hound back to Hell, and it couldn't have done a thing about it. Even demons can fuck up contracts.

The black hound's hackles came up in a rage-filled snarl, but it didn't even bother protesting. It was caught in the haste of its own negotiations, and it knew it.

Beyond the walls of our concrete arena, the storm sirens blared on, and the light trickling through the clouds was a vomitus green. The thunder was gone, chasing the front to the east. All that was left was the oppressive calm, the harbinger of something catastrophic.

Neither Estéban nor I moved. I waited, holding my

weight gingerly on my right leg. I could lunge to my left from there, and though my blood had soaked the torn denim of my jeans, I wasn't crippled yet. The kid stood to my left, a thrum of tension in my peripheral vision, maybe waiting for some signal from me.

I never had a chance to give it.

The hellhound sprang without warning. I dove right, Estéban dove left, and just like that we were separated. The black nightmare whirled, faster than before, proving it had only been toying with me all along, supremely confident in its own ability.

I couldn't get near it without meeting fangs, that wedge-shaped head snapping from side to side impossibly fast. Every time Estéban moved in behind it, it would spin, sending the boy darting back out of reach, then turn again to meet me coming. I got no more than a handful of glancing blows in, and I'm not sure the kid hit it at all.

Something tickled my cheek, and I realized it was a strand of my damp hair, stirred in the smallest of breezes. To the west, I could hear what might be the murmur of traffic on the highway, except for one crucial fact. The highway was directly to our east.

It was coming. The time for smart fighting was through.

There was no more dodging or feinting. I kept the pipes whirling and moved in. Black fog wisped away where they landed, and the demon was forced to put its full attention on me. One gleaming fang laid my knuckles open to the bone, but I kept my grip and used my other hand to clout the thing across the eyes. The copper scent of my blood was overpowering in the heavy air, and the quiet hum of traffic had grown to a tiny roar.

The hound lunged against my unsteady right leg, and it finally crumpled. *Traitor*, I thought, bringing my arms up to shield my throat. Instead of following to rip me to shreds, the demon let out a bellow of pain and spun, one massive clawed foot planting right in my guts. "Oof!" My breath left me in a rush, but I could see the handle of the machete sticking out of one muscled flank. Estéban had buried it almost to the hilt.

The hound forgot about me. I heard the kid scream as it lunged, and beneath that, the sickening sound of breaking bone. The black essence seeping from the blade trickled across the muck, wafting dangerously close to my legs. I scrambled, still on my rump, to get clear before that numbing blight could touch me.

Estéban screamed again, out of my sight, and the hound shook its head like a terrier with a rat. I grabbed for the machete hilt, and dragged myself to my feet with it, wrenching it free. The black fog poured from the wound, a deadly river flowing over the mud toward the unseen portal. The demon had Estéban's arm in its hideous maw, crushing the bone in those powerful jaws. Even then, the kid tried to fight, fingers gouging at the beast's eyes in desperation.

There was grit in the wind and it stung my cheeks. I would remember that later. Now, I only ducked my head to keep my vision clear. Grabbing a handful of mud-matted fur and stabbing the machete in with the other, I climbed those hulking shoulders, ignoring the burning cold that came as the blight ran freely.

The hound reared up to its hind legs, almost standing upright, and I clung tight, wrapping my legs around its throat. Estéban, wounded as he was, still managed to grab hold of a furry ear and yank, wrenching the creature's head to the side. It thrashed and writhed, trying to unseat me with no success, but managed to stomp right in the middle of the downed kid's middle. Estéban retched loudly, and I stabbed the machete in again for a better hold. For all those massive corded muscles in its neck, the demon dog could not turn its head to get at me, no matter how it snapped and slavered. "Yee-haw, motherfucker."

I raised the machete in one hand and brought it down at the base of the creature's skull. There was a satisfying crack of bone, but it refused to concede, bucking and flinging itself into the wall. My head cracked against the concrete, and I held on only through sheer stubbornness. The moment it landed on all four feet, I hit it again—and again. Each time, the river of blight grew, flowing over my legs where they were locked around the hound's throat. I may as well have been standing up to my knees in ice, the only consolation being the relief from pain in my right leg.

The creature quit snarling after the third hit but refused to leave its feet, drunkenly staggering this way and that. Four more blows were needed for the head to come free from the hulking shoulders. I went with it, tumbling over and over in the mud with the grisly trophy still held in one hand.

By then I could no longer hear the tornado sirens under the storm's roar. The head, a snarl fixed forever on its vicious muzzle, dissolved into blight between my fingers. I couldn't wait long enough to watch the rest of the body dissipate back to its hellish origins. There was no more time.

Estéban stared blankly at me with eyes glazed in pain and shock, and I grabbed his good arm, dragging him to his feet. "Run!" I screamed in his ear, but he couldn't hear me. I couldn't hear myself. The tornado was here, and we had nowhere to go.

The deafening roar blotted out all else. It became the be-all and end-all of our existence. Large chunks of gravel peppered us as we stumbled for shelter, wherever that might be. Something heavier hit the center of my back, staggering me, but I managed to keep us both moving. Out of the darkness and storm-blown debris, we crashed into a concrete barricade and simply couldn't see to go any farther.

Huddled at the base of the pillar, I tried to shelter Estéban as best I could, almost wrapping myself around him. Mira's spells were forfeit for fighting the demon, but I prayed to anyone listening that they'd still protect me from an ordinary, everyday tornado.

Sharp things bit at my exposed skin, drawing blood in what seemed to be a hundred places. The kid screamed. I think I did, too, until the tornado sucked away all air and the ability to breathe.

It felt like we were there for years, with nothing but noise and pain in that horrible vacuum. I wished for my eardrums to burst, just to relieve the immense pressure. Every breath was full of dirt and grit, and we choked and gagged on what little air we got. And just when I was certain we were dead where we sat, it was gone.

In the abrupt silence, I thought I'd gone deaf. Then I heard water dripping somewhere nearby. One beam of sunlight found us, amidst the mud and the shambles of concrete and twisted rebar. The breeze, once so punishing, flirted around us, smelling freshly scrubbed, like spring. I think somewhere, a bird was singing tentatively.

Estéban was curled around his injured arm, and I wasn't sure he was even conscious until he moaned and mumbled something in Spanish. "Hey, kid . . . You with me?"

He said something else, something I knew wasn't polite, but nodded, and finally raised his head. His skin was a sickly gray, his dark eyes wide and staring. I eased his hand away from his broken arm to have a look. The thick leather bracer had protected him from the ravages of fang and claw, but it was bent at a wholly unnatural angle.

"Boy, when you do it, you do it right, hey, kid?" I smiled at him, and he rallied enough to give me that "Are you nuts?" look. He was going to be okay. Getting to my feet, I decided I was going to be okay, too.

Sure, I felt like shit. Blood trickled down my stubbly cheek from a cut I didn't remember getting. My right leg was done with me, and refused to hold my weight. I was going to have scars down my left thigh, and the small vain part of me briefly mourned the marks. Luckily, I couldn't feel either of them, the blight-numbness extending almost all the way to my hips. The knuckles on my left hand were going to scar, too, but I flexed them and they still worked. Most important, I was alive and I had my soul. My right hand was bare of all marks.

As I glanced around the wreckage, I came to appreciate how unlikely that had been. The pillar that sheltered and protected us had been sheared off two feet above our heads. The shattered remnants were strewn about us, a jagged garden of concrete chunks and mangled rebar. Any one of those would have cracked a skull, ending all our troubles in an instant. Bless Mira and the powers that sent her to me so many years ago. "One of us is the luckiest sumbitch on the planet, Paulo—er . . . Estéban."

A gleam atop the broken column caught my eye, and I limped closer to have a look. Perched there, sweetly as a centerpiece, were two pale white river stones, shot through with clear quartz veins. Matching nothing else in the debris around us, they lay nestled together as if placed by a careful hand. I picked them up, rolling them over between my fingers. They were warm and dry.

I'm not sure about religion, or God, or where we go when we die. But wherever it is, I think it must be a good place. And I decided Guy and Miguel were there. I pocketed the stones, to be placed in my garden. I'd take my signs where I found them.

"Be at peace, guys," I murmured.

Estéban finally struggled to his feet and immediately blanched. "I'm going to throw up." And he did. I think he felt better afterward. At least, he had more color to his ashen face.

"C'mon, Paulo . . . er, whatever I call you. Let's go see what's still standing."

With my arm around his lanky shoulders, we hobbled out of the wreck of a parking garage, to find that Sierra Vista looked as bad as we did. The ground was littered with shards of plate glass, the storefronts gaping like toothless mouths. The cheerful neon signs were tangled in impossible ruins, if they weren't gone altogether. Water sprayed from a fountain that no longer existed, and only one hardy sapling swayed in the spring air. One building had collapsed in on itself, and I thanked the powers that be that the tenant hadn't moved in yet. Okay, so maybe sometimes I believe in God.

All in all, it looked like a war zone, Estéban and I being the walking wounded. I wiggled a finger through the shreds of my jeans and sighed. "Mira's going to kill me."

"Quién es Mira?"

"My wife. These were my good jeans." I was probably in shock, and I'm allowed a warped sense of humor. I just chopped the head off a hellhound that was trying to eat a seventeen-year-old boy.

"Jesse? Jesse!" Funny, that didn't sound like my wife's voice, but sure enough, a woman was frantically calling my name. Kristyn pelted toward us, multicolored hair standing at sharp angles like a terrified hedgehog. I wasn't even sure she'd known my real name, until that moment. "Ohmigod! Ohmigodohmigod! Did you *see* that?" For one horrifying moment, I thought she was going to hug me, and I braced for the excruciating pain. Instead she skidded to a halt, all but vibrating, she was so worked up, and blinked at our obviously injured state.

"Is that . . . blood?" Kristyn went as pale as Estéban and slumped toward the ground.

Somehow, I caught her with one arm. "Aw crap. C'mon, Kristyn. I can't carry you. Don't do this to me now."

She whimpered, doing her best to keep on her feet, but she was now covered in the very blood that had her swooning. My day just wasn't getting any better. It was Murphy's Law at its finest, right here. This crap only happens to me.

I glanced at Estéban and chuckled. Then he snickered. Then we both burst out laughing. Groggy, Kristyn eyed us as if we'd finally lost it. I guess maybe we had. But under the circumstances, I think it was excusable. We laughed until our eyes watered and we were gasping for breath. We laughed so hard it hurt. We were still laughing when the ambulances started arriving.

There was a minor incident when I refused to leave until I checked on my truck. It was going heavily against me, but about the time one paramedic had a syringe full of sedative pulled out, the other one relented. I was allowed to hobble to the parking lot, leaning on Kristyn, who seemed to have recovered her moxie.

My truck was there, all beautiful in her rain-washed glory. And miracle of miracles, she was untouched (barring all previous damage, of course). In a tornado's inexplicable way, the same forces that had trashed the shopping center had neglected the employee parking lot. All twenty or so cars sat there just as they'd been parked. I made a mental note to send Will and Marty back out to pick her up, then went along with my captors like a good boy.

Estéban and I had one brief moment alone, as the paramedics got us loaded into the same ambulance. He glanced at me, steadier now that his arm was secured to a board. "What happened to the baseball man?"

"Tell you the truth, kid? I don't give a rat's ass." And that's all I had to say about that.

23

They never found Nelson Kidd. I suppose it's possible the tornado carried him off, and we'll find his body years from now stuffed under some random rock by the terrible forces of nature. But I think it's more likely he just vanished, ashamed to face what he'd done. Ivan sent word out to the other champions. He'll never be able to pull the same stunt again.

Being the last person who saw him alive, I was of great interest to the police, no doubt aided by the almost–restraining order I had against me. Having two hundred thousand of a missing baseball player's dollars in my bank account didn't help, either. I spent the next two months answering questions of varying levels of accusation before a phone call from a former client (thank you, Mr. President) convinced them to look elsewhere. I heard later that his family had him declared legally dead. His grandson is now a very rich little boy.

The punch line of it all, at least to me, is that when Kidd said Verelli was tied up, he was being literal. The hotel housekeeping staff found the agent in his underwear, gagged with a sock and bound with miniblind cords. Someone managed to get a cell phone video of his "rescue," and that ran on the Internet for weeks, Verelli being paraded before the world in his tighty-whities and garters for all to see. I think I'm the only one who caught a glimpse of a black mark on the inside of his left arm. The video was poor quality, so maybe it was a shadow, or a cop's finger, or my own vivid imagination. Or maybe Mr. Verelli was more of a believer than he let on.

Though sweet Trav tried hard to convince the police that I was his assailant, I had an airtight alibi from half the population of Sierra Vista. In the end, he finally confessed that Kidd had beaned him with the clock radio and tied him up to get him out of the way. (Hey, I can't fault the old man. I wanted to shut Verelli up from the moment I met him.) Being caught in his lies pretty much ended his dream of painting me as the villain.

Unfortunately, that revelation cast suspicion on Kidd's mental condition at the time of his disappearance, which necessitated more legal dancing around to see whether or not I got to keep the money he paid me. I'm still waiting to find out if it's mine free and clear, and in the meantime . . . well, bills are piling up. That's the way things go. We're not even going to talk about the insurance company. They dropped me like a hot potato.

I came out of the adventure with seventy-two stitches in my left thigh, two in my face, and a torn gastrocnemius muscle in my right calf. Try saying that five times real fast. They glued my gashed knuckles closed. Oh yeah, and there was that case of mild frostbite on my toes (and Estéban's). Lemme tell you, that baffled them. Dr. Bridget was unthrilled, to say the least.

"God was watching out for you again, it seems." She gave me that withering female look, the one that makes you just want to crawl into a hole and die out of pure shame, whether you've done anything wrong or not.

I was put on bed rest. Within half an hour, it became couch rest, and in another ten minutes, it became lounging-on-the-patio-in-the-sunshine rest. I'm not one to stay flat on my back if I can help it.

My injuries did save me from spending that Saturday chopping an enormous tree into burnable chunks. It came down in my mother's front yard in the storm, and her birthday party turned into a lumberjack contest. I sat in my comfortable lawn chair, foot propped up on a log, and offered helpful suggestions to my brother and cousins on just how to best go about it. I thought Cole was going to kill me.

"I swear, big brother, somehow you did this on purpose, just so you wouldn't have to cut up this tree." Cole swigged from a bottle of Gatorade as he took a break from swinging his splitting maul. Despite the rather perfect spring day, sweat ran off him in rivers.

"You can't make this stuff up, little brother." I grinned at him and raised my beer in salute. He just glared daggers at me and went back to work.

Paulo—er . . . Estéban—was also spared the ignominy of physical labor. In fact, he got the hero's seat of honor for "saving" me from the tornado. I ask you, where's the justice? He seemed rather overwhelmed by my mother, who is a force of nature in her own right. Motherless boys of the world, beware. She can spot you a mile away. She has meat loaf, and she knows how to use it. I think we left her house that evening with ten plastic containers filled with various foods "absolutely necessary to a growing boy."

That growing boy also got to spend a good hour on the phone with his mother, most of it in such rapid-fire Spanish that even Mira had trouble following. It ended with tears I wasn't supposed to see, and our all promising to look after Estéban until he could be returned safely home.

The other phone call . . . Well, I claimed that duty for myself.

That night, when the house was safely locked and everyone else had gone to bed, I hobbled into my den and called Rosaline. She broke down and wept when I told her Miguel's soul was safe. I even told her about the river stones, and how I'd placed them at the feet of my little Buddha statue. Mira was the only other person who knew. Somehow, I thought the two women would understand.

"Gracias, Jesse. Muchas gracias, siempre."

"He'd have done the same for me." It was an uncomfortable call, despite the good news I was delivering. First off, I don't deal well with crying women. Second, I couldn't bring her husband back, even as badly as I wanted to. "Listen, if you ever need anything, you only have to call. You know that, right?"

"Sí, I know. You are an angel, Jesse Dawson. Do not let anyone tell you otherwise." We hung up after the usual exchange of greetings for the families, and I sat in the silence for a long time. Eventually, footsteps shuffled in the hallway.

"Is she all right?" Estéban appeared in the doorway, dressed in one of my T-shirts and an old pair of sweats.

I thought about chiding him for eavesdropping, then realized I didn't really care. "No. But she'll be better now."

He scratched at his hand, mostly encased in neon blue fiberglass. "Thank you for calling her. I . . . did not know what to say." He seemed to find everything else in the room more interesting than meeting my eyes.

He fidgeted with the cast on his arm, and I eyed him critically for a moment. "You're up late. Is your arm hurting? I can see if Mira has something for the pain."

That got the reaction I wanted. He straightened instantly, a hint of his usual anger flaring in his dark eyes. "I am fine. It does not hurt." He was lying, but it was a small balm to his bruised adolescent ego. I let it slide.

"Was there something else, then?"

His jaw clenched as he debated his next words. "Miguel thought very highly of you. I . . . did not believe him. I thought you were just another overhyped gringo."

I sat at my desk, watching him fidget. He blushed under my direct gaze. "And now?"

"I am grateful you were there. I would not have been able to do it alone." It came out in a rush, one single breath. Every one of those words had to hurt. A meaner person might have called him on it. I wasn't that person.

"Miguel was a good man, Estéban. He would have done the same for me."

"But I do not know that I would have. Before. I would now."

"You have a long time before you have to be making decisions like that. Just enjoy being a kid a little longer."

I don't know if he believed me or not. He nodded a little and shuffled back toward bed.

Ivan arrived on Sunday as he promised, to be greeted with a five-year-old's squeals of *"Djadko Ivan!"* My daughter could officially speak more Ukrainian than I. After taking a few hours to spoil Annabelle—the teddy bear was bigger than the child, I kid you not—we adjourned to my closet den to have one of those manly sort of talks.

He examined the pictures and books on my shelves as he spoke. "When you are to being more mobile, I would ask you to be coming with me to Toronto."

I nodded. "Guy's place?"

"Tak. I wish to find his weapon. It was not being sent to me, and so there must have been someone he cared about very much. We will to be taking care of them for him."

I nodded again. I was all in favor of a widows and orphans fund. "Yeah, I'll come with, no problem." I eyed my crutches. "In a week or two."

He turned to face me, idly flipping through the pages of the *Hagakure.* "As for the other request I have . . . The boy will to be remaining with you. There is no one left in his family to be teaching him."

Um . . . excuse me? That wasn't exactly a request by my definition of the word. "Do I *look* like Yoda?"

Ivan gave me an "I'm wiser than you" smirk. Nothing like having a six-foot-four Ukrainian standing in a tiny little room to stare you down—I need a bigger den for these conversations. "You will be good for the boy. He is to be needing discipline."

"I'm not training him to fight, Ivan. He's just a kid."

He raised one white brow at me. "When you were to being a boy, would you have avoided danger because someone was to be telling you, 'You are too young'?" He shook his head, amused. "It is better he is to being trained, before he is to be getting hurt on his own."

I hate it when he's right, and he's right a lot. I'm not sure how successful I'll be, though. To quote the venerable Yoda, much anger I sense in this one. Estéban is a hurt, angry kid. It doesn't make for the best learning environment. Then again, I wasn't so different when Carl took me in hand. It could work out—maybe.

Mira is adamant that the kid go back to school in the fall, and being as he is here illegally, she's started the process of getting him a student visa. He's now in residence in my spare bedroom, which has evicted Mira from her sanctuary. She says she doesn't mind, but I'm currently trying to figure out how hard it would be to add another room onto the house.

Though she wasn't consulted, Anna has made certain we know she loves having Estéban here. She always wanted a big brother (or jungle gym, and he serves as both). And he in turn seems rather fond of her. Coming from a huge family as he did, I'm willing to bet he misses some of the joyous chaos small children can generate. Enter Hurricane Annabelle, and problem solved.

Though I was fairly certain of the answer already, I did finally ask him about the blue Ford Escort.

He gave me only a puzzled look. "What Ford Escort?"

"The little blue car? Were you following me?"

He shook his head. "I have no car. I do not even know how to drive."

"So how were you getting to work?"

He shrugged his lanky shoulders at me. "I was sleeping in the garden area of the Wal-Mart. I scaled the fence and hid behind the shrubs." Well, that explained how he happened to catch me there.

So "teaching Estéban to drive" was added to my summer to-do list, and the blue car mystery continued.

It made me feel like a long-tailed cat in a room full of poisonous, radioactive, explosive rocking chairs. I keep a close watch on the traffic behind me now, and I have given up driving the back roads home from work. I've asked Mira to do the same. And call me sexist, but I'm kinda glad Estéban is at the house when I'm not there. Having a man (sort of) present makes everything okay, in some backward, male-dominated way. And I don't believe this is done, not for a minute. We'll call it hippie's intuition.

Viljo managed to get Grapevine up and functional again in fairly short order. The hacking attacks disappeared along with Nelson Kidd and the blue Escort, so Ivan's opinion is that the baseball player was responsible. I don't believe it for a heartbeat. Kidd didn't strike me as the computer whiz type, nor a man to attempt vehicular homicide. Thankfully, Viljo's got enough paranoia for an entire covert ops group, and our secrets are safe behind the equivalent of cyber titanium—at least as he explained it to me, but what the hell do I know?

Before he left, Ivan made arrangements for Guy and Miguel's territories to be split between me and the champion in San Francisco, one Avery Malcolm Vincent. Avery has a lot of work in Hollywood, with the starlets and rock stars. I get the businessmen and moguls from the East Coast here. Between the two of us, we'd manage the North and South, too.

I didn't know Avery well. We'd met twice, at Ivan's insistence. He was a clean-cut African American in his late thirties, more likely to show up to a casual dinner in slacks and a button down shirt than in my usual jeans and a T-shirt, and more likely to drink Perrier than beer. But after a brief phone conversation, we both agreed it would be better if we kept in closer contact from this point on, just to cover both our asses. I think I'll get along with him all right.

Being on crutches earned me a week off at It, too. When I finally returned to work, I was greeted with a techno remix of the wicked witch's theme from *The Wizard of Oz*, followed by AC/DC's "Thunderstruck." Kristyn thought it was hilarious. The rest of the kids eyed me as if I'd just crawled out of my own grave to sell goth apparel to the unwashed masses. Apparently, I was officially a badass mo'fo for surviving a tornado head-on.

Kristyn was only mildly unamused when I told her

I needed more days off in short order. I gave her some excuse about physical therapy, not wanting to explain why I was taking time to go hiking in the Canadian wilderness.

Ivan met me when I hobbled off the plane in Toronto, and after renting some gargantuan four-wheel-drive monstrosity, we headed north. Ivan seemed to know where he was going, so I rode in silence, the perfect passenger.

I don't know what I expected to find. A log cabin, maybe? Somewhere they walked out into the forest and made their own syrup? Guy's house was an average two-story home, probably enough for just him, on a rural road. I always pictured him as some kind of rustic hermit, living off the land, but his neighbors were within easy view with neatly kept lawns not too unlike my own neighborhood. We'd even passed a small grocery store a few miles back (well, kilometers, in Canada). It was bordering on suburbia.

Ivan picked the lock on the front door while I pretended not to notice and hoped Guy's neighbors did the same. I had never been arrested in a foreign country, and I was hoping to keep it that way. "What are we looking for again?"

"Photos. Letters. Anything that might tell us who he valued."

The house was abandoned, no doubt about that. There was no dust built up, no neglect visible, but it had that air, that cool, sterile emptiness that comes when no one lives there anymore. I took one look at the stairs, and volunteered Ivan to search the second floor. I'd graduated from the crutches to a cane, but I wasn't going to push my luck. Ivan assented with a grunt and disappeared upstairs.

Guy had lived simply, without much adornment. His heavy wooden furniture had the occasional plain cushion, and the cabinets in his kitchen were as ordinary as could be. There were a few wood carvings on the fireplace mantel, and one clock made from a slice of tree trunk on the wall, but other than that, there was nothing to speak to who he had been. Most definitely, there were no pictures of loved ones.

I wondered whether he had been lonely. Had he sacrificed companionship for the sake of his duty as a champion? I'd never be able to ask him.

While Ivan rummaged upstairs, I wandered out the back door. Here, at least, I found something more like the Guy I remembered. A neat stack of firewood lay split and ready for use next to the steps, and on the far side of the yard, several large logs awaited the same fate. See? I knew he was a lumberjack. He'd even left his hatchet buried in one of the logs where it waited for his return.

It took me a few moments to realize why that was wrong. I'll blame it on my largely being a city kid. The splitting maul, used to break the large logs into manageable chunks, leaned against the firewood beside me. Already, a thin coating of rust had started around the edges. One end of the neat stack had toppled over, weeds growing up between the logs. Someone who kept a house as neatly as Guy wouldn't leave a tool out to rust in the elements, or a job half done like this. He'd been surprised here.

My cane and I walked across the yard to retrieve the small ax, seemingly balanced on one sharp point in its chosen log. It took a couple good tugs to free it of the wood, so deeply was it buried. I hefted it in my left hand, feeling the balance and how the padded grip fit my palm. I was already picturing how to move with it in combat. This was no tool; this was a weapon—Guy's weapon.

"What are you to be having?" The wooden steps creaked under Ivan's weight as he joined me in the backyard.

"I found his weapon." I showed him the ax, and the old man frowned.

"Why would he to be having it delivered here, where there was no one to be finding it? I have given him instructions otherwise."

I ran my thumb over the ax, testing the edge to find it razor sharp, and had to smile to myself. I knew why Guy had disobeyed Ivan. "Because he didn't want anyone to get hurt, trying to avenge him. He was thinking of us." It was something I would have done, if I were alone. And that realization made me regret, more than ever, that I had never known him.

Knowing that someone would eventually come and claim the abandoned property, Ivan took Guy's computer when we left, preventing anyone else from accidentally (or purposely) connecting to Grapevine. I took his ax. I couldn't leave the weapon of a fallen warrior to be claimed by some amateur, or worse yet, to rust away to nothing. I made plans to hang it in my den next to my Japanese silk print. I thought it a fitting place.

All was well for about a week after I returned from Canada, and then Axel slithered back into my yard, literally. My attitude toward the infuriating demon hadn't improved much in the intervening weeks. I'd long since packed up the chess set and taken it inside. And since I just happened to have Estéban's machete close at hand, I snatched it up to behead the green garden snake.

"Truce, Jesse! Truce!" The little snake, barely more than a finger's width around, ducked into a gap in the patio stones.

"You stay in there. I'm getting some gasoline to roast your sorry ass." Honestly, though, hobbling my way to the garage wasn't the righteous exit I wanted to make, so I was fairly glad when he kept talking.

"Please, Jesse? I'm really sorry." He almost sounded like he meant it, too.

I peered into the hole, watching the tiny forked tongue flicker at me. "You knew he'd killed those men, and you let me walk into that. If I thought you'd stay in that body long enough, I'd make you into a hatband."

Slowly, the flat green head emerged from Axel's hiding place. "I couldn't tell. You know the rules. I tried, remember? I tried at the ballpark, and you just wouldn't give me anything I could use!"

"Then break the rules. Doing a good deed might not kill you, y'know."

The snake blinked at me, quite a feat considering snakes don't have eyelids. "Jesse, when it comes down to it, the only things between this world and total chaos are the rules. Don't be so quick to dismiss them." I raised the machete again, and he ducked back into the hole. "I said truce!"

"I didn't."

"Please, Jesse. I don't know when I'll be able to come see you again. There are things happening . . . down there. Bad things."

"You're breaking my heart."

The snake sighed, and his nonexistent shoulders seemed to sag. "Just . . . watch your ass, all right? I'd hate to see something happen to you."

"Before you can get your grubby hands on me, you mean?"

"It's not like that."

"It's not? Then why were you there the night I wrecked my truck? Goodwill and brotherly love? You were checking on your investment."

"That's what I'm talking about—"

"I don't care what you're trying to tell me. I don't trust you, and you aren't welcome here anymore. You will stay away from me, stay away from my friends, and my coworkers, and my family. Or I swear, by any god you believe in, I will find a way to end you."

"If you'd just listen for a second . . ."

"Don't make me say it, Axel."

"They're not going to stop, Jesse!" For a moment, I hesitated, startled by the sudden urgency in his voice (my voice?), and he plunged on. "All of this was just the beginning. They're not going to stop, and they don't give a rat's ass about the rules. That's what I'm trying to tell you."

"All of what? Getting run off the road? The computer hacker?"

"I've said too much already."

I made a grab for his scrawny little neck, and he squeezed back into the hole. "Who, Axel? Who are 'they'?"

He writhed himself into little green knots in agitation. "I can't *tell* you! Not without an exchange!"

"You conniving bastard. It always comes back to that, doesn't it?" There was only one thing he'd understand. "I banish thee, demon. Get thee hence!" There are things to be said about the oldies but goodies.

. He gave a small yelp and poofed, taking the hapless snake with him.

He wouldn't stay gone, I knew. He was strong enough that he didn't need summoning to cross over, and I was, after all, his soul to collect if he could. I would remember, next time, that he was a demon. It disgusted me that I even had to remind myself of that. I would never let my guard down around him again. There would be no more fraternizing with the enemy.

Annabelle came screaming out the kitchen door, Estéban right behind her in playful pursuit. Somehow I managed to avoid being flattened as they chased each other around the yard, and laughter reigned over my little piece of the world. Peace is fleeting, but oh, how sweet it is.

"Hey, watch that arm! I'm not paying for a second cast."

Oh, and for those who wondered, my mother loved her birthday present. Mira bought her a gift certificate for a day at a spa. It was, apparently, the perfect thing. Have I mentioned how much I love my wife?

ROC

THE
DRESDEN FILES
The #1 *New York Times* bestselling series

by Jim Butcher

"Think *Buffy the Vampire Slayer* starring Philip Marlowe." —*Entertainment Weekly*

STORM FRONT

FOOL MOON

GRAVE PERIL

SUMMER KNIGHT

DEATH MASKS

BLOOD RITES

DEAD BEAT

PROVEN GUILTY

WHITE NIGHT

SMALL FAVOR

TURN COAT

CHANGES

AVAILABLE NOW FROM

SIMON R. GREEN

DAEMONS ARE FOREVER

The second book in the series following *The Man with the Golden Torc*.

Eddie Drood's clan has been watching mankind's back for ages. And now he's in charge of the whole kit and caboodle. But it's not going to be an easy gig...

During World War II, the Droods made a pact with some nasty buggers from another dimension known as the Loathly Ones, who they needed to fight the Nazis. But once the war was over, the Loathly Ones decided that they liked this world too much to leave. Now it's up to Eddie to make things very uncomfortable for them—or watch everything humanity holds dear go up in smoke.

R0027

THE ULTIMATE IN
SCIENCE FICTION AND FANTASY!

From magical tales of distant worlds to stories of
technological advances beyond the grasp of man, Penguin has
everything you need to stretch your imagination to its limits.

penguin.com

ACE

Get the latest information on favorites like
William Gibson, T.A. Barron, Brian Jacques,
Ursula K. Le Guin, Sharon Shinn, Charlaine Harris,
Patricia Briggs, and Marjorie M. Liu,
as well as updates on the best new authors.

ROC

Escape with Jim Butcher, Harry Turtledove, Anne Bishop,
S.M. Stirling, Simon R. Green, E.E. Knight, Kat Richardson,
Rachel Caine, and many others—plus news on the
latest and hottest in science fiction and fantasy.

DAW

Patrick Rothfuss, Mercedes Lackey, Kristen Britain,
Tanya Huff, Tad Williams, C.J. Cherryh, and many more—
DAW has something to satisfy the cravings of any
science fiction and fantasy lover.
Also visit dawbooks.com.

*Get the best of science fiction and fantasy
at your fingertips!*